BREATHLESS

Anne Swärd

BREATHLESS

Translated from the Swedish by
Deborah Bragan-Turner

MACLEHOSE PRESS
QUERCUS · LONDON

First published in Great Britain in 2012 by

MacLehose Press
an imprint of Quercus
55 Baker Street
7th Floor, South Block
London W1U 8EW

First published in the Swedish language as *Till sista andetaget*
by Svante Weyler Bokförlag, Stockholm, 2010
Copyright © Anne Swärd, 2010

English translation copyright © 2012 by Deborah Bragan-Turner

Translation sponsored by
SWEDISH
ARTSCOUNCIL

A CIP catalogue record for this book is available
from the British Library

ISBN 978 0 85705 103 5

10 9 8 7 6 5 4 3 2 1

Designed and typeset in Collis by Libanus Press, Marlborough
Printed and bound in Great Britain by Clays Ltd, St Ives plc

To Nadja
To Samuel
In memory of L.

Sunshine hours

Every day she sat in a deckchair on the veranda, counting the hours of sunshine, drinking iced water, dozing. Trying not to think about cigarettes. The sweet smell of fresh tobacco, the smooth taste of smoke, the delicious rustle of a newly opened packet of Silk Cut and the sensual warmth that filled the mouth. Pregnant with a giant apricot, that was how she looked. Her taut, rounded stomach was covered with down and had a springy resistance when the father-to-be and his brothers poked their filthy fingers at it. It smelt of sun-warmed, harvest-ripe fruit, how they wanted to take a bite, but she stopped them: No! Not quite ripe yet. Three more weeks in the sun. *Three weeks?* They had been patient an eternity, how could they stand more of this waiting? But she pushed him and his brothers away, they would have to be content to watch and wait. For a little while longer the magic fruit belonged to her alone.

She sat there and saw her stomach darken, swell, stretch in a high dome towards the light. Rejoiced in the last luxuriant warmth of summer, tried not to think about cigarettes and the future and him. The other one. For love is a *folie à deux*, she had read that somewhere. And now she knew it to be true from her own experience, and the worst thing was that all it took was for both of them to be slightly crazy – together, the whole thing became utter madness.

Her infatuation had grown until it lost its softness and her stomach likewise. She looked on them both as if they belonged to someone else: the lunar mountain that rose up above her hips, and the ravine of ill-starred love, so deep she could not see the bottom. Pull yourself together, she said to herself. Get a grip, get a grip . . . do not think about him. But whenever she tried not to think about him, there he was in her thoughts.

Love is something one is stricken with, like a fever or bankruptcy. No, it was a fever that laid waste to her body, however hard she tried to cool it down on the outside. Love has no laws, veers between lovers as it pleases. She hated him. Loved him. Loved him so much that she hated him. His mere existence was bad enough – so close that some nights she thought she would go mad; indeed she was not sure, perhaps she had already.

The veranda became her home that summer, the rest of the house was too warm, unthinkable to spend the nights indoors, when the heat had crept in through the asbestos roof and transformed the top floor into a dry sauna. The stone walls had the warmth of the entire summer stored up in them, impossible to breathe inside, instead David had made a bed for them in the corner of the veranda that was shaded in the morning. They slept close together on a mattress to the sound of the sparse night traffic on the motorway in the distance, the rasping calls of the tree frogs from the overgrown dam behind the house, now and then a goods train and a solitary nightjar over the field. Even in her dreams she tried not to think about him. It did not work, however hard David held her to him. However hard she had exercised her willpower when she went down into the cellar to fetch beer, even though she was terrified of bats and knew that they were hanging from the low ceiling. This was so much more difficult, her will was not strong enough to withstand the thought of him.

At night David's presence felt soothing, his arm around her stopped her floating away, out into the cold dark universe, her stomach like an inflated helium balloon. But during the day she sat alone, proud and dignified, and wanted to be left in peace. Shooed him and his brothers away when they sniffed about her like dogs. Did not need them any longer, did not want their hungry looks, their curiosity. As if they believed she was the bearer of a secret, when in point of fact anyone could tell what was on its way: an apricot, king-size. She was becoming incredibly big.

The due date passed by days and weeks. The bulging fruit grew more and more overripe. Her navel, which once had been a little white bud, spread into a rose of gossamer skin and turned brown in its innermost folds. Her legs, which she could no longer see, filled with water, and a river delta of veins branched out, distended, snaking down her inner thighs.

Björn, grandfather-to-be on the father's side, gave her Tiger Balm to rub into her swollen ankles, but she could not reach down, all distances and proportions had shifted and he had to do it for her. She allowed him to do it, as the act of tenderness it was. Felt like Farah Diba on her peacock throne, although her own feet hardly smelled of virgin milk, they were black and cracked after a whole summer barefoot. Idun, grandmother-to-be on the father's side, had sent off for the latest firm moulded bras from Swegmark mail order. She had never really bothered about bras before, but was informed by the future grandmother that from now on she had no choice. It was not just her stomach that was growing, had she not noticed?

"Will you stay like that afterwards?" David said and nodded towards her new and different charms.

"I should hope not," she said, having no desire to carry them around for the rest of her life and satisfied with the manageable size they had been hitherto.

Despite her new weight, she had enjoyed the long and sultry summer, in her strange state she was above all trivialities. Heat, hunger, boredom, agitation, flies, none of the things that usually irritated her could confound her now. She had never given birth before and so she was not apprehensive. It was natural, she thought. Animals do it more or less *en passant* and she had always thought of herself as an animal, a fox, lithe and instinctive. They just do it and then they go off hunting again – and this was how she imagined it would be for her too. When it was time, if she could manage it, if it did not go too quickly, she had decided to conjure up the picture of the vixen giving birth alone in the cool darkness of its lair.

She devoted much time to her efforts not to think about cigarettes. In particular not Silk Cut, the light tobacco with the faint smell of bacon. If she had not weighed three hundred kilos with legs like mangrove trees she would have been able to stand at the side of the motorway at any time of the day or night, hitchhike to the coast, take the ferry over the Sound, buy a packet and hitchhike home again. How dangerous could it be? Expectant mothers had smoked forever, as far as she was aware. Why had so many things suddenly become dangerous now, that were not dangerous before? In all probability because one decade was about to end and another to begin, one could feel a kind of optimistic mobilising in the air. Was it ethical? At any rate she had no desire to participate in it. Wanted to be left in peace with her usual cigarettes and habits. It was only when something was forbidden that one started thinking about it the whole time.

The days grew hotter and drier until in the end they passed into something resembling autumn. Harvest was the word used to refer to this season, it will come soon, she thought. The longer an apricot hangs on a tree, the easier it falls. Björn, father of the father-to-be, had three apricot trees trained against the sunny side of the house, and at this particular time in late summer the fruits were so distended, so sweet, so ripe, so ready that just a look was enough for them to loosen and land in one's hand. Things happen when the time is right, even a non-believer could be convinced of that.

While she waited she took pleasure in the last warmth of the year, gathering it up as one gathers one's strength, without knowing how badly one is going to need it.

It was a protracted delivery.

The child that came out at long last looked nothing like a shiny rose-pink apricot covered with golden down, more like an Eskimo. The feeling that it had been worth it – the months of waiting, her body's drastic transformation, the fear that took hold with the very first contractions, the reckless drive to the maternity clinic in thick fog, the unspeakable pain, the feeling of abandonment, that she was the last living soul on earth and lay there all by herself in a strange delivery room in a deserted hospital and gave birth as best she could although she had no idea how to give birth to a infant, and the lies afterwards when everyone declared that she had not been alone, even though they had no notion how alone she had been – the feeling that it had been worth it did not emerge straightaway.

When the killer whale baby finally rolled out of its mother after three days like a gigantic ball of pain, she stared at the result with shock. It should have been a boy. Someone who looked like the father. Since he was the one who had made something start to grow inside her, uncontrolled, then at least what came out should have certain similarities with him, the originator. But no, first it was a girl, second . . . hair as dark as if it had been dipped into a bottomless lake.

Later, when it was the new Pappa's turn to inspect the harvest's yield, he stared too. The girl resembled no-one, least of all him, but not her mother either. He did not utter a word, overwhelmed by the seriousness of the moment or perhaps by disappointment. All the others on both sides of the family were various shades of Nordic blond. The nurses did not react until they saw the child in her father's arms, but it had happened before, what with all the new foreign workers in the area. And sometimes babies were born with coal-black hair that discreetly fell out after a few weeks. After all, it was man's ability to adapt that meant he survived.

The obstetrician washed his hands somewhere in the background and maybe he was thinking once again that his job really was donkey-work rather than craftsmanship: women who screamed and kicked and calved as if there were nothing human left in them. Like this one.

"It was a big stomach for such a little one," he said, without turning round to reveal whether he meant the mother or the child, probably both.

The mother recovered but there was something frail about the child. It was not really a perfect baby, rather pale, rather weak, grew feebler as the days passed, the blood counts were too low, a clear case of anaemia. Against her black hair and dark glistening eyes, her skin had a pale blue pallor, the paediatrician thought they should give her a transfusion. But the mother did not want him to stick needles and tubes into the little mite and so he reluctantly gave the child a few weeks to improve.

Jaundice at the clinic and a ban on visiting. The two families stood in the hospital grounds and waved when the mother lifted up her daughter on the balcony. A pale, dark-headed infant was all they could see at that distance. Everything in miniature apart from the eyes, unless it was just the colour, dark sea-green, giving the illusion that they were huge.

Maybe it was not a miracle, but it felt like it – the situation improved. Even though the birth certificate was just a piece of paper, it did verify that her daughter existed, this pale little thing lying under the hospital blanket and squinting out at the dazzling September light. It was to be Angela Rafaela. "Eh?" the new Pappa said doubtfully. But it had already been decided, once the thought was formed it could not be withdrawn. It ought to have brought bad luck. Angela Rafaela after the archangel Raphael with his powers of healing, because here was a child who had healed herself and there was reason to believe that some higher authority had had a hand in it. Or perhaps just the tip of a wing, but it had made all the difference.

"She has to have a name that people can pronounce as well," the new Pappa's mother said.

"O.K. . . . *Lo*," Mamma said, irritated. Was that simple enough? She was clutching at anything and the name Lo, which means a lynx in Swedish, had just popped into her head.

"Angela Rafaela Lo Mård? That sounds crazy," Pappa said.

That people would just call her Lo Mård scarcely made things any better.

How could anyone think he had the right to interfere in what her child was going to be named – she had no intention of taking back the name she had just given, that would be tempting fate, like sucking the life out of the tiny nostrils.

"David, it's already decided," she said. "Next time you can give birth and choose the name." While she had been sitting in the deckchair, nurturing the baby inside her all summer, she had been reading Anaïs Nin's erotic diaries and her full name, Angela Anais Juana Antolina Rosa Edelmira Nin y Culmell, was unashamedly long.

But at least Grandmother was satisfied that the name they would use would be Lo. It was easy to remember, and that was the most important thing about a name after all.

———

I was baptised on the Feast of the Guardian Angels in October 1969, a year of hope with a slight hubris in the air. The moon was not quite so far away, it shone with the same desolate light, but now that it had been touched by men it seemed less remote in the planetary darkness. The year of the moon landing was, according to my father's mother, the last year that man could still surpass himself in anything other than stupidity.

My first memory is of a bright light shining straight at me. I always thought it was the sun, but it must have been the lamp in the ceiling seen from below as I was passed from arm to arm in a kitchen full of people. So many arms and yet I did not feel trapped. Such a strong light and it shone just on me. The adults warmed their hands on me, sniffed at my neck to drink in the aroma of new life, kissed me one after the other as if I was a holy relic in a shrine.

No-one could understand how I had come to be, in what dark corner of the large house it could have happened, the house where my parents and their brothers and sisters lived like one family. They just had to get used to the idea. My young uncles and aunts pulled me from all sides. I was not supposed to have been there, but now that I was, dreams and hopes were spun around my dark head, something of which I was fortunately unaware. I was not to trouble myself with anything other than existing. A ship so overloaded with expectations was to be a vessel too oppressive for a small child.

Tender roots in the new earth, in the rich black soil, so unlike the barren ground they had moved away from. My small roots would bind them to the place where they still did not feel at home in their own right. Someone had to be born here so that the others could hang on to the birth certificate's clear proof of belonging. The adults must watch closely over me so that no harm should come. Protect, nourish, raise, make me house-trained, set one or two extendable boundaries and look the other way when I overstepped them. As soon as I was big enough I would slip away to escape the affection. I needed it to be there, just so long as I could stand still long enough to accept it.

*

Born under a lucky star, according to the story they told me. Someone pointed out the Lynx constellation in the northern hemisphere, I loved standing out in the yard with Pappa's brothers when they were in that mood, magnanimous, when they would look at shooting stars and dream of getting away – back home – where they really belonged. Sometimes they could be depressed and light-hearted at the same time and then the starry sky was the only thing that helped. Every now and again they were in high spirits and acted like men from the Ministry of Silly Walks. On those evenings the stars did not matter to us.

I was happy as a child. And if I was not happy, I did not realise. If something was wrong, I did not see it, I thought that what we had was happiness. The short-term kind that darts between trees is perhaps the only kind there is. I was happy as long as I could run free, happy in my puppy fat, happy when I was lying under the bed eavesdropping on my young aunts who spent a whole summer talking about nothing but sex, happy when Pappa's youngest brother Rikard chased me through the arboretum, even though I knew it was not as much fun when he caught me. I never saw that happiness was so brief, because it came at such short intervals that I scarcely noticed the gaps.

About the time on the veranda, about the art of not thinking about the forbidden, I still knew nothing.

———

"Beware of love," Mamma said as she sucked the poison out of my swelling foot, spat a long yellowish jet into the grass and rinsed her mouth with milk.

Love and snakes.

Love, snakes and the motorway.

Love, snakes, the motorway, the lake.

Bats.

High-voltage power lines.

Horror films.

"What about dogs?" I asked.

"Them too."

"Nothing else?"

She raised the axe. "More?"

"Yes."

"Undercooked chicken. Bacteria," she said and swung the axe with all her strength so that the pieces of birch wood shattered. The strength in her arm muscles was not to be trifled with.

"And vole fever," she added.

"Vole fever doesn't exist down here, Mamma. It's only further north."

"And the rest. Watch out for the rest," she said.

I wrote it all down in the green Chinese silk book with the ferrous smell of melting snow and blood between its pages. The book for beautiful things and dangerous things, I just did not know which were which yet. Fear is something you have to learn, if you are not born with it, Mamma said. I had to be protected from myself because I did not have an ounce of fear in my body.

"You would go along with anyone at all without something inside you telling you to stop. Do anything you like, get into real trouble." That was not true. I never got into trouble.

Mamma tried to teach me what fear was.

Pappa tried.

Both my grandmothers and grandfathers tried.

All my aunts and uncles.

And Lukas.

No, maybe not Lukas. But the others tried.

Yes, Lukas did as well. Trust your fear, he used to say. The kitchen full of nose blood. Run, Lo, run . . . I did not want to run, but I did. It was not my blood, not my kitchen, not my fear.

Brush Fire

One dry, aimless day in an infinitely long summer, a brush fire broke out beside the railway that carved through the landscape. A landscape already scorched by the sun, my landscape, open and gently sloping down towards the lake.

It burned in the field of barley and along the railway embankment, smelled of singed weeds and tar, white-hot rails, blackened barbed wire. Insects and field mice burned. The earth burned. The blackthorn bushes crackled, the turkey sheds smouldered and screeched. Something was changing, a feeling of security melted away, a different mood would take its place.

News spread as fast as the fire. It was in the middle of the factory holiday, most people were at home and rushed up from all sides. When the whole village was standing ready along the edge of the field it looked like a civil defence exercise, were it not for the terror in people's eyes. The flames advanced rapidly in all directions with the help of the wind, if it was allowed to run its course the fire would soon reach the houses. The fire brigade took its time, it was a much drier summer than usual in the middle of harvest, perhaps there were fires in several places at once. But we could not wait, the fire would not wait. Mamma and Pappa's mother started to break off large branches along the embankment for all the helping hands. Cooperation and working together were needed now – just like the old days, one of the elderly people said.

Everyone in my family was there, and I wanted to be there too. At first they tried to push me out of the way, but soon it was all they could do to keep the fire in check and they were no longer aware of me. I ran back and forth with water like all the others. Saw Mamma go dangerously close to the worst of the fire, saw Pappa's brothers help to smother the flames with military blankets and tarpaulins. Two tall women, my father's sister and my mother's, walked along the embankment stamping out the embers in men's high wellington boots. Pappa's father Björn and Mamma's father Aron worked side by side with quick, jerky strides, like brothers in identical overalls, but Grandfather Björn was taller by a head, as enormous as the bear he was named after. They wanted to show that they were just as capable of work as their sons and they had begun to create a firebreak in the field so that the blaze would lose its hold. I saw Mamma's mother standing on the side of the hill cradling an empty zinc bowl, as if she did not know why she was standing there. As if someone had tricked her into thinking that she could direct the teamwork from up there, just to keep her out of the way. Pappa had burned his hands and was being bandaged up by Mamma's brother, who ruthlessly ripped wide strips from Pappa's favourite shirt to protect his damaged palms. My mother's sisters were links in the long chains of people passing buckets of water out of the nearest houses from hand to hand.

The fire spread along the side of the hill as if it would never be halted. Working against the wind we tried to limit the disaster until at long last we heard the sirens approach.

It was dangerous to get in the way of the hard jets of water, everyone drew back. All except one. A teenage boy I had already noticed as the only one who went nearer to the fire than my Mamma. At times he almost seemed to be standing in the flames. When everyone else had taken a step back he continued his monotonous fire-fighting. Mamma shouted a warning to him, but he took no notice. She managed to shove him away from the flames, but he was straight back. She grabbed hold of him tighter and screamed something at him in the voice she always had when she was afraid. Then she hit him, but he did not react, just pulled away and carried on. She took hold of him and shook him, as if she was trying to wake him out of a spell. He broke loose again, but his strength was gone and he sank down on to the charred grass as if all the energy had emptied out of him in an instant.

From manic activity to complete stillness in a few seconds. He just lay there, black from his hair down to his gym shoes. I had never seen a dead person, but he did not look alive. Smoke could poison you, I knew that, during the last autumn storm Mamma and I had helped Pappa's father clean up in the arboretum after the wind had been through it like a tornado and when we had burned the branches the smoke made me sick and I had thrown up half the night.

Pappa's father led Mamma away through the crowd. I went closer to the unknown boy to see if he was breathing. His chest inside the sooty T-shirt seemed to be gently rising and falling, but for safety's sake I sat a little way away from him – if he stopped breathing I would call Pappa. My father had once breathed life into a child who had died. This was clearly no child, but Pappa was the only person I knew who could wake the dead. Once, he had caught sight of a girl in the weir next to the factory. She had managed to pull herself to the edge, but she was not breathing. Pappa said that he had seen my face in hers as he gave her the kiss of life. From then on I knew who would save me if anything were to happen. Until Mamma's sisters said that that was not the whole truth. Certainly my Pappa had brought *that* girl back to life, but once long ago he had not been able to save the one whose name we could not mention in case Mamma's mother heard it, the youngest, the one who fell through the ice.

After a very long time the stranger opened his eyes and with difficulty he sat up. I should have left, but when he looked at me I could not. Pappa had given me a carton of milk that was good if you had inhaled smoke, I took a couple of sips and gave the rest to him and he took it without a word and downed it in one.

When I asked him which of the people there were his family, he said that there was no-one. I could not think of a single person in the village who was missing, all of them had come out of their houses to help.

"Don't you live here?" I said. He nodded and indicated towards the lake. There was no house there. He was just pointing over an empty field. I stood and screwed up my eyes in the sun. Had there been a house there that had burned down?

"Can't you see it?" he asked. I sneaked a look at him to see if he was pulling my leg. Strained my eyes, stared at the place he had pointed to, but there was nothing there.

If that was where he lived, why had he tried to fight the fire here and not from his own side? As if he had tried to put out the fire in the wrong place altogether. I explained which people in the crowd were my relatives, all except for Mamma, did not want him to know that she and I were related. I had never seen Mamma like that before, never seen her hit anyone, apart from once when she was alone in the cold-storage room with someone, I did not manage to see who, probably Pappa, the incident was so bewildering that I almost forgot about it.

His eyes widened at each mention of the twelve I identified as my family.

"What about you? Do you live on your own?" I asked.

"No, of course I don't live on my own," he said, without looking at me. "I'm only thirteen." He spat into the grass, black and red.

But I did not think that was so.

He gazed out over the field, as if he wondered himself where his house had gone, but seemed to be in no hurry to rush home and make sure that his family was O.K.

"What about you then?" he asked. I am sure it was obvious, but I still could not tell the truth. Pappa used to say that I was older than I looked, Mamma did not agree at all, I was just quite small. "How old?" the boy said again, measuring me as he looked. Not much to measure, I had not even reached the age of seven. Instead of answering I asked him where he lived – truly. Then I suddenly felt his hard hands take hold of me. I lost contact with the ground, without warning he lifted me right up until I was taller than him and there . . . far down the slope, sheltered from the wind and people's view by high trees, was the house. Beyond my horizon, far beyond the limit Mamma had set for me to roam around on my own, almost down by the water's edge, the widening of the river, round like a lake, silver-blue, with two narrow streams that meandered further north and south.

He set me back down on the grass, I straightened my sleeveless dress that had ridden up and got creased and had the marks left by his black hands. Felt my face tighten with soot and heat.

*

As soon as the worst of the disaster had been averted, speculation over what had caused the conflagration began. Or who. Arson, Mamma believed. Sparks from the train line, Pappa said. Dry grass that spontaneously ignited, Mamma's sisters thought. Arson, Pappa's father agreed – it had begun to burn in several places at once, natural fires seldom follow such a rapid pattern. Mamma's father thought it might be a bit of everything, it was a fire-summer, a snake-summer, a summer of parched and overheated emotions. I said nothing and no-one asked me what I thought.

Through our combined endeavours the fire had been brought under control and put out, but the danger was not over. The ground glowed with sealed-in heat, the fire could creep along the roots and stay alive for days and restart at any time. Watch had to be kept on the field all through the night. The thirteen adults who under normal circumstances kept an eye on me must have been too preoccupied or exhausted to bother whether I was in my bed or not. The rest of the night I sat with the unknown boy near to his house wrapped in a heavy saddle blanket that smelled of Calor gas and old stallion, filled with new, unfamiliar feelings.

The fear that the underground embers would suddenly flare up again kept me awake. His presence as well. Was he one of those you had to be wary of? I was not sure. The fire, the dark, the tiredness, the stinging in my eyes, the sense that I had to look after myself now, that no-one would protect me so far away from my usual territory. Independent overnight. No-one would recognise me when I came home, *if* I ever came home. It seemed unreal that I had had a family at all, I felt so grown-up, so far from home that I lost sight of my old life, the house, the arboretum, the cars in the yard, the tall white birch, my hiding place. Where this endless night would lead I had no idea. For the first time in my life alone with someone I did not know, beside the forbidden lake where, it was said – I knew this even though I was only seven – people from the village had deliberately gone under. One or two from the neighbouring village too, as the river was deepest here, where the channel had burst, as it were, and flowed out into what we called the lake.

Where he lived was still the only thing I knew about him, in the house where no light was turned on the whole night. He went into the garage and found a blanket for me when he heard my teeth chattering in the darkness, but he did not go into the house, despite hunger, despite thirst. I did not know what his name was, only how his hands felt when he lifted me up off the ground, the smarting of the tender skin of my armpits, a cold tingling in my stomach. He did not fetch a jacket for himself, never felt the cold, he said, just sat on his heels, huddled up, and smoked as if he did not have enough smoke inside him already. When he offered me a cigarette I understood that life would never ever be the same again.

The only things I had smoked before were chocolate cigarettes and even that I had done in secret. I could not say no, what would he think, that I was a child? I did not want him to light it for me, just sat there, tightly wrapped up in my blanket like a stuffed cabbage leaf and carefully held the cigarette in my hand. Thought I would save it, as a mark of . . . something. It was the fact that he had asked me that was important.

This was something I would always remember. The only thing I wanted to wipe from my memory was the sound of the birds on fire, but that was hard when the smell of them hung over the field. The turkey sheds were already in flames when Mamma managed to open the padlock and the birds that were still alive flew out like blazing torches and set fire to the corn where they fell.

The whole village was shrouded in a stench of the charred remains of living creatures. The pain in my lungs helped to keep me awake. To sit with a stranger and say nothing and feel cold and keep sneaking a look at him and then at the glow of his cigarette and know that our job was so important that we had to make sure that the whole village did not catch fire, made everything easier to bear. Including the longing for home I felt when I saw the bats silently swoop after insects above the lake.

He did not ask what my name was. I told him anyway.

"That sounds like a boy's name."

"No, it's the name of a beast of prey," I said.

"Yes, yes. I know. I know all about beasts of prey," he said and looked at me sceptically when I related what Mamma had once told me. That one autumn when the ice froze earlier than usual up in the north, where my family came from, a she-bear walked out to one of the rocky islands and went into hibernation. When she woke up in spring the ice was gone and she was caught in a trap. Men went out in boats and looked at her in awe. In those days a bear was an exceptional sight up there and she was a magnificent specimen. Then they shot her, because they were hungry that spring after the war and everyone knew that it was the same bear that had killed my great-grandfather, so his family received the biggest share of the meat.

"A bear's not a beast of prey," he said.

"I know, but that was the bear that killed my great-grandfather who gave Pappa's father the name Björn. And it was Pappa's father who gave Mamma the name Karenina. And Mamma who gave me the name Lo."

"Oh, right," he said, and looked at me quizzically. "Are you going to smoke it or can I have it back? It was my last one."

"I'm going to," I said, "but not at the moment."

Lukács Zsolt. That was what he was called. Or rather . . . Zsolt Lukács – a misunderstanding that occurred long ago when he arrived here at the outset with his father. As far as he knew his father had written his name down on a piece of paper that he left with the day nursery staff the first time he left his son with them – without realising that in Sweden the forename is usually written first. When he collected his son later the same day everyone called him Lukas.

And Lukas it remained. It was a funny story, but he did not tell it as if it were funny. He did not mind the mix-up, he said, Lukács had been his mother's surname, that was why he liked it. And when he pronounced it in Hungarian it sounded like lo-cat. A number of times during the night he had to go off and be sick after all the smoke he had inhaled. He had gone nearer to the fire than anyone else, displaying a defiance that reminded me of that dangerous look in Mamma's and Pappa's eyes when they threw themselves into the surf at the sea. Again and again into the waves, into the flames, as if each time were the last.

He knows all about beasts of prey, I thought, as I watched him dry his mouth and sit down again. I realised that he was the one who had started the fire. I did not understand why. Sitting on the burned-out field on the lookout for signs that it was starting up again, I was suddenly aware that he hoped it would.

The sandy field, the heat under the soles of our feet, the smell of burned flesh when we ran. If the fire had not started, I would never have encountered him. When I returned home that morning I knew scarcely any more about him than before we had met. Not much was said during the night, but the fire had burned all the way between our two houses and that had altered everything.

At home in the dawn, blue with cold and altered, everyone was still asleep. I slowly washed my hands with Grandmother's lily-of-the-valley soap, the rest of me was so black I would probably never be clean again. Crept down in the bed between Mamma and Aunt Marina, tried to steal some of their warmth under the blanket without waking them with my ice-cold hands and knees. I wanted to face both of them, could not choose which and lay on my back instead. Mamma's sleep was troubled, she tossed her head back and forth so that her long hair became more and more entangled on the pillow.

When the family assembled on the veranda for a very late and silent breakfast, I behaved as if nothing had happened. Everyone looked pale, the mood flat. Pappa's hands were wrapped in clean new bandages, he fumbled and grimaced and swore and his mother and Mamma's sisters had to help him with his coffee and porridge. He looked as though he enjoyed being waited on from two sides, his father teased, no-one else said anything, there was a gloomy atmosphere around the table. The subject of the fire had been exhausted long before. All that remained was to eat in silence and then to go down and look at the devastation.

I could not tell them that I had met someone who had offered me cigarettes and seen the sun rise from another world on the other side of the field. I was hurt that no-one had even noticed my absence. But belonging to everyone in a way meant belonging to no-one, at night I often wandered round between the beds and any one of them could have thought that I was sleeping with one of the others.

Just as the guilty return to the scene of the crime, all the villagers returned to the burned-out field. Perhaps it had all been a nightmare, but no, it looked as though war had rampaged along the field of barley and the railway line. The wind had died down and the sour smell of smouldering vegetation hung stubbornly over the black landscape. No-one spoke, there was nothing to add, except possibly a cautious word of thanks directed obliquely upwards – that despite everything the fire had been halted before it reached the houses.

The boy who said he was called Lukas was there as well. He stood slightly aside and hung onto his rusty bicycle, with a look I did not really comprehend. I glanced back, but did not go up to him, stayed with Pappa's brothers and counted charred electricity poles along the embankment. Could see that it was best to keep everything to do with the night of the fire a secret. Growing up meant not saying all you knew, not always following the impulse to tell everything that filled your mind.

The rain finally came, a day too late. Grime over everything that had burned. The impression that something had threatened the village gave a feeling of solidarity in misfortune, even if it did not last.

Boys' eyes

We lived at the edge of the village in a district with no name, where beauty and wilderness began. The sloping fields of corn and the sky, the forest of bats and the power station. And the lake which was not a lake, just as our village was not a proper village in that it did not have its own name. It was an unwanted growth or maybe a free zone with its own laws, or lawless, depending on your point of view. We lived at the place where three silver trails ran together – the river, the railway, the motorway – where the world began or ended, that also depended on your point of view. Lately I have started to think that nearly everything is connected to this.

The secret about him I had to keep better than any secret I had kept before. I had never learnt the secret about secrets, apart from what I hid under Mamma's wardrobe where she never vacuumed: a worn-out hunting knife, a bottle of Paco Rabanne aftershave, the steel guitar strings I could not resist unscrewing from Rikard's guitars, a porn magazine with pressed butterfly wings and chewing-gum wrappers. And now the cigarette as a relic amongst the others in the dust.

Until now I had been able to go from one to another of the family's thirteen adults and pour out everything I wanted to without anyone tiring of me. Now I had fallen through the rabbit hole into a world I could not speak about. Lukas had said that that night was a baptism of fire. I did not know what that meant, but he said it as though I would clearly understand, that was all that mattered.

A few days after the fire, I walked down the gravel track to his house by the lake. Through the trees, with leaves as dry as sloughed snakeskin, I caught a glimpse of him with someone I assumed to be his Pappa. He was at the top of the roof, his Pappa down below on the step. Appeared to give his son an order, though I did not hear what. I went closer. So accustomed to bringing a smile to the faces of adults that the indifference in the man's eye when he turned made me feel uneasy. He said nothing, it was so quiet I could hear the snakeskin leaves rustle. Lukas gave me a quick glance before he turned away. I spun round and walked up the hill towards home without looking back.

People round here are different, hard to make out, Mamma's father used to claim. And that was not a good thing – to be different – it was preferable to be the same. Like us in our family. It was true that Lukas had said they were not from round here either, but they were from another foreign place and differed in another way.

Boys' eyes, boys' hands, boys' smell. I was not afraid of him, the feeling was more like the one I had when I was at the lake. It was bottomless. So swampy that you never knew if there was something under your feet or not. Not exactly frightened but disturbed by the fact that from the very first day at school he stood in one corner of the enclosed yard and looked at me as if I had something he wanted. It was obvious he did not intend to come up to me and take it, like the older boys, with a modicum of force. Not him. No threats from him, he just watched. As if he had all the time in the world to wait. Eyes like suckers, though not moist and warm, but reserved and yet still insistent. I kept far away from the spot he had earmarked for himself, but his gaze cut right through the schoolyard. He was alone like me. No, more alone, so alone that no-one even quarrelled with him. He did not look as though he kept to the wall because he was afraid of ambush, just that he had laid claim to the patch and sat on the back of one of the benches looking at nothing in particular. Or at me.

A few weeks later, when he happened to be behind me in the lunch queue, I noticed that he still smelled of smoke. It was hard to believe it could be from the railway fire, but I had not heard any talk of another fire since that one. I had been bathed immediately in heavy-handed fashion by Mamma's mother and she promptly threw out my clothes, it was impossible to get rid of the smell of sulphur pervading them. She often flung things out and bought new, a phobia of everything that did not smell immaculately clean. She used to scrub Grandfather Aron in a hot bath every afternoon when he came home from the leather factory. Clean clothes were lying ready for him on the bed and then it was time for the afternoon shave, a custom that lived on from the past, from the north where he always had to have a protective layer of stubble when he went out into the harsh cold in the morning. Going out to work newly shaved in minus thirty degrees meant instant frostbite.

"You have a strange accent, where do you come from?" Lukas had asked me towards the end of the night of the fire. He spoke a husky, soft, slow Skåne dialect that poured like maple syrup into the darkness between us. Outside the family I had scarcely met anyone before I started school, but I knew there was one world at home and another world beyond.

At the grocer's Pappa would pretend he understood, whilst mumbling to me that he did not grasp a word of it and how long did you have to live here before you could understand this impossible language? Mamma did not pretend, she said "What?" after every sentence until they became irritated with her and thought she was making fun of them. I did not understand everything either, but it was not me they were talking to so it did not matter.

"Ripberget," I said. True, I had never lived there, but all the same that was where I came from and my language too.

"Dialect," the boy corrected me. "You don't speak a language, you speak a dialect."

"O.K., but it's a different country anyhow. Two thousand kilometres away," I said, making a sweeping gesture somewhere towards the field as I was not sure which direction it was in.

"Me too. Two thousand kilometres. But that way," he said, pointing in the opposite direction.

Snow patches, wind-exposed slopes, cloudberry ants, burned forest land, ore fields, bare fell above the tree line, clearwater lakes. These I had heard about since the day I was born. " . . . Clearwater lakes, if only I could describe them to you, but you can hear in the words how pretty they are, Lo?" When I closed my eyes on Pappa's knee I saw them quite distinctly, one lake behind each eyelid, as clear as crystal.

"Halstrad whitefish," Mamma said. "Over an open fire down by the water. Better than anything you can ever dream of if you've never tasted it." If I really concentrated hard I could taste the sooty flavour.

"In summer you can sometimes see bears roaming around in the big expanse," said Pappa's eldest brother. "Most often alone, bears are solitary creatures."

"Soli-what?"

"Lone wolves," Mamma explained. "Like your grandfather." I opened both my eyes.

"Is that why he's called . . ."

"No, no, your grandfather's mamma gave him that name because his Pappa was killed by a she-bear just before he was born," Pappa's mother said.

"And bog myrtle vodka," Mamma's mother interrupted, and blew her nose into the tissue she always had up the sleeve of her cardigan. "Bog myrtle vodka and bleak fish under the birch tree by the river," she went on. "That's my dearest memory from home." She pointed to the silver birch casket where she kept this memory. I opened the lid.

"But it's empty."

"I know," she said, nodding, and did not care to explain further, it was typical of her to say strange things that you had to try to understand as best you could.

"The cabinet's empty, the emperor's naked and you lot are all homesick!" Pappa's father's voice was heard suddenly from the hammock. We had hoped that he was asleep, but he never slept. And he hated nostalgia. Ripberget and Laxberget were just romanticised translations of Kiirunavaara and Loussavaara, as they said at home. Homesickness, as persistent as piles – he blamed everything on that. It was one thing to move house, Pappa's mother objected, to move your roots was quite another.

"The dark, the cold, the unemployment, the mosquitoes? Is all that to be forgotten now?" Grandfather asked. A feeling of disquiet spread around the table on the veranda. Pappa stood up and left, his brothers contented themselves with staring at their plates. Grandfather pierced

34

me with his eye over the edge of the hammock. "Don't listen to them, Lo, it's pure hogwash, we come from a land where no-one can stand still. You get eaten alive. Swarms of mosquitoes suck your blood until you lose your reason, if you ever had any. As long as you keep moving you can survive, but any man who has to stop to eat, have a pee, sleep . . . God help him. Set birch-bark alight in a tin bucket and lay it in the grass, that's the only thing that helps. And not even the thickest grass-smoke works on those blood-sucking monsters. No place for sensitive folks, Lo, no place for the likes of you and me."

I did not know who to believe, if the Promised Land were here or there or somewhere else entirely. According to Pappa's father it was here, in the warm south, in the land of rich earth and short winters. He was never heard to say he wished he were back there, like the others. I was happy too, but that, Pappa assured me, was because I had never seen anything else.

It could not only have been the never-ending winter darkness or the unemployment or even the mosquitoes that had made them move, there must have been something more. Perhaps the girl whose name you could not mention, the youngest one who drowned. If her name could not even be mentioned, how could they continue to live in the place where it happened? To see that water each day and not know if it was a lake or a grave they saw. Everything must have lost its beauty after that, or at least have a bitter tinge, nature's cruel indifference.

After the fire, silence soon settled over our village once more. Everyone retreated to his own side of the overgrown hedges. It was not like at home, Pappa's mother let it be known, where garden boundaries did not exist and you went to see people when you felt like it, went in without knocking, helped yourself to something to eat and lay down for a rest on the kitchen sofa while you waited for the owner to return. All my pictures of what the family called home had been painted by someone else. A ptarmigan is a bird that can be snared in the snow and eaten, with a wild and bluish taste, that I knew, but I did not know what it looked like when it was flying or how the snare worked in reality, if they were caught by the neck or the foot and which was worse.

His dark eyes turn blue when it is cold. But I do not know that yet, the night of the fire was a state of emergency and since then I have just seen him at a distance. The age difference should be enough to keep us apart. He is almost an adult, at least not a child, not in my eyes.

The very first afternoon that I am going to walk home from school by myself, he coasts up beside me on his man's bicycle, slightly too large for him, so close that I think I can smell the smoke from the fire again. Instead of increasing my pace I slow down, walk so slowly that he finds it difficult to keep his balance on the bicycle.

I do not reply. He does not ask anything either.

I do not know where he wants to go, only that I should not go with him.

I go slower and slower until he wobbles right into me. The handlebars go straight into my face, it hurts so much that I cannot even cry. I am normally paralysed at the sight of blood but this time I just clench my teeth, struggle to my feet and start to limp away. It is raining and my shoelaces, my favourite skirt and my minuscule ponytail are soon hanging down. I hear him come after me on his bicycle, which has a new squeak, and he says something about sorry and bloody well didn't mean it and wait. When he catches up with me he takes hold of me round the waist and lifts me up roughly onto the crossbar. "Hold on," he says. As if I had any other choice, he has already started pedalling.

Your life flashes before your eyes when you die, Pappa has said, though how should he know that? As we sway through the traffic at top speed, the voices of my family flood through my mind. The boy rides twice as fast and half as steadily as Mamma does. I shut my eyes and get ready to throw myself off, but I stop myself at the last minute, at this speed . . . I would kill myself. After what seems like an eternity he brakes so hard that the gravel scatters, I want to look and yet do not want to, do not want to see where he has brought me and what is going to happen there. Not until I hear a familiar dull chopping noise do I open my eyes.

I should just run in and not say that it was his fault, because then it would be too bad for . . . I cannot hear if he says "you" or "me". His voice is drowned out by another that is shouting my name. Mamma with the axe. Striding through the grass and wearing an expression that warned she was expecting the worst.

"Is *she* your Mum?" he says in a strangled voice and takes a step backwards.

Did he really think that he would be able to drop me off at my house unseen? There is always someone here who will see. Mamma stares at my blood-stained T-shirt, then at Lukas and then back at the blood. Holds me so hard she seems to believe she can stop the red that is oozing from my mouth all mixed in with saliva. Pappa's father has appeared behind her and examines my mouth decisively. Says

37

that it is only a bite, admittedly right through the lip, but only a bite nevertheless, and a bite means that the teeth are fine. Children bleed a lot, they have to, he says, so it cleans the cut and prevents blood-poisoning. Mamma is not listening, just glowering darkly at Lukas as if she thinks it was he who bit me.

"Take it easy," Grandfather says. Then, turning towards Lukas, who is already on his way, "You! Hey, you're going nowhere. I want to talk to you." But there is something about him . . . the way he just defies Grandfather, throws his leg over the bicycle and sets off down the hill while Grandfather stands there, disarmed, glaring after him.

My mouth is throbbing and bleeding and has a thick taste of iron. I feel sick. Not so sick that I need to throw up, but still I bend over the burned September grass and force out a bit of school lunch so it splashes up over Grandfather's feet. It has the desired effect, they stop watching the boy, let him disappear while they look after me. Streaks of blood mingle like red worms in the grey fishy sludge. I squeeze out a few tears as well, which fall on top with ice-cold precision.

So cold that I do not recognise myself. Rather a feeling of not being able to touch the bottom, of having gone so far out into the lake and only imagined that I had something under my feet.

No, and again no.

Keep away from him.

Do what we tell you, do just what we tell you, this is not negotiable.

Up until this point I had lived surrounded by love without rules. Never a no, and then all of a sudden as many no's as there were adults in the house. The freedom to roam and do as I wished was abruptly over.

At night I cannot sleep, mental growing pains, my thoughts run in circles like flies until I fall asleep from exhaustion. Evil under the surface, winged devils, sunken laughter, the accustomed paths through my territory are full of cracks, but I am not afraid of them, what scares me is the attraction they hold.

———

He is taller than me by two heads. He can cover my hand with his so it disappears. His wrists are twice as wide. Is this the problem? I do not get a proper answer from Mamma. On the other hand, I can spit much further than he can; Mamma's sister Katja, my instructor in superior spitting techniques, has taught me how to spit and how to kiss. When it comes to holding our breath underwater, it is a draw. It is true, when we are standing in the sun, I disappear completely in his shadow and he can pee much further, I do not stand a chance in that, and when we arm wrestle as well, but he does not make a big deal of it. There are more differences than similarities, but it is the differences that please us. I should not have repeated the X-rated stories to Mamma, she immediately suspects where they come from. About the nightingales who sing most beautifully when they have had their eyes poked out. Lukas does not treat me as a child. He does not take it into account.

"I have something I want to show you," he says one day, pointing towards the forest of the bats on the other side of the lake. For me the forest is still just a dark silhouette further away than I have ever been. A boundary, beyond which I cannot imagine what is waiting. He looks at me as if he has set a trap out there or discovered a secret grave or an abandoned fox cub we can tame.

"Come on." I am stubborn, but Lukas will not give in. "You'll like this, I promise." I do not think much of his promises, but I let myself be persuaded in the end. I am able to ride on his pannier rack until the greenery becomes too dense, then we hide the bicycle in a blackthorn thicket and continue on foot. I follow his white T-shirt through the almost impenetrable foliage, a guide leading the way across the rugged terrain of pungent giant caraway and scrubby bay willow. An oppressive heat that forces your eyes out of their sockets. Sometimes I lose sight of him and I have to stop and listen.

Halfway we have to pass through the dead part of the forest. I have never set foot here before, even with him. Lukas comes to a halt, before taking a first step in amongst the silver-grey trunks. A sense that the ground under the leafless trees is poisoned. I grip his top and hold on tightly as I follow him. The naked elms, ghostlike in death, will be easy victims if there is a bad storm. Lukas nimbly dodges the huge skin-coloured moths between the stumps, I stick close behind him to shield myself. Even before we have made it through I start thinking that we will have to go back that way as well, before darkness sweeps in over the lake.

After the dead forest the vegetation becomes thick once again, a sweet and indefinable scent of wilderness. In the midst of the undergrowth there is a large enclosure with guinea fowl, forgotten, no-one seems to have passed this way for a long time. Lukas wants to release them, but he cannot open the iron grille. Scared by our presence they flap against the wire netting in a hopeless attempt at flight. We move on and there it is, overgrown and camouflaged by nature – the house Lukas found when he was trying to keep out of his father's way. The pearl fisher's house.

*

He needs me. Someone small and flexible has to climb in through the broken window to open the door from the inside. I shake my head.

"Yes, Lo."

"No way." Not for anything.

"Sweets?" I hesitate, is there anything I would not do for sweets? Negotiation has begun. Lukas lifts me up at the window, it looks like a horror film in there. Curtains of cobwebs, a rank smell of mould, darkness locked in long ago. I refuse.

There is a dead body in there. There must be. Otherwise how could the key be on the inside? Lukas cannot answer that, instead he brings out a bag of cough sweets, prepared for me to be awkward. Still no. Not so difficult, cough sweets taste horrible. He takes a bubblegum out of his other pocket. I shake my head firmly. He holds out a whole handful. Nope. Then he produces the entire bag. When it comes to bubblegum, I am weak, and why should he not take advantage of that? However much I go on about it, Mamma never lets me have any because it always ends up getting stuck in my hair. I snatch the bag and, with my mouth full of bubbles, I begin to wriggle in through the opening Lukas has lifted me up to. I scrape my back and whimper, but Lukas just pushes me forward. Too late to change your mind now, he says, I have already stuffed three pink pieces of gum into my mouth, so now I have to keep my side of the bargain.

As soon as my feet hit the ground I hurry to unlock the door and let him in. The cobweb-curtains sway, I stay close to the open door. Stand there chewing and blowing nervous bubbles, pretending to keep watch while Lukas checks round. Things we have never seen before and

41

cannot fathom what they are. Things we do not know if we should be frightened of or not. It takes a while before we realise that the odd-looking bits of rubbish hanging from the ceiling are dead bats that never woke up from their winter sleep.

It smells like another country in there. Not that we have ever, apart from Lukas' first dim recollections, been in another country. But we imagine it would be like this.

The house is small and dark like the innards of a clam and has been empty for so long that the hinges have rusted up and creepy-crawlies have taken over. The amount of dust, like a thick layer of radioactive fallout, indicates that no-one has set foot in here for a very long time. Traces of scampering mice and outspread wings of owls in the dust on the floor. Drifts of droppings, moths and dead wasps along the walls.

Everywhere these remarkable things on dusty cluttered shelves. Tiny skeletons of animals we do not recognise, a lacquered box with razor-sharp knives, beautifully ornate chopsticks. Ancient crumbling incense cigarettes that according to Lukas are infused with some sort of drug. That does not stop him smoking them, the sweet stench of exotic cigarettes, their strength sapped by lying forgotten for decades, but still with the power to intoxicate, at least enough to make him spew in the sink.

There are so many strange things to smoke, so many foreign places to make your own. This is a place made for hiding away, a refuge from curious eyes. Despite the mummified bats on the ceiling, we go there. Despite the giant ghostlike trees of coral in the windows where the spiders have spun new webs on top of old. And under the floor, no, we cannot even begin to think about what lies under the floor. The pearl fisher's forsaken loves, Lukas says.

We have heard about the pearl fisher, no-one seems to have known him but everyone knows stories about him. How he journeyed to Japan to try his luck in the pearl waters there, only to discover that the Japanese pearl fishers were all women, so much for his macho adventure.

We try to make the space our own in a clean-up operation. We sweep in a frenzy, haul out the heavy rugs and wash them in the lake, and then the Japanese quilts, which float like marbled paper in an oil bath before they fill with water and sink. Clear out the flues to the stove as well as we can and test it with a fire, unaware that we are sending smoke signals to the entire village from our secret den.

This place unnerves Lukas, and yet he wants to come here. The derelict house has something going on in its walls, something crawling and breathing, but nevertheless this is where we head for all the time. At my house there are too many people all over the place and Lukas is far from welcome. The list of objections against him is long and Mamma's patience short. Lukas' home, on the other hand, is so empty there is nowhere to hide.

Every morning I wait for him at a different spot we have decided on the night before, according to an ingenious system no-one would be able to discern a pattern in – just as the points in a constellation resemble nothing unless you already know what they are supposed to represent. Sometimes I wait under the wrong tree or behind the wrong greenhouse, dovecote, garage, in the wrong out-of-the-way spot by the lake. But he always finds me in the end. The village is not very big.

*

Below the pearl fisher's house we can bathe without being seen, concealed by a dense thicket of waterside trees. The land around the lake is covered in a thick growth of bay willows, water plantains and wild angelica shielding us from view on all sides. As long as no-one comes up close we will not be discovered. You have to be careful not to become entangled in the plants growing wild underwater. They seize hold of your legs and hold you down under the surface. The water snakes. The slow-swimming adders.

Mamma is looking out of the window. She has done this the whole time we have been sitting in the empty classroom that smells of glue, book dust, mother's sweat.

"There must have been a mistake."

"I don't think so," the teacher says coldly.

I say nothing. Make an effort to sit still even though I can see out of the corner of my eye that the door is ajar. There is a way out, a means of escape at any rate.

"A misunderstanding," Mamma tries again.

"The only misunderstanding here," the teacher says slowly, "is Lo's."

Difficult to sit still on the sweat-slippery stool but I try at least not to look provocative, because provocative is what the teacher calls me and is something she cannot stand. When I asked Pappa what it meant, all I could grasp was that it was something you should not be.

"Not at your age," he said. "You can wait a while for that."

"We have never had a first-year playing truant before. But this . . ." – the teacher performs a peculiar wriggle of her upper body in an attempt to adjust her bra unobtrusively – ". . . young lady does it like a fully fledged high-school student."

Mamma's gaze rests somewhere out in space, I look at the teacher, who in turn looks at Mamma. No-one's eyes meet, and it is best if it stays that way.

"I think Lo has totally misunderstood what compulsory school attendance means. Do you know what compulsory school attendance means in Sweden?" Without taking her eyes off Mamma, she directs the question at me. I shake my head. "No. There you are. Just as I thought."

"But for goodness' sake, she's only seven," Mamma objects weakly.

"That's what I'm saying," the teacher replies. "If you play truant like this at the age of seven . . . then it can only get worse. There are *statistics* to prove it."

Accusing blue eyes in the stale air of the classroom. I look at the teacher who looks at Mamma who looks at a crow who is sitting high up on the frame of the swing.

"You and your husband had better make clear to your daughter what's important. Otherwise there's no point in her making an appearance here for the rest of the term. Her unpredictable presence just unsettles the rest of the class. In the autumn perhaps we will let her start the year again." The crow lifts its tail, shits, screeches and flies away.

"Well," says Mamma, as if this was a sign, "in that case we'll go. Come on, darling, I've got an appointment at the hairdresser's in a minute." But no-one is going to escape so easily. The teacher wants to talk to Mamma alone. "Lo stays here," says Mamma, not wanting to be left alone with the teacher.

"No she does *not*," says the teacher. All that remains is for me to leave.

That Mamma has already lost is obvious by her humiliated silence. As I slide off the sweaty plastic seat it makes an embarrassing noise. Just want escape from the classroom with its bad feeling and lack of oxygen, out to Lukas who is probably prowling around outside like a criminal. He is the one they are going to talk about now. He is the one who has made me into a fully fledged truant at such a tender age, that is the last thing I hear the teacher say before I race along the corridor and out to freedom.

Lukas is sitting on the fence between the playgrounds, idling away the time. The older children are not allowed to enter the area for primary children, so he is sitting there without letting his feet touch the forbidden ground. The tractor tyre smells of burned rubber, I spin round and round on it until the heavy chains creak.

"Come on," he says, but I have just finished spinning and cannot stand up. When I bend my head backwards the clouds above me are sucked together in a swirl.

I know that they can see us through the window. You are going to get into so much bother, I am thinking, and maybe I say it aloud, because Lukas suddenly looks as though I have struck him across the mouth, although it was meant as a warning and not as a threat.

"Who has hit you?" I usually ask when I can see that it has happened again. One should not ask, but I am just a child and so I do. Lukas on the other hand is old enough to know that it is best not to answer. Anything you say can be used against you. At school no-one seems to have the courage or the desire to touch him, so it is not difficult to work out where the bruises come from.

*

46

"Lukas is twice your age, why aren't you with your classmates?" the teacher had asked while we sat waiting for Mamma, who was late for the meeting.

"But they're *children*," I exclaimed.

"Yes, but little one, so are you." Perhaps. But I have never seen it that way. The first thing I felt when I came to school was shock – thrown in among my peers, in the midst of a pack of wild dogs, all snapping at each other's legs. Compared to them, Lukas felt the same age and less intimidating.

He was old enough to go into year seven that year, but he had been moved back two years, a hard nut to crack, they could not put him in the special class for maladjusted children since he was not a trouble-maker – it would have been easier if he had been a troublemaker. Fighting at break-time, cheeky to the teachers, if he had had any obvious problems, difficulty sitting still, for example, but no, he has no trouble whatsoever with that. Sits absolutely still on the bench, does not move a muscle, regrettably he does not move his pen either and never puts up his hand. Cannot learn a thing. At home, perhaps, but what he learns at home is of no use when he comes to school.

When Mamma eventually comes out, her curry-coloured towelling tank top is sweaty under the arms and her eyes are dull with migraine. Takes an unopened packet of cigarettes from her shoulder bag although she stopped smoking ages ago. Summons me to her with a single glance. Lukas has slipped into the shadows and cannot be seen. Not a word from Mamma as we pedal home, she is in front, slipping slightly from side to side on the seat of her jeans, as the bicycle is adjusted for Pappa's mother. Mamma is tall, but Grandmother is taller. And I am small and at the moment I am trying to make myself smaller. From now on I have to toe the line, do as I am told, no more no less, not cause more awkward meetings. Next time it will be the headmistress, the teacher had warned.

Crisis meeting in the kitchen, everyone has to be there apart from me. Unaccustomed to closed doors, I wail and kick at it until Pappa's brother Rikard, who as a rule is always on my side, comes out and picks me up in both arms, carries me away and flings me onto the television sofa.

"Stay!" he hisses, as if I were a dog now as well. If that is how he wants it ... I think, and try to bite his hand, but Rikard pushes me over as if I were weightless. "Don't move an inch," he warns, "and I don't ever want to hear that Lukas' name again." I have never seen him like this before, I sit still out of sheer surprise and feel the blood pounding in my ears.

Mamma is also changed. A different tone. The difference between blank shots and live ones.

"I love you, Lo, but not when you lie."

"I don't lie!"

"Not when you lie, I said." She punishes me in the worst possible way – by withdrawing her love. Does not comfort me when I begin to cry.

"You should beware of lies, they are dangerous. Little caterpillars that lie never get any wings."

"I'm not a caterpillar!"

"No wings, Lo, just think about it."

———

Lukas had arrived in the village the year before I was born. He could remember almost nothing about his life before this, and what I had done with my time before I met him – that part of my life had already faded from my memory.

"Why are you so dark? When all the others are so fair?" he asked. "Where do you really come from?" He thinks it is unfair that he is the one called darkie, when I am the dark one of the two of us. In summer his hair is bleached until it is nearly blond, it is just his eyes and his name and the fact that everybody knows. My origins are just as distant as his, but only on a map. It is not completely true that all the others are fair – in every class there are children belonging to the Greek workers, with names as long as the night goods train. But those children have each other. They are obvious, belong together, keep together.

Our home is not here, but the most important thing is that it exists. It is a conviction we help one another to sustain. Since neither of us knows what it looks like where we really belong, we can imagine these places how we want. Sometimes they merge together into one. I have never been where my family comes from and Lukas has no memories of where he was born, on the outskirts of Budapest, only a few hazy details out of context. A blue glove, warm bread, a fox in a trap, blood in the snow, one or two words from a nursery rhyme or a swearword, he is not sure. Unsorted, unusable moments, a sensation in the stomach, mouth, nose, not really a smell or a taste, just a vague feeling.

At his house they never speak about what they have left behind. Have no language in common, his Pappa has mastered only rudimentary Swedish and Lukas even less Hungarian, just the very simplest of phrases. Such silence between them at the meal table, they have never

49

spoken to each other, scarcely know each other, father and son, two wastelands.

Lukas does not go near my house, knows that he is not welcome. Instead every day is filled with lies for his sake.

Beware, Mamma says. Boy's eyes, boy's hands, boy's smell. Love and the other lies. Especially love, whose poison is like a snake's, goes straight to the heart with no time to cause pain, suddenly you are lost. I always wondered who she had cherished with that sort of love.

Karenina

My Mamma with seashells in her ears, no make-up, her long body constantly moving, sweat glistening at her armpits, narrow waist, broad bottom, flared Lee jeans, strappy platform clogs. I loved her as a capricious wind that comes and goes to suit itself. It was Rikard who taught me to cycle, Marina who taught me to swear, Lukas who taught me to swim and roll cigarettes, Katja who taught me kissing and long-distance spitting, Grandmother Idun who taught me to paint my lips and click my fingers to "My Funny Valentine". Mamma taught me nothing. Not even to look out for all the things she was afraid of.

She did not turn me away, but was merely out of reach the whole time, even when we were together. A perfectly normal mother except that she smoked Silk Cut that you could only buy on the ferries over to Denmark. Pappa was also quite normal apart from the fact that he could walk on water, however thin the ice was.

Together they made up a sacred circle of four: Idun and Björn, Anna and Aron. Grew up together, always lived together, before the children, with the children, with the tar-boiling, hay-making, forest, mine, railway. When my parents and their brothers and sisters were teenagers and Pappa's father had the idea for the long move south, the two families did even this together. Everything they owned was packed up in the same way they lived: mixed together and shared, secure and cramped.

They bought the place unseen – the house by the undulating Skåne field, the largest they could find that was fairly reasonable. The houses were twice the price of those in the north, which Grandfather Björn took as a sign of what a promised land the south really was. Not cheap, but promised.

And so it came about that all their savings were suddenly tied up in a place they had never even seen. In addition they had been obliged to take out a loan so big that Grandfather Aron could not sleep at night. He had never been in debt to anyone before, had been brought up that way and thought of it almost as a sin. To buy a house unseen, that was madness . . . madness, according to Grandmother Idun. She was usually the one who made the decisions, but not this time, otherwise it would not have happened. The idea that they should move was Björn's, the man she loved for his ideas, but he did not usually carry them out – this time was different, he said, the children's future.

Before they packed up their joint van-load of furniture and set off on the two-thousand-kilometre journey south, someone had to go on ahead and reconnoitre. The house had to be renovated, but they did not know how much needed to be done. None of the sons could take time off to accompany Björn, instead it was my Mamma Katarina who volunteered. Björn was doubtful, but Grandmother Idun persuaded him. Katarina was as strong as their own boys and besides she was the most practical of the youngsters, it was just a case of setting her to work, she was used to lending a hand.

Idun had spoken. And so it was.

*

The train across the country took a day and a night. Neither Grandfather nor Mamma had travelled so far before. He had been involved in laying tracks, but had never actually made a train journey anywhere. And neither of them had the faintest notion that where they were going to move to was so tremendously far away. He had wanted to travel alone. Why had Idun insisted? They sat in silence all the way down to the Västerbotten border, then Mamma fell asleep, fortunately. With her head against his shoulder, which embarrassed him slightly, but at least he was relieved that the silence between them had a natural cause.

The house was far from what he had imagined. If this was what they called "in need of renovation", then they had entirely different standards down here. A cellar of standing height rather than a crawl space. Extremely well insulated with proper synthetic material, not just air gaps and sawdust. Björn went from room to room and breathed in the feeling of newness. Modern materials and kinds of wood that smelled different. A dining room . . . that was a word to savour – redolent of punch. Big enough for them all to be able to eat together for the first time, as long as they bought a larger table. Fitted carpets in the bedrooms so numerous that they would not have to sleep more than two to a room. The ground floor the size of a small cathedral. Practical, ceilings high enough even for Björn, Idun and their tall sons. Massive double-glazed windows that let in so much light, not what they were used to: temporary secondary glazing that always misted up in winter.

Björn opened the window onto the garden and flicked out the flies lying sluggish and well-fed on the sill. He had never seen fatter flies.

And there it was – the arboretum – the reason he had fallen for this particular house. The impressive collection of exotic trees, at least they were exotic to him, born beyond the tree line. They spread out coquettishly in front of him. A Garden of Eden. Paradise.

Katarina following at his heels, just as dumbfounded, went to stand next to him at the open window. He wanted . . . to say something, but he was speechless. It was not like him to be so weak and sentimental. Perhaps because he had taken off his shoes and was barefoot like a child. When he had had the chance for the first time in his life to experience the feel of a fitted carpet between his toes, he had unlaced his boots and let his big white foot sink into the unresisting softness. He really did want to say something. Something that was worthy of the situation, but he could not. And it did not help that she stood there so close to him, her sandals kicked off too, her hand raised. She held her slender brown hand before her like a delicate and exotic leaf, as if trying to touch the magnificent arboretum from a distance. He hoped she understood what a kingdom he laid at her feet.

This was what all their children deserved. They had not grown up in luxury and affluence, far from it, but the future was theirs, he promised her. As far as he knew all the children had originated in the warm flour-smelling bakehouse, at the side of the house that the families had rented together for many years. So was it chance or delusions of grandeur that made them choose regal names for their firstborn? But who has a greater right to cherish dreams than those who possess nothing, had not he and Idun always dreamed of being able to give their eldest son Erik all this? And Anna and Aron had undoubtedly held the same hope for their Katarina.

There she was now, Katarina, like a vestige of the old in the midst of the new. It must have been to do with the change in the light. Something that rendered her a little like a queen, looking out over the new landscape as if in two minds whether it was worth conquering or not. An ice-queen, coldly distant, or maybe just exhausted after twenty-four hours on the train. Her scent of birch and melting snow. Surrounded by the unfamiliar, she smelled of home.

"Queen Katarina," he laughed. She had not been following his thoughts and gave a start at his laugh. Watchful, looked at him as if she thought . . . that he was flattering her? Or the opposite, that he had caught her red-handed committing the mortal sin of pride – standing there, hand raised to the mirage beyond the window as if imagining that all this was hers and hers alone. Did he want to bring her back down to earth with his sarcastic "queen"? She lowered her hand, but as he glanced at her, her distinct profile was no less majestic.

"You know who you're named after, don't you?" he said. No, she did not know. Did not know who he was talking about, even though she had spent several years longer at school than he had, serving no purpose at all.

"Russia's greatest ever ruler, Catherine the Great. A conqueror." She mumbled something inaudible in reply, still suspecting that he was making fun of her, that he had picked up on her weak point, her vulner-ability, and he wanted to put her in her place so she did not get ideas. Conqueror? Why did he call her that?

It was not time to go to bed, but she had unrolled the sleeping mats and the old military sleeping bags on the floor, to serve as their beds until the furniture arrived on the van. And she had been out and bought something for them to eat and candles and a pack of beer at the grocer's shop, which was almost closer to the house than the outside privy was back home. While they ate, Björn continued to talk about Catherine the Great and she resisted the urge to ask him to listen to her instead. She had things to say too. She just had not found the right words yet.

This tsarina, who had clearly made a big impression upon him, had conquered vast territories on Russia's account. She had three children by three different men, presumably none of whom was her husband – she had simply had him assassinated after he had been crowned regent and then she took the throne herself and reigned for another thirty years over her huge empire, Björn related, opening another beer.

They had come to a promised land, everything would be better here, he assured her, as they sat in their makeshift sleeping quarters with the military sleeping bags, it was just like during the war, only without the war. What did he mean, "everything", she wondered, she did not think there was anything wrong with their life at home. What were they lacking?

"Light, warmth and hopes for the future, Katarina, for a start . . ." A winter in Skåne is as short and mild as a holiday – without the temperate winter there would be no arboretum.

"What's an arboretum?" she asked.

"It's a tree-universe," he said. "A universe of trees." That evening they went in for the first time, among the tall trunks that made even Björn look small, despite his stature.

*

They fell asleep and awoke in a different state of happiness, but with the same feeling of elation. He rose quickly to see if the arboretum was still outside the window. It had not been a dream, the trees were where they should be, all the different species he had never seen before and whose names he did not know.

The house needed no work, they could take some time off, relax, bask in the sun for the remainder of the time until the others came down from the north. The only thing they had to do was to buy a scythe to cut the grass and buy a good book on trees so that they could guide the others around the grounds, point out sugar maples, black poplars, empress trees, everything that was now theirs. Björn had thought they had bought a house at great expense, now it turned out they had acquired a paradise for next to nothing.

Jubilant, he lifted the newly awakened Katarina as if she were a slender birch pole and waltzed her round the room with long jerky steps.

She weighed nothing. A tiny waist like Idun's before the five children. He could have danced with her until darkness settled over the fertile fields of early summer, if she had not been so dizzy that she crumpled into a laughing heap on the floor. A princess on a pea in a punch-scented dream about a proper house. Her clearwater gaze. He felt young himself, was laughing too, it had been a long time, but he could not help it when he looked at Katarina sitting with glowing cheeks. Shy all of a sudden, even though she was the boldest of the four girls, more like Idun than her own mother. Her blue skirt had ridden up in the careless movements of the dance and she tugged at it. Such recklessness. There must be something in this new world that was making them like this. Intoxication that went straight to the senses, bypassing reason. The air was already pulsing with cow dung and buttercups whilst at home winter was scarcely over. If anyone could see them now . . . They would think that the buttercups, the cow dung, the change of air, idling about like this, sleeping like vagabonds until late in the morning, the shift from late winter to early summer, all of this had gone to their heads. Decompression sickness. The danger of stepping too quickly into the light. Giddiness. Blinding.

He was unaccustomed to it. Perhaps that was all. He had never been alone with any of the girls and now they were almost adults, especially Katarina, at seventeen the eldest. A young Idun, tall, strong, lucently fair, her skin like birch. Powerful arms. Strong neck. Cold eyes. Like morning water, he thought. The sensation of waking up too quickly when you plunged into her gaze. He had always sobered up when he looked into Idun's eyes. But Katarina's eyes did not have the same effect on him, they made him confused, not clear-headed.

Idun was the same as ever, only not quite so translucent and her strength had passed into a kind of heaviness. He did not lie when he said that he loved her more with every child. But differently. Because Idun *had* changed, for her each child was a whole new experience. He did not share this feeling, for him it was just more of the same.

There were days when he wished that he remembered. He had asked her "Do you remember?" and Idun had smiled wryly and said how could she ever forget? And then he had been too ashamed to ask her to share her memory with him, however hard he tried he could not recall their first meeting – the crucial moment. Perhaps there was no crucial moment, but he imagined something, yes, against the light in a cloudberry meadow.

He remembered her forever. She had always been there, as natural as breathing, you did not think about it all the time, but you could not survive without it. Sometimes he wished he could recollect how it had been when he first fell in love with her, there were days when he really needed that memory.

Why are you telling me all this, Katarina thought, but she allowed him to continue, buttercups, cow dung, change in the air, light – something made him see her differently, she knew, indeed seeing her at all was different. Speaking to her. He had never done that before. She had the feeling that he walked round the many rooms of the new house looking for her as soon as she was out of sight. And when he disappeared into the arboretum for a long time, it was she who searched for him, she went through the trees calling his name, as if she really missed him.

The house felt immense during the time they spent alone together waiting for the two families. In order not to feel completely useless they refined the dream before the others arrived, made a few small repairs that were in fact unnecessary, took care of the vanload of furniture that had been sent on ahead. Sat on the veranda in the evening and enjoyed the calm before the storm, the absence of mosquitoes and the presence of one another, the unfamiliar smells from the arboretum of balsam poplar and eucalyptus.

"If your love is unrequited?" she said one evening when they had unrolled their sleeping bags and were just about to go to sleep. Her voice rose cautiously at the end, making the words a question. He looked at her in astonishment. What in heaven's name did she think he knew about all that? She had fallen silent and blown out the candles in the beer bottles, their only source of light here where, in contrast to home, nights in early summer were dark.

"Well, then you take the name Karenina like in a Russian novel about impossible love . . . and then you put up with it . . . until it passes," he said.

Put up with it until it passes? Was that all he had to say?

Put up with it until it passes . . .

Did he not understand? Was that really the only thing he could advise her to do? He knew nothing about Russian novels. Had just happened to see the copy of *Anna Karenina* that she was reading in the evenings and picked up the name from the back of the book. He knew nothing about anything. Unrequited love included.

Breathless

To your last breath, Lukas said. It was September and all the most important things that have happened to me have always happened in September.

We lived on the outskirts, a district that was not called anything other than the outskirts. Where the field sloped abruptly and the world came to an end. Or began, it depends, just as the lake shifted and changed the whole time. Now it had begun to take on a September colour, September was my month and at this time the water was my colour. When memory has lost its shape, colours still shine clearly. Lukas' eyes were black as river pearls, when it was cold they turned blue, the Japanese rice cooker dirty pink, the mosquito net grey from many summers' insects.

There was a strong smell of angelica in the late-summer air. The flies that had lapsed into a coma during the hottest weeks had come back to life and become annoyingly intrusive. And they buzzed round Lukas in particular.

"To your last breath," he said, but I was not so sure.

"It's dangerous," I said, a pointless objection, a lame protest, he just shrugged his shoulders at my warning.

I did not intend to stop him, nor to go with him.

"You'll have to do it yourself," I said.

"Sure. You'll never be a real man, you're too cowardly." Mild scorn in his voice and I thought maybe so, maybe he is right – or I just did not have enough desperation within me. This water was too deep for me, I would have no chance even though you could see how much the lake had shrunk in the summer heat. Anyway I did not want to be a man, I wanted to be a woman. This was what I thought, but I did not say.

I disappeared into his shadow, he had shot up that summer and I had not kept up with him. He had had an erection for several days, he said. It was as if something had locked, a mechanism that had got stuck so it was impossible to bring it down. Now he had it in his head that it would help to swim across the whole lake underwater, hold his breath and count, focus on survival. He looked at me enquiringly, but to be honest I had no idea whether it would work. Perhaps it was good to give his blood something else to do instead of collecting in one place in his body, causing problems. But he had to do it himself, with my tiny leather pouches for lungs I would sink like a stone halfway across. And his erection was hardly going to go away because I held *my* breath, was it? If we had shared the same bloodstream, but we did not. It was what he wished for, that we two should be one, we were not, just as our village was not a proper village and the lake was not a proper lake, only a place where the flow of water swelled and the river spread out, deep like a lake.

I had a rough idea how it worked, even though I did not have one of my own. It was not mechanical, as Lukas seemed to think. It was blood that made it stand straight out in his blue boxer shorts. Or possibly an evil spell as punishment for paying it too much attention, some things do not thrive on attention, that was what he used to say to me. I looked at it, as if it was an overexcited puppy that someone had played with too much.

"Don't think about, it'll go."

"I can't *not* think about it, I can *only* think about it. It hurts, don't you understand!" He had flies round his mouth and something in his eye made me feel uneasy, made me scratch away at old insect bites just to distract myself from the feeling of powerlessness, not my own, but his.

I lowered my gaze and stared at the problem. Hurts as in a sore that he has picked at? When I said that he gave me a murderous look. He reached out for me at the same moment I turned my back on him, groped in the air a second too late.

"The only sore I have is you," I thought he said, but perhaps I just imagined it, he often said that I imagined things, and now I had reached the house and opened the door that was hanging askew on its single hinge. The pearl fisher's house, our hiding place. A well-kept secret tucked away in the thick greenery by the lake.

The day had been doomed from the moment I opened my eyes and things had only got worse. Stifling when I awoke and deadly silent in the house that normally never slept. Chat, laughter, squabbling, Grandmother Anna's clatter in the kitchen, Mamma's chopping, Grandfather Björn's voice penetrating everything, my aunts' music, cars in the yard, all the familiar noises and every now and again something I did not recognise, something that made me prick up my ears and sneak closer. But this morning only quiet. As when a persistant wind suddenly abates and the silence is so palpable it can be heard, with a sound all of its own. I fumbled for Mamma and Aunt Marina on either side of the bed, although I was aware they could not be there because I could not hear them breathe.

Hello, here I am all by myself in bed and it is my birthday, I wanted to shout, but to whom? The house appeared to be deserted. I waited for the morning light to travel over the cloudberry-patterned wallpaper. When it seemed that my humiliation was complete, I rose to look for them, confront them, demand congratulations, banana cake, restore order. Went from room to room in the large house without finding a living soul. At last I heard faint sounds outside the open kitchen window, voices, muted, as if they were each talking into a plastic bag.

There was a gloomy atmosphere around the garden table. I had never been to a funeral, but it must feel like this, the air heavy to breathe. I saw in Mamma's face that something was very wrong, she had never been good at hiding things and now she was not even trying to. Sat with her legs curled under her on the cane chair, red with weeping. The others looked odd, this did not seem like a day of joy at all, a day to eat banana cake for breakfast. I had not seen Mamma's face like this since Pappa left. She was smoking, although she had stopped ages ago – no-one would forget the dramatic finale when, to prove that smoking was over forever, she had thrown out every ashtray we had in the house, including the blood-red crystal one she had been given by Pappa's father. An exaggerated gesture, and what was it worth now? It is possible to smoke without ashtrays, and she did. The saucer in front of her was piled high, despite the early hour. Pappa's sister Marina had also lit a cigarette without any protest from her mother, and Mamma's brother Isak was sitting on the back of the chair with his dirty boots on the seat, another thing no-one objected to, murmuring:

"It's bloody awful. Bloody awful, and that's a fact . . ."

I sat on the window sill, no-one taking heed of me. A wretched circus monkey in front of a miserable audience who would not even look at me. But what about *me*? I wanted to shout. It is actually my birthday today . . . we usually have banana cake . . . But the sight of Mamma filled me with a knot of anxiety that only she could evoke. Instead of saying anything I leapt through the air and landed crouching on my heels in the middle of the table. It was intended as a pleasant surprise, but Mamma did not even raise her eyes. I did not notice how the others reacted, because I only had eyes for her, all my attention directed to her half-closed eyelids and smoking mouth. She was the centre of the distress, there was no mistake about it, and it reminded me of something I did not want to be reminded of on any account.

Rikard shooed me off the table like one of the irritating flies in the September heat. Mamma lit another cigarette as Marina in one deft movement drew me to her. She held me hard and in a practised manoeuvre lifted me on to her lap, even though I had shot up that summer, all arms and legs, and could scarcely fit on her knee any longer.

"Is it something to do with Pappa?" I whispered in Marina's ear. She blew the smoke past my face and brought her lips close up:

"No, for once it's nothing to do with your Pappa. But you must leave your Mamma in peace today."

"What about the cake?" I pleaded, and she laid a finger on my lips, it stung like a nettle.

"We'll sort it out, hush, don't be such a baby."

———

The only thing to suggest that it was a group of the living and not the dead who were gathered together under the wild damson trees was the smoke from Mamma's cigarette. From a distance it looked like a séance, uncomfortably quiet, almost frozen. I observed them from my swing in the tall white birch, waiting for something to happen. No-one bothered about me, the wind was rising, the swing was squeaking – Pappa should have fixed it but he had left a long time ago and now there was no-one to repair things and make them work smoothly.

It began to feel like the garden of death, but I did not know who had died. No-one answered my questions, as if I too were talking into a plastic bag and the questions stayed inside it. I should just take the bicycle and clear off, if you were invisible, you might as well disappear. I went inside and packed the essentials, the secrets in the dust: the hunting knife, the steel guitar strings, the porn magazine, the aftershave, the cigarette, still unsmoked since the night of the fire. Took the bicycle that Pappa had left behind, it was far too big, I had to ride at a slant under the crossbar. And although it was downhill all the way along the gravel track between the fields of stubble, it was very difficult to pedal.

I used to imagine that the lake was an enormous eye, the only visible part of an even more enormous underground creature. The beautiful, terrifying giantess Hyrrokkin, who one day would rise up and surprise us all, distort our perspective, dislodge woods, factories, roe deer, houses and fields of corn, which would collapse into the crater where her body had lain, and she would just walk away. She belonged to a different and a better world, like Lukas and me, had just rested here a while and would leave devastation in her wake.

It was Pappa's father who had told me the story about Hyrrokkin. He was interested in mythological women, particularly the demonic ones with extraordinary powers: Jezebel, Lilith, the sisters Fenja and

Menja who made the sea salt-water. He liked to watch Mamma when she was chopping wood too, with her shirt-sleeves rolled up and her hair Medusa-curly with sweat, a cigarette in the corner of her mouth when she thought no-one could see her. Hyrrokkin meant smoke, Grandfather said, and I had seen smoke rising out of the earth at dawn, especially over her eye when it was turned to ice in winter. Now she was tucked up under the ground, invisible except for her mirror-like eye. You could bathe in it if you dared. It was not for the faint-hearted.

Her eye was gazing right at me, with a beguiling look that enticed me even from afar. The dark sky gave the surface of the water an uncommon metallic green shimmer. This scene bestowed on the lake that was not a lake the greatest beauty, but there was almost no-one who ever bathed here. There were rumours about people who drowned themselves and people who were drowned. I was so young I had only vaguely heard them, but I had been warned numerous times about the lake – like everything else Mamma warned me about, I did not let it seriously affect me. Lukas. Goods trains. Lies. Balls of lightning that hurtled over the fields in pursuit of the one spot to strike. Not easy to find that one point in a place where everyone made strenuous efforts not to stand out. If I ever ate chicken at someone else's house, I had to cut right to the bone to satisfy myself that it was properly cooked. Mamma had showed me how to check, I only wondered who that someone else could be, whose house I might eat in? We never mixed with anyone, only kept our own company. Thirteen people in two families, like the Taikon family, but without the fun, without the horses and music, Rikard said. Anyway, to go to someone else's house and eat chicken was a still just a dream.

*

I did not see Lukas until he emerged from the overgrown thicket by the lake. At first I did not recognise him, he was wearing the same expression as Mamma. Who died, I asked. It must be someone Lukas knew, judging by his wretchedness.

"Dead? What are you talking about?" he said with a grimace.

His erection. It hardly explained the funereal atmosphere at home, but did account for his pained expression. It had been like this for days and was not a laughing matter . . . he sounded more disgusted than triumphant, although under normal circumstances such a thing would not trouble him. He took his hands away from his crotch, and, as if I looked disbelieving, he made a pointed gesture.

"See for yourself!" All he was wearing was his shorts, and they had an alarming bulge.

"Will you feel it? It's sick." I shook my head.

"To hell with it then," he muttered, "maybe you don't believe me . . ." I did believe him, saw his desperation, I was ten years old and yet I knew more than he did about certain things, despite his sixteen years. Unlike Lukas, I had someone to ask, he had to discover everything by himself. However he did sometimes play up his lack of understanding to diminish the age difference between us.

"Can't it be emptied?" I asked cautiously.

Lukas pulled an exasperated face: "I've tried that."

"That's not what I mean, I mean empty it of blood."

He looked at me with a mixture of distaste and consternation. As far as I was aware it was blood that made it stand up and so emptying it was perhaps the only way. He shook his head, sceptical.

"Blood's all connected up together in the body, it's just one

68

system, like, one single lot of blood . . . You can't empty one part of your body without emptying the rest. You'd bleed to death."

For all I knew he might be right, but his own tactic sounded just as dangerous: to swim the whole length of the lake under-water without coming up for breath once. You can breathe in your imagination, he maintained, right up to your very last breath, for there is always a last breath, even in your mind.

After a while he entered the pearl fisher's house, where I was stretched out on the bed waiting for him to think better of it. I was far more concerned about him diving right into Hirrokkin's eye than about his erection, which after all could not last forever.

He found my hastily packed canvas bag next to the bed.

"Have you run away from home? Couldn't you have brought something to eat?" he said, as he rummaged through the contents, flicked through the porn magazine and then fished out the holy cigarette from our first meeting, and before I had time to open my mouth, he picked up a lighter and lit it . . . it burned like tinder.

"And what the hell are we going to do now?" he said and blew the smoke hard at the ceiling. I shrugged my shoulders.

"Dunno. It's my birthday, but why should we worry about that?"

"I mean, what are we going to do about this?" In a forced manner he indicated towards his stubbornly swollen prick – there were many words for it but prick was the ugliest and most ridiculous and Lukas said it all the time, which gave me the feeling that he did not like it.

After searching among the books under the bed I found an old medical book that I had looked in many times before. I blew off the dust and opened it at a page with pictures that looked as though we could be on the right track. Lying on my back I read it silently to myself first and then out loud for him:

"Erectile dysfunction." I raised my eyebrows questioningly, but Lukas was stamping up and down on the spot and appeared not to have heard of it.

"Priapism?" I carried on.

"Uh, I don't understand a single word of this stupid language, get to the explanation."

"Urological emergency," I continued to spell out. I had always been a good reader, even when I had no notion what it was about.

"But skip that bit, get to the point – further down, further down ..." I let my eye skim over the text. Lukas' mouth was twisted in torture, as if his condition from one moment to the next had become unbearable.

"Prolonged and painful erection not caused by sexual arousal. The causes for this condition may include: leukaemia, psychoactive drugs, anabolic steroids, recreational drugs such as alcohol and cocaine, protracted sexual activity, a burst artery in the scrotum ... scrotum?"

"Yes. Don't know. Haven't a clue," he looked pale and signalled to me to carry on.

". . . bite from a black-widow spider, tumour, carbon monoxide poisoning, spinal cord injury or lacking diagnosable cause. The problems are due to blood trapped in the erectile tissue. An erection lasting more than four hours is deemed to be a medical emergency."

Lukas was no longer complaining, he nodded at me to read on.

"Four hours, it says. How long did you say it's been like this?"

"Days, on and off," he said staunchly.

"*Days?*"

"Yes, for a while it seemed to be getting better, but then it got worse again."

"But listen: the condition requires immediate medical attention, to prevent scar formation that could result in permanent inability to maintain an erection." I looked at him as he stood in front of me, legs wide apart, with the face of a maniac.

"Immediate medical attention, it says here. Doesn't that mean . . . today?" I traced down the page with my finger, searching for the answer: "Treatment involves draining the blood by inserting a needle into the penis."

"Aagh!" Lukas looked as though he was trying to cast off something that had scalded him, but his hands were empty and it was a pitiful, disembodied gesture.

"The area is numbed with local anaesthetic and the blood is drawn off from . . ."

"No thanks!"

". . . from the erectile tissue until the swelling goes down."

"Can you stop!"

"Wait. There's an alternative: ice can be put on the perineum to reduce the swelling. Perineum? What's that? Well, you can put ice on it anyway. Climbing stairs is sometimes effective as the exercise can send the blood flow to other parts of the body."

"Shut up now," he groaned and sank to the floor, but I kept on reading.

"In serious cases prolonged accumulation of the blood can lead to necrosis, spontaneous tissue death, gangrene. Fully developed gangrene cannot be cured. In cases of dry gangrene the affected tissue falls off of its own accord. In cases of wet gangrene the affected area must be amputated, i.e. a surgical removal of the penis, known as penectomy."

Lukas' face turned pale green, with his hands at his crotch he stood up and backed out of the room, moaning.

Stairs and ice – he had no choice.

———

Mamma had warned me about Lukas ever since the fire in the village. He was not welcome in our home, preferably not to be seen at all in my vicinity. But there were no stairs at his house and no freezer with ice either, so we had to get into our house unseen. While I made sure it was safe, he started to race up and down the steep stairs between the cellar and the floor above.

"This feels like . . ." he looked as though he would be prepared to have it amputated after all, ". . . a sadistic joke," I caught him say on the way down.

"But is it working?" I asked impatiently.

No-one trusted him, and now he was running up and down our stairs half-naked and could be discovered at any moment, but it was this or a needle in his penis, that was the choice. I saw his lean sun-tanned back disappear up the stairs. A back I knew so well and yet it often seemed so unfamiliar, as changeable as his face. When his height increased, out of control, last spring, his body had not managed to adjust its proportions. He was in disharmony with everything, as if there was no longer enough room in his body, as if he had stretched out rather than grown. Become a tall thin shadow of himself, almost worse than Pappa the last summer before he left.

*

"How does it feel?"

"Sore."

"But has it got softer?" I asked next time he passed me as I stood on guard on the landing. He thrust his hand down to see.

"Has it hell."

Ice was now his only hope. If the stairs were hard work, the ice was humiliating. Lukas was doubtful, but in the absence of ice cubes I had already fetched two bags of frozen mushrooms and stood in the food cellar with them dangling from my hands. He took off his trousers, I told him to put them on again, it would be cold enough without putting them directly on his skin. It would be no consolation if he brought it down and it suffered frostbite in the process.

"O.K., but I'm doing it myself," he said dismissively, jumped on to the freezer, frowning with pain, and accepted the packets of mushrooms.

It was probably the thought of the penis amputation that helped him to endure – shame and ignominy, as well as pain. The cold appeared to aggravate his suffering instead of relieve it. Like cures like, was Rikard's standard response when something had to be remedied. He had for a long time wanted to be a boxer, but he had such thin skin, his eyebrows could not take it. The boxer knows nothing of the dancer's pain and the dancer knows nothing of the boxer's discipline, he claimed, you should respect what you do not understand. Like now, how it was feeling for Lukas. I could see that it was hurting, diabolically, but perhaps that was a good sign, if Rikard's cure logic was correct. We did not have time to think it over, we just had to try and see.

To begin with nothing happened, time passed and still nothing happened, and then . . . to speed up the proceedings Lukas pulled down his shorts and put the deep-frozen bags of mushrooms right on his crotch.

With that Marina arrived.

She was suddenly standing there in the cellar door, carrying an armful of hammock cushions rescued from the unexpected cloudburst, staring at us. The rain had made her mimosa-yellow cotton top see-through, one of her breasts was larger than the other, she was wearing nothing underneath and I was struck by how remarkably like Pappa she was, apart from the breasts. I had never noticed it before, but with her medium length hair now wet and pushed back off her face she was so like him that I gasped.

Mamma was upset when Pappa left, but his sister Marina was the one who was angry. How she shrieked at him in the kitchen. Marina's screaming was the most terrifying of all the things that happened at that time.

Now with a violent push she threw the cushions aside and snatched for a weapon. That turned out to be a vacuum cleaner hose, an old-fashioned chrome model, lethal. Without a word she raised it up towards Lukas, in attack or in defence, it was impossible to say. The bags of frozen mushrooms slipped from Lukas' hands on to the stone floor with a muffled sound. His shorts were still hanging round his ankles as he sat and tried to take in what was happening, the iron pipe, the expression on Marina's face . . . If I could have moved, I would have pulled them up, but I was just as transfixed.

All the evil energy in the room was directed towards Lukas, she did not even look at me, just made a vague gesture that I should move away from him. But I could not.

"I haven't done anything," he said. You only put soap on hands that are dirty, as the saying goes in my family. Marina . . . I saw the chrome pipe gleam in the light from the fluorescent strip when she swung it round in the air to build up speed. She was going off the rails, she must be. Hyrrokkin had drawn herself up to her full height.

Instead of covering his penis, which was still standing straight up, embarrassingly swollen, Lukas raised his arms to cover his face. As if he seriously did think that she would hit him. She would never do that. Even if she *was* losing control. Not Marina . . . was the thought in my head the second before she did it. Hard. Right at Lukas' face with an awful thud. A shrill sound like the call of a bird of prey escaped from my lips. He groaned softly. If he had not been so used to protecting himself at home the blow would have knocked him to the floor. The sound of the metal against his armpits was harsh and very painful.

While she was reloading her iron pipe he finally seemed to grasp the seriousness of his predicament, jumped down from the freezer, pulling up his shorts on the way and, crouching, started to move towards the open door, to the garden and freedom. The torrential rain outside almost drowned his voice as he rattled off what sounded like a stream of accusations and apologies. Marina was standing in his way. Let him go, I was thinking, just let him go . . . afraid of what he might do otherwise. But she looked more furious than scared, blocked the doorway, raised the shining chrome pipe towards him again. Capable of anything at all, it seemed, as if she really was someone else.

When he, with the speed of a fighting dog, grabbed hold of the vacuum cleaner tube, I saw the fear in her eyes. Marina had never been hit before, Lukas was used to it. When the shock of the surprise attack had subsided, she would soon lose the assailant's advantage.

Mamma's sister Katja had explained about the use of sound

75

cannons to disperse rioting crowds, they were as effective as water cannons, and now I climbed up on the freezer and yelled as loud as I could in an attempt to defuse the menacing situation. Lukas had just succeeded in wrenching the weapon out of Marina's hands and lifted it up towards her to gain free access to the door, when Pappa's brother Erik appeared in it with Katja immediately behind him. Without waiting to take in what had happened, they overpowered him. Suddenly it all unfolded like an unreal film: Lukas on his knees on the concrete floor with Erik on top of him, a hard kneecap in the small of his back, it looked horrible and quite unnecessary as Lukas was completely still.

"Are you O.K.?" Marina nodded in reply to Erik's question. I wanted to say that it was *she* who had hit *him*, even though it was Lukas who happened to be holding the weapon when they came in, but I dared not open my mouth, suddenly felt very sick. When everything was quiet in the room, a musty odour of half-thawed mushrooms mixed with mouldy winter-apples and caustic soda from the adjoining laundry room filled the air.

The chrome pipe was a side of Marina she had never revealed before.

"Take him up to the kitchen," she said, and without demanding a word of explanation Katja and Erik obeyed her command. Lukas offered no resistance when they pulled him roughly away.

Leaning against the freezer, Marina gasped for breath. Looked as though she was trying to find herself again, after she had been lost, or perhaps she had actually for a while been changed into somebody else. A stranger had possessed her body, that must have been what happened.

"Lo . . ." she began, but broke off and started to pull at her top that was so yellow it almost smelled of mimosa. It was hopelessly out of shape, she could not straighten it, Lukas had pulled it to one side when he tried to disarm her. One of the seams was torn and it had the mark of his hand on the front between her breasts.

"You're coming with me. Now!" she ordered and dragged me up the stairs.

Mamma was sleeping. We had to tiptoe around the house and there was no opportunity for a noisy interrogation in the kitchen.

"What's wrong with Mamma? Who's died?" I asked.

"Jean Seberg," Erik said. Who? Was it someone we knew? But he was not listening, he stood by the sink unit holding Lukas in a harsh grip and said that we were going to take this matter to Lukas' father. And *that*, he intimated, was just the beginning.

No, not Lukas' Pappa, not Gábriel, to drag him into it . . . my family had no idea.

———

There was one other place where I belonged, a place I could disappear to whenever I wanted to. A snow kingdom far away, vast, imposing, silent, desolate, wild. A landscape where there was only one season with a short interruption for a summer soon over. Completely different from here, where the past was overlaid and obliterated by the oppressive scent of growth, stagnant heat, flies, the lake's jade-green eye staring unceasingly at us.

Escorted by Pappa's brother Erik and sister Marina we walked down the gravel track to Lukas' house in deathly silence. The late summer sun going down over the fields, on the day that never had been a birthday. I thought all along that Lukas would run off, since Erik was no longer holding on to him, but sooner or later he would have to come home, so what was the point.

The person they said had died – the whole time I was thinking of her – was the only one who could have saved us from this. If the others, like Mamma, had been more concerned about her death and less about Lukas and me, we would have got away with it. They would not have had the energy to turn everything upside down, as if a disaster had befallen us in our food cellar.

No-one in my family apart from me had ever been in Lukas and Gábriel's house. I tried to say that it was no use talking to Lukas' Pappa as he could not speak Swedish, but they thought I was trying to help Lukas out of fear. I was – but not because I was afraid of him, I was afraid of what was going to happen to him. *Anything you say can be used against you.* Lukas must have had that line in his head, because he did not say a single word in his defence.

"Say something!" I whispered to him.

"It's better," he mouthed and nodded in the direction of his crotch.

"Something else. To them. Lukas . . . Please . . ." But he just shook his head. It was futile, who would believe that story?

It had passed, his stubborn erection, but what help was that when one problem just led to another? To be caught red-handed, instant evidence, that was all my family was waiting for. Proof that he was anything but an innocent friend, that what had seemed fairly harmless about him when he was thirteen, had grown into something danger-ous now he was sixteen. We were eyed with suspicion the whole time, we could never relax, our games became an act and that took away the pleasure, took the playfulness out of playing. If neither of us let go, we would both sink. To the last breath, I recalled the phrase now, it came from a film that ended with one person betraying the other, I had never really understood why.

Gábriel stood in the door and watched us approach.

"*I'd like to live in Mexico. I hear it's so lovely,*" I whispered, to ease the tension. Lukas laughed. A clipped dry laugh. Erik gave him a shove, as if to emphasise that soon he would not be laughing, he could be sure of that.

The bruises on Lukas' body were the only testimony to his father, otherwise he was seldom seen. Sometimes on his way to or from work with his bicycle, or when he made repairs to the house, affected by rot; it was so close to the water that the floors were always damp, just like in the pearl fisher's house. Once in a while he would sit on the wooden porch and watch the kites or turn on his radio, tuned in to wavelengths we did not understand.

"*I'm a real scumbag. . .* " Lukas whispered out of the corner of his mouth as we slowly neared his house.

"*What does 'scumbag' mean?*" I whispered back. He laughed again and received another irritated push, this time from Marina:

"You bloody well *won't* laugh, do you hear?" she hissed.

In the final scene of the film "Breathless" the man is running, shot in the back, the bloodstain spreading across his white shirt, until he collapses. She is behind him – she who has informed on him to the police, in spite of love. It is silent when he falls, just the look on her face as she bends over him, watching him die in the street. "I'm a scumbag," he says, before closing his eyes with one hand and drawing his last breath. "What did he say?" bewildered, she asks the policeman who has just shot him. "He said: 'You're a scumbag'," says the policeman. Then – her empty gaze into the camera: "What does 'scumbag' mean?" before she turns away and the screen turns black.

What the final scene was actually about, I could not understand. Loyalty, guilt, but how they related to each other . . . Now at any rate I felt like her, traitor and executioner in one, as if I had hauled Lukas up the steps where Gábriel had just opened the door and looked questioningly at his son. How do you measure silence? It was so quiet you could hear the clouds moving above us. Until Gábriel said something in his own language. Lukas' hand made a vain gesture towards the cigarettes in his pocket, something he often did when he felt under pressure, but he was only wearing those threadbare shorts. He looked as though he was freezing, held his arms round his body.

"What did he say?" I whispered.

"I don't know. He always talks like that when he's angry," Lukas said under his breath so only I could hear.

———

"Do you sleep with a lot of men?"

"Not so many."

"How many?"

I hold up seven fingers. "How about you?"

"Me?" Lukas sounds surprised at being asked.

Gestures quickly with the fingers of one hand . . . twenty-two.

The bedroom scene in "Breathless" was my favourite. It was best to do it with the hat and the cigarette too. We had to manage with Grandfather

Björn's old Stetson. Jean Seberg playfully tried on Jean-Paul Belmondo's gangster hat, while he lay on the bed smoking. Lukas said that I had Jean Seberg's dimples. Her eyebrows as well. And something about the way I looked. "'60s rebellious youth", it said on the video case. Without really knowing what it meant, we acted it out as faithfully as we could. Lukas' role was an antihero, it said; this thought appealed to him, a hero who was anti everything.

"I'd like to live in Mexico. I hear it's so lovely. When I was little Dad would always say: we'll go there next Saturday. But he'd always forget," I mimicked.

"I bet it's not great at all in Mexico. People are such liars," Lukas' turn, "it's like Stockholm." – "Stoekkoelm", he was imitating Jean-Paul Belmondo – "Everyone who's been there says: the Swedes are terrific, I had it three times a day. But I went there and it isn't true – they're not like they are down here – and they're just as ugly as Parisian women."

"Swedish women are very pretty," I objected.

"No, no, perhaps a few of them, but not all. The only town where all the girls are beautiful – without being gorgeous, but charming, like you, where fifteen out of twenty girls have something special – isn't Rome, Paris or Rio de Janeiro, but Lausanne and Geneva."

I remembered her now, Jean Seberg, Mamma's favourite actress, she was the one who had died. On a street in Paris. No blood, no audience. For real. Lukas and I had borrowed "Breathless" from Mamma's collection with a handful of other films and watched it on the rental set at Lukas' house. Saw it so many times while his Pappa worked his shift at the factory that we could not fail to learn the lines. *"Do you sleep with a lot of men?" "Not so many." "How many?" Seven fingers . . .* One time I wanted to swap and say Lukas' lines, but he was not keen.

Following an overdose of sleeping tablets Jean Seberg had been found on the back seat of her car after she had been missing from her apartment for eleven days. Eleven days. The car had been parked the whole time on a busy Paris street without anyone noticing her – how could that be possible? How can you live in a town like that, *were* there even towns that were so big that somebody could lie dead in a parked car for nearly two weeks without anyone walking past and wondering? Had no-one seen her, or did no-one care?

Mamma had heard a report of her death on Swedish radio on the morning of my tenth birthday, so I had not imagined the funereal atmosphere in the house.

A son. Her farewell letter was written only to him. Not to any of her many husbands, it does not matter how many of them there were, the letter was still only written to her son: "Diego, my dear son, forgive me, I can't live any longer. Understand me, I know that you can, and you know that I love you. Your mother who knows you. Jean." I knew just enough English to understand her parting words. "Forgive" and "understand me" and "I love you" were not the most important – the most important were the last words . . . "Your mother who knows you." It was so unbearable to think of him, so sad, and at the same time – a twinge of jealousy when I considered that my Mamma would never have written that to me.

Almost anything at all can look like a crime if you consider it in a certain way. A dead woman on a back seat, Lukas and me in the dark cellar, they condemned him without a trial, at once forbade him to go near me. We did not see each other for two days, no-one allowed me to slip out, Pappa's brother Erik declared that he was going to keep a check on every step I took, every step Lukas took as well – somehow or other, when he had forbidden Lukas to come within sight of our house. After Erik went back on the day shift he had no chance of carrying out his mission. I would escape and Lukas would search me out again . . . However hard they pushed me, I was never going to betray him like Jean Seberg betrayed Jean-Paul Belmondo in "Breathless".

Innocence

Whenever I travel by train he comes to me. A haze that rises in my memory. Trickles out even if I attempt to seal it off with sleep or conversation. Perhaps a visit to the restaurant car with a glass or two of wine and a book that would usually sweep me away from this world. I do not know how he can sense that I am on a train, but he does and that is when he appears. The railway separated our houses, the endless night trains, the slow goods trains pounding towards morning. Every time I go by train I travel back into memories, childhood, through summers and winters, skirt lengths, hair styles, chewing gum that has lost its flavour. I shut my book, it is not worth trying to read now, the sky is ablaze with yellow and a colour I cannot name. I am crossing from loneliness into loneliness. Loneliness is only a lack of companionship that one must grow accustomed to, until it becomes a companion in itself.

Travelling by train at night is a journey towards light. Trains that convey so much sleep across Europe. At daybreak I go out into the narrow corridor. The compartments are in line, like oxygenless pigeon-holes for eight people. I stand there with the morning smokers and the old folk in crumpled suits and shiny synthetic dresses, who, like me, always wake in the hour before sunrise: the suits, the frumpy dresses and me – a small, sleepy, tragic troop.

I like being alone amongst other people, exactly as I am in the stifling compartment with room for a large family or eight strangers. Opposite me a newly breastfed baby is sleeping. I cannot hear her breathe, but I can feel the gentle rhythm of peace surrounding her in the dimness. And the mother, slowly falling asleep, between deserted villages and sparse forests, the roe deer of dawn here and there in the mist. Hungarian, Slovak, Polish countryside, they all merge together after so many hours on a train, the child on the seat, Lukas' face, the coral landscape, sunken ships whose hulls resemble the hollow chests of gigantic whales with ribs eaten clean by shoals of silvery krill. The skeletons radiate light even in the darkest deep. The reflection of all one has left behind, with or without regret.

If I dip my hand into the tangled threads of memory, the first thing I come to is the fire. The fire that perhaps has spread further in my recollection than it did in reality. The fire, and in it Lukas.

———

It is a summer of extreme heat. Forest fires have broken out in eastern Europe, an electrical storm has caused hundreds of fires that are left to burn unattended. After the driest spring for over a hundred years, enormous stretches of land are now burned out, the lack of rain combined with dry thunderstorms has created a smoking inferno.

The paediatrician I slept with last night in a room facing the busy street has still not come down for breakfast. Not that we slept much, no doubt he will spend the whole day in bed, exhausted. Positions I did not even know existed; I tried to relax and be compliant and not suffer from nausea when he turned and twisted me this way and that. Felt like the white foam on the dark surface of a wave that forced and pushed beneath me. My skin an almost sickly white against the

85

blackness of his. In the background the pulsing of soul music. *"That's how you like it, huh? That's how I like it, babe."* If only life could always be like this, could fit together like a supple pair of hips: *huh? Yeah . . .* Like our hips, almost moulded to each other. He was heavy and though I have a weakness for the boyish type, it is still good to go to bed with someone you can really feel.

"Do you often go with strange men?" he asked.

"Not so often."

"How often?" I held up seven fingers. The speed of my reply made him laugh. Seven hundred . . . was what he seemed to think.

Now, from the speaker in the dining room, Marlene Dietrich's seductive voice that must have been left on the night before. It is not suitable breakfast music. I keep an eye on the door where guests, hungry and replete, come and go. Is he going to miss his conference today? Yes, at any rate he will miss breakfast. Should I wake him? No, I am not his wife. He had no wife, he said. But he liked married women. Innocence made him melancholy.

Lust for men and fear, perhaps they are feelings within me that cannot be separated, it is men who have to be distinguished one from another. But how does one know? How does one see? The signs? Do not suspect someone without cause, but making a mistake can lead to disaster. It is easier with all the other things Mamma warned me about, motorways are all dangerous, it is possible to drown in every single lake, snakes can be divided into poisonous and non-poisonous, but men . . . you simply do not know. Have to live with the uncertainty. As I recall she did not warn me about strange men or unprotected sex, like other mothers did. Just about love.

I resolve to place my trust in someone, then I will try to see him in that light. Without trust one is dead, or might just as well be, but too much trust also carries the risk of not surviving long. Men who cannot take a no, men who have never taken a no, or men who have decided never again to take a no, that they will do whatever they like with the next girl who says no.

The television reports of the fires last night made me restless. I went out after dark, the town was feverish, Friday evening, hunting season, high heels, whites of the eye glowing, smashing glasses. I do not like this frenzy, actually, prefer daylight, normal days in normal places, chance meetings when one least expects them. But every so often I feel like being wild with rouge plastered on my cheeks. Slip into a bar convinced that someone is sitting there waiting for me.

It was pleasant talking to an American, to be able to speak without thinking. It started with one glass that soon became two and then three, I threw caution to the wind, the barriers came down and all my secrets spilled out, unimpeded. Perhaps because he did not seem to be listening very carefully. He was not going to correct me if I contradicted myself, nor demand explanations, just listen and forget. Appeared to have heard all the stories before, from his position behind the bar in an Arizona desert, I imagined, where he stood pouring out mescal and listening to the world's troubles. And I could see what he thought of me ... a poor lonely lady of the night, all dressed up and nowhere to go.

His features were sharp like a cock-of-the-rock, as if his blood was a mixture of all the minorities, until he became everything and nothing, free. A man who can ride but cannot swim. A man who can score a bull's eye at any distance, but cannot distinguish one woman from another under his nose. Grand Canyon, Lake Como, I thought when I saw him, Oakland, Idaho. A typical man. They do not exist, and yet there he was. Looked like someone who would get caught in a loop on the lonely, lonely roads that stretch into infinity in the American Midwest. Paediatrician, he said, in Manhattan, though now he worked for Médecin sans Frontières. I could see my surprised expression in his gleaming black eyes. He had come here for an international conference on noma infection, taking place in the town this week.

"Noma infection?"

"You don't want to know."

"Yes, I do."

"No, you don't. Believe me." Noma was God's punishment for mankind, especially children. He pronounced the disease with a capital letter and God with a small letter, perhaps you reach that point when you have witnessed enough suffering. We talked about the fires instead.

Trust or alcohol, something made me start talking. He did not drink himself, refused when I offered him a glass. Normally I do not trust men who do not drink, especially if they are sitting alone in a bar. But from time to time exceptions have to be made, the fact of the matter was that he was far too good-looking for me to leave.

"I'm a doctor, I know what that stuff does to your brain." I knew as well, but that did not stop me.

"I would like to live sober and die drunk." So would I, but how can you know when it is time . . . I want to be prepared.

"Aren't you a bit too young to be taking death so seriously?" he asked, lighting a cigarette.

"Aren't you a bit too old to be concerned about your future brain capacity?" I asked. He was handsome, but certainly over fifty.

"You little rascal," he exclaimed, amazed. I am not usually good with older men, I never know how to deal with them. They are so sensitive, I am always hurting their feelings. But I was enjoying this.

"You black marauder," I retorted. Heard him draw breath. It was in the balance.

If he could call me a little rascal, I could call him a black marauder. As he was a paediatrician he must be accustomed to charming insults and anyway he knew exactly how handsome he was, was no doubt always gathering nurses like ripened grapes and could do with a bit of opposition, someone who did not just fall into his hands.

"What do you want?" It seemed he had not made up his mind to leave, but was giving it serious consideration. I was not in the habit of being quite so blunt, but since he asked me, I did not beat about the bush.

"O.K.," he said, "but we can talk first." Talk? Of course . . . I have nothing against talking. I was not the one who had to get up early for a conference. He ordered a cup of green tea for himself, I ordered a glass of slivovitz.

"You'll have to pay for that yourself, I never buy women alcohol." And innocence made him melancholy? He was full of contradictions. I paid for mine and we talked about the fires. I told him what I had heard as a child, how long a fire can continue to burn underground, the smouldering roots giving no outward sign of the catastrophic damage being caused.

Unfamiliar forests

I have been warned about unfamiliar forests, full of hidden dangers, the importance of staying close to home where the situation is known. I have never followed that advice. As soon as a place begins to resemble a home, I move on. Objects are so alien. People too, the more one gets to know them. The view over a strange town from a room rented for the night gives me a sense of calm. I feel most at home when I am somewhere else. Away from my belongings, away from those I love. Could be in any town at all and feel the same loneliness. Yearn for a place that does not exist. Home is where each person's own smell merges into the smells of the others, there is no such place for me.

I travel without an aim, but I have read somewhere that all journeys have secret destinations of which the traveller is not aware. April, the cruellest of months, there are no sunglasses dark enough for the spring light on the streets of Kazimierz. I look straight into the sun and do not care if someone is sucked into my eye and burned to ash.

There are as many dogs roaming loose here as there are domestic ones, the tame ones prowl around with their tails rigid, constantly on their guard. The wild ones are placid, taking no notice of humans. The dogs doze in the afternoon sun. It is a beautiful day. Time is running out, somebody or something is approaching, a breeze stirs along the ground, the dogs' eyes roll in their sleep. The stray mongrels are just one incidental piece of the street scene, they could rise to their feet at any time and move somewhere else, quick to react to impulses of need and flight.

Fall asleep, forgetting who I am, wake up as someone else, with another face – go out to buy a new pair of boots and throw away the old ones – I do this on the third day. Dark red with brightly coloured flowers embroidered on the leg. A tingling in the tip of my tongue, like a secret message. A good day. I can feel it. A good day, a good spring.

With every step I am reminded of my new footwear, the hard leather is gripping my calves tightly, but it is not uncomfortable. Sense a new level of awareness, unnerving and at the same time arousing, as I follow the river downstream, the morning still young.

The faces of the women in this town have so many aspects. Most beautiful of all are their early morning faces, closed and serene like sleeping birds, walking along the river, ready for the punters who have to fix new boundaries between themselves every day. Traces of the night's love encounters on their bare necks, oval blue blotches that cannot be washed away but have to be covered with make-up before they can climb aboard the trolley buses and the trams on their way to work. I wanted to be one of them and now I am. Learn to keep pace with the gentle flow of the water, adjust to the women's ways and move-ments, blend in. The only thing distinguishing us is language, but during the silent morning walks along the river bank, nobody notices. I can feel the change in me this town is causing, the light, the men, the women.

Sit for a while by the river and rest my feet, aching from the new boots. See a man at the edge of the water sharing out food from a plastic bag to some of the stray dogs. A performance, how he tries to direct the group to prevent the pushy ones taking everything and leaving nothing for the lowest ranks. He shouts something to me and smiles. I smile back and indicate that I do not understand, and that just makes him repeat the sentence, louder, as if that would help me. Then he tries to drive away his four-legged friends and approaches me with half the troop still circling round his legs.

I stand up, there are a lot of them and they appear more wild than tame.

"*Nie mówie po polsku,*" I say.

"That was perfect Polish," he says. Of course, but *I don't speak Polish* is the only thing in Polish I can say.

"English is O.K.," he smiles, "and I really like your boots."

The psychopath is often charming, generally has success with the opposite sex. I cast around in my memory. Dogs . . . Do they like dogs? Do they like to feed abandoned animals? To give them a feeling of power . . . no, I do not remember. He comes nearer, walking as if he owns the diminishing distance between us. When he extends his hand and notices that I hesitate, he wipes off bits of the dogs' food on his trouser leg and offers it again. *The psychopath often has children with several women. The psychopath seldom takes his own life, since he does not have strong feelings of regret or failure.* Why must the psychopath always be a man? And why must he always come up to me? What is it about me and maniacs? Where is the power of my attraction in their eyes? I want to know . . . so that I can do something about it, is it the colour of my lipstick or my habit of watching people too unashamedly, averting my gaze a fatal second too late?

*

"I'm Jiri," he says, shooing away the dogs.

"Lo."

"What does that mean?"

"Wild cat," I reply.

"Wild cat . . . In what language?"

"Mine."

"Ah, in *your* language. You've got your own language? Wild-cat language?"

He himself looks rather wolf-like. Predatory teeth, amber-coloured eyes, grey suit. The suit, is it ironic? It must be. He is wearing it with trainers. Perhaps he belongs to the category of intelligent lunatics, attractive psychopaths, treacherous high-risk projects.

"You're popular," I say, nodding towards the dogs strutting round his feet.

"Yes, I've spoilt them, or rather . . . bought their love. I bet yours can't be bought, eh?" he says and shakes out a cigarette.

Indiscretion is the order of the evening. Too much vodka in a dingy bar by the river. Too much darkness, too much river, too many of Jiri's friends, too many strangers, too many men. Too many languages – English, German, Russian – which in drunkenness merge into Polish, Swedish, Slovak. In the end people cannot even speak their own language, we just laugh and in so doing we understand each other for the first time that night.

When I try to slow the pace he smiles at me. He says his name is Jiri, but his friends call him something else. You can always drink three glasses, he says, three before, three during, three after. I can trust him because he has a hell of a long list of academic qualifications.

"Before, during and after what?"

"No idea, it's just a saying," he laughs. I have heard that in these parts they use vodka as a contraceptive . . . not before, during or after, but instead. He does not laugh at that. Alcohol can be the subject of jokes almost everywhere, but not religion and not sex and definitely not at the same time. Why do I never learn? I know his sort, who take themselves very seriously under the thin mask of intelligent irony. I have a certain weakness for them and that irritates me. A sophisticated layabout, sexy but graced with ironic taste in clothes and a soft spot for hungry abandoned dogs, what promise does that hold? For all I know, we may well sleep together before the night is over, but one thing is certain – we will not joke about it.

I begin to think that we will never shake off his friends, but suddenly they are gone. Jiri makes sure that we are alone, stops a clapped-out car on the street and pays a young man to take us to his lodgings on the other side of town. We are too drunk, sleep first and have sex later, making us feel less like strangers. As if we had been together before, but no, I would have remembered him, he moves in time with the breeze, the most sensual rhythm.

No-one has to have everything, but everyone has to have something. It might only be a fragrance one has never smelled before. Beautiful Slavic features. Handsome neck. Worn-out shoes that look as though they have walked far. Dark humour. A face exceptionally open. Exceptionally shut. A photo of children next to his heart. A story to tell. A weak point. A flaw. I do not know if any of this is really him, but the fact that I cannot put my finger on what I find tempting about him, is the tempting thing.

"You fire into the blind spot between the eyes," he says and marks the spot with two fingers against my forehead, as if he wants to anoint me or execute me or both at the same time. "The heavy body falls," he mumbles, "it's slack." I am not sure what he is talking about, although his English is good I do not understand what he means. The walls of the badly lit one-room apartment are dripping with damp, like the inside of a glass jar. It is meagre accommodation for someone who works at the university, as he claims to do, devoid of books too. Salt-mines, steelworks, I think when I see his hands. He is better looking without the suit, before a world opens up of . . . I wish I knew what it was called in his language: pleasure. I run my hand over the network of small hard muscles in his back. Dung-clearing muscles, he says. He has to go home to work on his parents' farm as soon as he has some time off, his father is getting old and has been blessed with only one son. Five daughters and only one son, and, what is more, he does not want to take over the farm. A minor catastrophe.

"I could help them financially instead of going home to toil away in their muddy fields. But it's not a question of money. Do you understand?" I understand precisely. He rolls on to his back and pulls me down on top of him, alleges that I was murmuring a name in my sleep, could I be married? Without waiting for an answer, as if it is not very important, at least not more important than hunger, he gets up, restless, and disappears into the corridor. Returns from the floor's communal kitchen with his hands full of bread, lard, pickled cucumber and beer.

Most people play their best cards first, so why not part then with the illusion intact? An illusion is not exactly a lie, it is its own truth, a short interval while the oxygen lasts in the floating bubble. A man who is pleasant one evening is indeed pleasant in that place and at that time, even if in his normal life he is despicable, before and after that evening, always has been and always will be despicable. He shows his best side – offers it to me – before the smell of sweat penetrates the smell of aftershave. And now and then I may prefer it that way.

Sex is sometimes the price you have to pay for the delight of seducing a man. Sometimes more, sometimes less. Make him fall, preferably slowly enough to see it happen. Was Venus ever afraid when she lured men? But she was not a normal woman, was not subject to normal laws. She enticed men up on to her mountain and seduced them. Mound of Venus: the raised, hair-covered part above the pubic bone in a woman. In this perilous place all her men fell victim.

As soon as Jiri is sleeping soundly I creep away, back to my hotel room.

The last thing I notice before I drop into bed is a growing dark cloud outside the window, as if an enormous sack of thousands of bats had been emptied over the hotel's pointed roof. Then everything is black. Not a darkness that eyes become accustomed to, no, pitch-black like closed-down factories at night, like the lake back home, at its deepest point.

Axe

"You've slept with every one of the men, haven't you?" Mamma says and lifts the axe.

"Yes," I reply, "but only once." She lowers the tool and shades her eyes with her hand, they are almost white in the bright light. "Apart from with the great love of my life," I add. She weighs the heavy axe in her right hand, wary.

"How many times did you sleep with him, then?" She raises the deadly instrument again and swings it over her head with such dexterity that with the first blow the birch log whimpers and splits and leaps away, hitting the wall of the woodshed with a dull thud. My Mamma with an axe, a scene that always scared me as a child. She was terrifying even without an axe.

"Don't come back saying I didn't warn you," she mutters. I instinctively flinch as she lifts the hefty axe once more. I wish I could blame her, I really do, but the truth is for the whole of my life she has warned me about love.

She looks as though she would like to laugh but has forgotten how. Instead she takes aim again, stretches and applies her now failing strength. She is still just as skilful, her technique does not let her down, but she lacks the weight and speed required for the axe to do its job effectively.

She was chopping wood when her waters broke, and when Pappa

left. Chopped. Every time. When someone died, when someone deceived her, when I moved, when she caught Lukas and me in the act, when she and Pappa's father had argued. When she was sad she took the axe and went out. I was used to it. The noise from the woodpile was the beat that accompanied all disasters, large and small, as I was growing up. I knew what a catastrophe sounded like. Heavy, slow, ominous. When I left the village the sound of the axe accompanied me.

She is in her element cutting wood, the steel that cleaves the air that cleaves the tree that cleaves the silence. I have always liked watching her while she chops. There is something alarming in the sight and at the same time awe-inspiring. If something were to happen, an outward threat of any kind, it would still be she who would protect me, and not the other way round. With every stroke I am convinced of this. A mother-goddess in a struggle with her demons, spider woman in her most terrifying form. Mamma would like to weave the web of my fate – like the cosmic spider drawing all humans together with umbilical-cord thread, entwining them into the huge pattern.

"To belong to everyone is to belong to no-one," she reminds me.

"I know."

"Do you?"

"Yes. But that's how I want it." Now she lays down the axe and rubs into her aching hands the same mink fat she uses for her woodcutting boots. It is universal, like everything else in her life, it would not surprise me if she fried herring in it too. She does not ask who he is, the love of my life, the one who dazzled me so completely. Perhaps she thinks she already knows, in the way that mothers believe they know because we once shared the same bloodstream – they never let us forget.

"I can't understand how you manage it. Honestly, girl, what sort of stuff are you made of?"

"Some kind of hard timber from the north, I imagine."

"Silver birch? With titanium screws in that case," she says sourly. Her eyes: twinkling blue. I try to be truthful with her, even though I know that she does not like it and she does not want to understand.

"What do you actually want from them? All they'll bring you is emptiness, that's what I think. What one gives you, another will take away." I am determined not to be provoked, but it is already too late. "You were given too much love when you were little," she adds and shoots an impenetrable look in my direction through the yellow lenses of her dark glasses. They look ridiculous. Hope she takes them off if anyone comes, whoever that might be . . . "Too much love. That's the reason," she repeats.

· "The reason for what?"

"The men."

Yes, I do sleep with every man, but not with just anybody, only with the ones I have selected, and they are a tiny percentage of all the men who cross my path, and then . . . well, then I leave them before they have a chance to display their less attractive side, which often means straightaway. What do I want of them? Not faithfulness under a cloud of creamy white tulle, at any rate. Not the Hiroshima four-poster bed, not the padded Alcatraz cell.

And what do they want of me? "Fascinating", "special", I hear more often than not – that means I am not pretty. I am not one of the most beautiful of women and that gives me a broad spectrum of potential men to choose from. Stunningly attractive women often seem so alone, it is only when they are tipsy that men dare to approach them. Or when the men themselves are tipsy and looking to offend them in some way.

Whatever Mamma believes, I select them with great care. Of course I have made mistakes, but that can happen in choosing one only – a misjudgement or bad luck can lead to a lifetime of regret. I once met a man who despised all the women he could not have, almost as much as he despised those he could have. But I cannot make all men scapegoats for that.

"Be careful," Mamma warns in her icy dialect. If she can no longer be my guardian angel, she wants to be my bird of foreboding. "Life's not a carnival, Lo." I know. But maybe it can be. A man who smells of Jicky cannot be utterly without hope. Or Eau Sauvage, Équipage, Hypnôse. Ozone perfumes are the ones I rely on most, the brackish, sweet and salty unisex fragrances, water scents. The animal, glandular smells like musk and civet make me more cautious, it has to be very late and only certain sorts of nights.

"Some day your past's going to come back to haunt you. Somebody who took it harder than you thought. Men are . . ."

"Dangerous?"

"Romantics," Mamma says and fixes me with her eye through the yellow glasses. It has grown cold. We have moved into the kitchen, she fills the pan with water and fumbles for the coffee tin in the cool cupboard. "Romantics, Lo. You ought to know that. And yes – that sometimes makes them dangerous." I know that her loyalty to me is great, but it cannot be sought. Now she suddenly looks hard, turns on the gas, strikes a match. I always hold my breath when she lights the gas stove. She refuses to replace it, if she is going to die, she will go up in flames, not fade away. *I have only daughters, God, my God, why have you forsaken me?* laments a woman on the radio. Mamma is listening. "Daughters," she mutters to herself, "greater happiness and greater sorrow." That was what her mother always said.

You cannot just toy with them and quit when you tire yourself, one day it will turn out badly. Marsupials . . . that is what Mamma calls them, but she is a marsupial herself, she carried me, I may have clambered out of her pouch early and taken off, but sometimes I long to be back in her protective presence again.

The red zone

I met him on the tram between Buda and Pest that spring when the catalpa trees flowered too early and the month of April was so warm that by summer it would be unbearable to stay in town. He was the last one to squeeze on when it had already started to move. My eye caught the paisley pattern on his shirt, only madmen go barefoot on a tram, I was thinking when I saw him hanging on, his hip against the chrome post, drinking from a bottle and smiling. What was he smiling at? Nothing in particular . . . just a smile? He lit an imaginary cigarette and suddenly I had a sneaking suspicion that I had caused the smile. Discreetly I wiped my lips, perhaps a little of the paprika filling had ended up outside my mouth as I ran across the street from the market hall to the tram stop with my warm Hungarian bread.

Nothing is quite like the light in April, not in this town, Budapest at this time is like a mirror, the sort that lies and tells you than you look better than you do. We were travelling right into the shining brilliance over the water of the Danube. The last thing I saw before my vision was flooded with white was a drop of lemonade trickling down his smooth sun-tanned chin. I wanted to catch it with my tongue while he was dazzled, but we were already through to the other side.

The first thing I could distinguish when the brightness dimmed was his hand. An animal, presumably a dog, had disfigured it. Small stumps remained in the place where his fingers should be, but his hand was so deformed it could scarcely be called a hand. He dragged it nonchalantly through his hair, I could not help watching, wondering how it would feel to be caressed by a hand like that, if it had any sensation left in it, feeling. Perhaps his hand had not forgotten – life before the accident – what it was like to experience the tiniest details in your finger tips.

I searched for something else I could let my gaze rest on. Round his neck he wore a loosely knotted tie with the Taj Mahal embossed in the fabric. I have never seen such a handsome man with such awful taste in clothes. Perhaps I was wrong, but it seemed as though something burned within him, from his hand right up to the intense look in his eye.

We rode in a wide arc through the town. Lukas' town. I tried to imagine him standing on a street corner, but I could not picture him, he did not fit in here. Then we travelled back over the river and by the time we stepped off at the last stop it had turned to autumn, or it felt like it, cool, with a hint of rain in the air. Him and I and a whole crowd of youngsters of different sizes on their way to school in newly pressed uniforms. The children went in one direction, he went in the other, I went the same way.

The smell of lilac at the wrong time of year disturbed and confused me, until I saw the soap factory. He walked slowly, as if wanting me to keep up, past the factory towards the block of flats in its shadow. We cut across the empty gardens of the estate and when we emerged at the other side the buildings came to an abrupt end. Flat fields covered in weeds quite unlike the ones at home stretched out towards the motorway in the distance.

Where was he going? The gauge was registering in the red zone. Never go with any man who obviously wants you to go with him. But I had not yet developed a fear of strangers. The rain was so light it was hardly noticeable, just a film of moisture on the forehead and cheeks. He raised his shoulders in the thin shirt, increased his pace and by a field that appeared to be lying fallow, overgrown with thistles, he stopped without warning and turned round.

"What do you want?"

I did not want to look at his disfigured hand, but it was impossible not to, as if it were whispering: ". . . Hey, you . . . yes, you . . . Look at me. Don't be afraid."

It should be possible to spend a day or preferably a whole week in a new town without going to bed with someone. On a purely theoretical level I know it is feasible, but single men in the transit hall, freshly showered men in the breakfast room, the backs of beautiful heads at the check-in desk, someone's profile in the lift mirror, a smell along the pavement or on the tram, that is all it takes.

Men with grandiose dreams. Men with dogs. Young men who drink too quickly, older men with eyes like desert islands. The ones who shoot from the hip. Soft-hearted killers. Men in exceptional circumstances. Men with style. Men without. Men who do not know what they want or why. Or men who know exactly. It is not that they are all walking around waiting to be seduced, but if the opportunity presents itself, I do not see what would stand in their way.

"You're peaceful when you make love and violent when you sleep," someone said.

"Your laugh's like a wave-machine, it makes me seasick," said another.

"Come," said the black marauder. And I did.

The rest of the weekend we spent in his summer cottage just outside Pest. Roasted last year's remaining chestnuts in sooty tins on the wood stove and ate them piping hot out of their skins with salt, drank moonshine strong enough to put a wild boar to sleep. It was not a dog that was responsible for Miklós' ragged hand, it was a machine at the soap factory. When he touched me I felt calm. His hand did not feel repellent, just different, softer than a child's.

There was something soft about his mouth too, like biting into a plum overflowing with pungent dark red juice from his generous lips as they grew more and more red. His mouth breathed: "Bite!" And I bit. Fleeting shadows moved across the cottage wallpaper, the clouds rolled by.

"You know Eskimos," he said suddenly, when we were back in bed after eating all the chestnuts, even the charred ones, to quell our evening hunger, we did not lack food, but a feeling of being full. "To increase the strength and endurance of the sleigh dogs, they used to leave a bitch tied up for the wolves to mate with," he said. On top of him, I was quiet. Outside the French window darkness had fallen over the garden, all that could be seen were the outlines of handprints on the inside of the dirty window pane. Lots of handprints, as if someone had tried to get out. "And they let the cold take the girls," he continued. "They laid them in the entrance to the igloo where they soon froze to death. Two out of three newly born. But only in times of necessity. In the summer they built a little stone grave by the tent and put the girl in there to die. If it was spring or autumn they suffocated her with a sealskin. Some lives had to be sacrificed so that the others could survive – always the girls – because they could never be hunters."

His eyes were still as soft, his eyes and voice as well, but something else had altered. Something within me.

Fear is like an animal. In fear we are changed into a creature with four legs, feeling the chill beneath our paws. *Come*, he whispered. *Go*, I said to myself. Trust your fear. Go now. Go.

———

The smell in the room had changed from pleasure to discomfort, I recalled it from somewhere, childhood, frogs rotting in the rain, a sweet urine-like smell.

"Be quick," he said, when I spluttered that I had to go out. Bloody unnecessary right in the middle of it, seemed to be his opinion. The lie was fairly transparent, but there was no time to consider, he had said that the old water closet inside the house was broken, you had to go out between the gable end of the house and the empty dovecote. "Hurry up," he said, in spite of the fact that hurrying was the only thing I could think about, anxious that he would sense how cold my body had become, how white, how bloodless, how rigid with fear.

And then, as if he had suddenly changed his mind, he held on to me. Not with the soft, damaged hand that I liked, but with the other, less sensitive one.

"Your bladder must be as small as a bird's . . . What did you say your name was?" His fingers tight around my wrist, he must have felt that it was frozen to the bone. I tried cautiously to wriggle free and said my name again. It was not difficult. Two letters. I do not understand why he could not grasp it. He had already asked me several times, as if he were not satisfied with my answer.

We had laughed and toasted one another and I had lost count of how many glasses I had consumed of his aromatic home distillation as it went down the decilitre line on a plastic jerrycan without a label. Now for the first time I could taste it, sharp like a cut in the throat. What had he given me – liquid insecticide, weed killer, diluted rat poison? Any of those toxic substances that are readily available in a house in the country.

"You're cold," he said, "freezing cold. What is it?"

"I need to . . ." searched for the word in German, but it was gone ". . . let go!" I pulled away and as soon as my hands were free I dragged on what I thought was my dress. It turned out to be his shirt, but there was no time to change, I just stumbled away through the darkness without looking to see if he was following. I had tunnel vision, tried to take my bearings by the light, but it was black everywhere. As I groped my way along the walls I found only locked doors.

I had swallowed his rubbish, laughed my most childish laugh, seduced and allowed myself to be seduced as if life had taught me nothing. His tongue in my mouth, my hand in his shorts, more spirits in the glass, falling on my back with him on top of me, just as drunk . . . or only pretending to be, maybe he was stone-cold sober the whole time? Alert and focused, right behind me now – just wanted to give me a head start to increase the thrill.

I banged my hip on something hard without feeling any pain, fumbled further along. Thought I heard him say my name, but it might have been the wind, it was rising and the gaps in the walls of the wooden house made it sound like a broken instrument the wind blew through. Finally, at the end of the kitchen, I found a back door with a key in the lock. The night air hit me, I breathed in the oxygen, an impression of just having surfaced, and carried on out into the overgrown garden. The briers ripped the thin material of the shirt. I wandered around in circles until I knocked against the metal railing at the boundary of the plot, climbed over and hastened further into the unknown darkness.

I have no stamina when it comes to fear, it drained away from me as I was running. I came to a standstill in the middle of the desolate field. A meaningless flight with no-one in pursuit, a quarry who stops in the midst of the hunt and wonders why she is fleeing. Felt empty, disorientated, slightly stupid. The wind was cold, my mouth tasted of sooty chestnuts and smoke from his mouth, a trace of blood. Without fear there was nothing to drive me. I crouched down to catch my breath, felt lost, no longer sufficiently agitated for fear to outweigh tiredness, longed for a bed, any bed, my warm hotel bed or his lumpy mattress. Just to give in to exhaustion, shut my eyes and fall asleep. In my imagination as I ran, the motorway in the distance with its sporadic night traffic had been my salvation. Now that I was standing close I did not feel so sure. I might get into the wrong car, anyone at all could pick me up, there was nothing to say that I was safer out here than in the house with him.

Of all evil things he is not the worst, I thought. From a distance the summer cottage looked like a sleeping hare alone under the night sky. Blue smoke indicated that the stove in which we had roasted the chestnuts was still burning, a rustic idyll shrouded in the peaceful darkness of spring. Somewhere far away the sound of a nightjar. From a distance everything beautiful, simple.

I turned back.

When I reached the fence I saw him standing by the French window in the bedroom, waiting, naked with a towel round his hips and even when he pushed open the door and stepped out into the garden, he did not appear to see me. For a long time he stood listening, instead of calling for me. Was it in these parts that there were bears who went right up to the houses and ate out of the rubbish bins at night? I had heard about it, thought that must be what stopped him shouting for me. Or perhaps the knowledge that there were those giant bloodsucking bats that . . . no, surely it was not here, but further east in Transylvania? Probably he had just forgotten my name again. That was why he was standing in the dark, waiting. I could make him out clearly in the faint glimmer of light from the bedroom and despite the distance I could see how the wind took hold of the towel he had twisted round his hips, lifted it up and exposed him before he had time to cover himself. As if he sensed that someone in the surrounding darkness could see him.

Upright between the tall trees, half naked, calm, he seemed so much less than the man in my head as I ran away. The alarming disquiet in bed, the sudden uneasiness under my skin, what had triggered the reflex of fear? I was there of my own free will and enjoyed being with him. It was not the place, not the situation, not him. He was a careless lover, but I liked him. And his spider-hand had enticed me, caused me to notice him and want to know who he was. How it would feel to be caressed by it. But he had two faces, as different as his hands.

*

In every culture throughout every age the same ritual: a feared animal is worshipped in order for it to be appeased. The more one fears man, wolf, bat, spider, the more one idolises them. I once had a phobia of spiders, especially the large, hairy variety. Made up my mind that their bite was deadly, but that was just as superstitious as the belief that the bite could be cured by an exhausting dance, the trance-like tarantella. The venom was quite harmless and most spiders' jaws were too weak to penetrate human skin. But what good did that do? To know. Not even when I read that spiders have a heart did my fear of them diminish. Fear is fear, irrational and persistent. Intense, manipulative. Fast working. From one second to the next you lose your balance. You have control for as long as you can keep it, then it has gone, slipped through your hands like a slippery piece of soap; and when you have lost control, the only thing that remains is fear.

My fear of spiders may have caused the problem in bed, desire and fear, sometimes they run into each other, mixed, confused, impossible to separate. The Eskimo girls were certainly responsible, stories I had heard when I was a child, pestered to be allowed to hear them . . . until I found out how many sleepless nights they would give me. That in the past in times of necessity they suffocated their new-born daughters – that your own family could do this, turned my whole world as a girl upside down. I could not stop thinking about those little girls, how their tiny round legs jerked until they fell to the sides, loose, under the sealskin closed so tightly over their mouths.

———

When we arrived at his isolated retreat in daylight, I had not noticed any other inhabited houses nearby, only a few derelict buildings. We had taken a bus and then walked a long way through the countryside, peaceful and deserted, to reach his remote summer residence.

"What are you thinking?" he asked after a long silence. I scarcely knew where I was any more, or if I would have any chance of finding my way back to town by myself. He sounded wary, perhaps he thought that I disliked this neglected area that made the prosperity of Budapest seem very far away. But in my eyes this scene was grudgingly beautiful, a childhood landscape I had not encountered for a long time.

He walked down the middle of the gravel track, no car passed, no person, we were alone with each other and a hawk soaring over the field. The mangled hand between us a reminder of everything I did not know about him yet.

He regretted his decision. It was obvious in the way he did not look at me. He could have tried to hide it, but he did not. From the moment we got off the bus he had been silent, maybe thinking how foolishly impulsive it was for the two of us to come out here to his summer cottage together, as if we had both forgotten where we were supposed to be going that day. We knew nothing about each other and could only communicate after a fashion. Not that language was a problem, he had worked on building sites in Berlin and Nuremberg, so his German was better than mine and English filled in the gaps for us both. But we had no idea at all what we should talk to each other about.

He had not asked a single question about who I was, wanted to know nothing about me other than my name. And what did I really want to know about him, besides how his deformed hand would feel on my skin?

*

His cheekbones reminded me of Lukas'. A face that could instantly change from hard to tender. I loved the way the light affected Lukas' face, but he would not have liked to hear me say that, compliments were always an exaggeration and exaggeration made him embarrassed.

"You're pretty," he said – I remember it, because he said it only once.

After leaving the bus a long way out of town, I had not heard so much as a dog barking, not even from afar, no sign of life anywhere. As if this area had been evacuated and left to the birds of prey. Just as I was growing accustomed to the impenetrable silence between us, it was shattered by his question. What was I thinking about? Women with faces translucent with age, how my throat was sticky with dust from the road, that somewhere round here Lukas had been born, that there was a strong smell of wild rosemary along these roads, his injured hand, smooth with a new layer of skin, right next to my hand as we walked. But mostly I was thinking about snakes, that we were walking through typical snake terrain, that I have never liked snakes, neither before nor after I was bitten as a child, that they are the only thing I cannot disguise my fear of.

My limited German was not adequate to explain all of that, so instead I asked him what he was thinking.

"That I've forgotten your name," he said, without looking at me. I followed his gaze and caught sight of the hawk again. It was gliding nearer. Characteristic buzzard movements, slowly circling high up, the very behaviour that usually indicates the presence of snakes. The hawk might mean that the place was teeming with suitable food, or that the situation was under control, that somebody was doing his best to hold the reptile population in check. But my fear needed no proof, just one buzzard circling over fields in this way, the summer-like April warmth bringing them out of the holes where they have kept themselves alive all winter with the heat of each other. I often saw them down by the lake when I was a child, black adders, where did they go? When I was a teenager they had disappeared. Or had I lost my eye for snakes?

Lukas maintained that they gave birth to their young. I could visualise it, a nightmare of unrestrained adders reproducing fully formed new adders. It was some hybrid thing, according to Lukas, producing eggs that they hatched inside their own bodies. Most of all I was frightened of snakes underwater. Both adders and grass snakes were excellent swimmers and often went out into the lake to catch small fish. You had to be faster than your own shadow to avert that threat. You needed the right amount of fear to be as fast as that. I was paralysed.

"Are we there yet?" I let my eye sweep along the gravel track to discern any suspicious twisting and slithering movements, noticed a sudden cold wind blowing in towards town.

"There," Miklós said. I gave a start, but it was not a snake, it was the house. A peeling turquoise summer cottage with shutters closed, partly hidden by shrubs and soapwort growing wild all over the garden. "Come on," he said and vaulted over the rusty gate. I hurried after him, relieved to be close to safety.

At the bottom of the steps he stopped. In the sharp midday light a snake was lying on the top step, warmed by the sun. A sort I did not recognise but evidently he did, because his bearing changed in an instant. He was moving so slowly he appeared to be standing still. The snake lay coiled up, amassing heat, waiting. He took hold of a fallen branch – had clearly done this before. With the skill of an expert he caught the creature and flung it at lightning speed in a high arc into the thorny bushes by the gable, unlocked the door and showed me in.

———

There was nothing sensational about his face, when I caught sight of him on the tram. Discreet and ordinary, I have always had a weakness for ordinary faces. It was not his hand that caused me to notice him, but his smile, unnerving like everything else that breaks the pattern when you are confined with strangers. First the smile, then the hand. Recoiled, could not conceal it. An instinct for trouble. It was obvious that he could see how my pupils dilated and how involuntary distaste made me press my back into the plastic seat and in my embarrassment bite off too large a piece of bread. No doubt he was used to all possible insensitive reactions, but can one ever get used to arousing unprovoked repugnance in others? My eye was drawn back to his hand, the fleshy pink tarantula that he pushed through his hair in an attempt to straighten his windblown locks. With a hand like that perhaps you are extra scrupulous about other details.

When I was a child I saw many men who had lost one or more fingers when they got in the way of an axe, the blade of a saw, a roller, chain or bad-tempered sow, had gangrene or frostbite. But this hand is not slightly maimed, it is mutilated beyond recognition. And yet . . . where there is aversion there is also desire, his hand attracted me, appealed to something within me that had not been stirred before.

When I creep back into the house he is asleep. Or perhaps pretends to be sleeping and wakes up, turns over and calls me to him. Once distaste has merged with desire and mingled together, it is difficult to separate them. I ought to go, leave this place, I am thinking as I walk towards his bed, and as I crawl between the sheets with him, willing and yet unwilling, and even more as he lays his hand between my shoulder blades. I do not want him to feel the bulge there, the raised back of the reptile that is fear.

Suspicious, he asks me where I have been . . . gone so long. Must have got lost, I answer. Impossible to get lost in a garden this size, fenced in as well. Bad sense of direction, I say vaguely, hear how idiotic it sounds and add something about vision being impaired in the dark. Then he feels my muddy feet under the cover.

"There's no mud in my garden, you were out in the fields running away, weren't you?" I shake my head but he can feel the holes in his shirt from the blackthorn bushes and asks if I was trying to clear off. I say I was not. "You're lying." I do not deny it. The scratches hurt when he pulls me towards him. On the wall above his head a quotation has been pinned up: *I never forget a face, but in your case I'll be glad to make an exception.* Groucho Marx, I think as he enters me.

Dawn is beginning to break, a cold mildew-blue light is spreading over the walls of the cottage. He holds my face between his hands, the whole one and the impaired one, bites my neck. His hands have a smell that make me recoil before I realise what it is, that it is myself I smell the scent of. The smell of me on his hands, from before when we made love.

We are always someone else when we make love. Another, beyond ourselves. Whenever I meet somebody like him, I have the need to find the other in him, andros, the man. The one he becomes when he makes love.

Neither neither nor nor

I liked sleeping with Lukas, our secret sleep. In the middle of the day in the pearl fisher's house we let the hours slip past, float away until darkness fell. We drifted, surrendering, along the verge of wakefulness, half-sleep, sleep, dreams, unconsciousness. He lay on my arm or I lay on his, and I tried to imagine that he had had that look long before he met me. That actually it had nothing to do with me, that it was not my fault that he had such a look in his eyes – as though something was missing – every time he looked at me.

Bodies. Physical contact. In the end it all revolves around that, when you have spent so much time in each other's company that there is nothing left to say. Lukas' nakedness did not excite me, nor did it bother me. I was as familiar with it as I was with my own. Just a body, no surprises from one day to the next. Some variations according to the season, a little bit more fat beneath the skin in winter and a little thinner and more languid in summer. And then that other change, not cyclical or connected to the time of year but more irreversible. From child to teenager through a long drawn-out adolescence, and for Lukas the change to an adult body. So slowly that you did not see it until it had already happened.

As long as I remained in the body of a child we could continue to be friends, but when I let it go? It had to happen one day, and when I could no longer call myself a child, everything would be more complicated.

Lukas seemed to be waiting for that. He looked at my slender hips.

"Haven't you thought about starting to grow yet?" What? Did I need to hurry? I took his hands away.

"You must be the smallest in the class." I was not. There were even some boys who were smaller than I was. Compared to them Lukas was a skinny giant with hands like horse-chestnut leaves and a pack of heaving muscles under his skin. He lifted me up in the water and flung me out of my depth so that I would learn to swim.

Sun, sleep, play. Summer existed just for us, and we existed just for summer. As long as we had each other, we had everything. Grasshoppers dipped in wild honey, left-over food smuggled out of the house. Drink out of the rainwater butt, shower in a downpour of rain. Sleep. More than anything else, we slept, our secret sleep, Lukas could never sleep enough. I had to learn to like it as well, or at least to be patient with him. Lie beside him and study the rhythm of his slow breathing, the sleeping presence of his warm, outstretched body. As time passed I thought he became less and less like a hunted dog. We thought we were safe when we went around, unsuspecting and spontaneous, near to the line without overstepping it, we just pushed it ahead of us, neither neither nor nor.

"What's happening? Where do you get to when you suddenly disappear? What on earth are you doing?" Mamma said, in the big sunglasses that made her look like a deadly hornet, especially in that striped top, so baggy at the neck that you could see down between her breasts.

"All sorts. Playing."

"Just think, *The Communist Manifesto* and *Alice in Wonderland* were written at about the same time," said Pappa's father, who was sitting in front of Mamma's bookcase, carefully passing his finger over the spines.

"All sorts. Playing," she mimicked. "You're not meeting that Lukas, are you?" Her pupils contracted. I avoided her eye.

"That Lukas, is his father's surname really Puskás?" Grandfather's voice sounded almost respectful when he pronounced the name. What? Mamma asked unkindly. Puskás . . . one of the world's finest football players of all time, in the '50s when the Hungarians were the best, the Magnificent Magyars . . . had she never heard about them? Mamma shook her head. She did not like anyone touching her books, and she definitely did not like talking about Lukas. Her pupils were as tiny and piercing as pinpricks, like the time when Lukas was messing about with his canisters of laughing gas, though if anything Mamma was about to go up a gear rather than down.

"And what has that got to with anything at all?" she asked, maliciously.

"I just thought they might be related."

"As if that would help," Mamma said, cutting the conversation short.

Mamma was the only one in the house to have a bookcase, even though the books only filled one shelf. Grandfather had some books in a wooden box under his bed, as if a proper bookshelf was something alien to him. In the pearl fisher's house Lukas and I found twenty identical mouldy black leather volumes, arranged alphabetically. A pattern. The way Lukas' brain worked, it had to see a pattern, every coincidence had a deeper meaning. It *had* to form a whole, the threads of an invisible spider's web that held the chaos of existence together. He wanted to try to piece together the world around us, to make up a

118

picture that at least made some sort of sense. A picture of what, I asked, but he did not know yet. My job was to decipher my way through the text, while Lukas explained to me what I had just read. He was bad at reading, but he knew a lot, mostly the sort of thing he had picked up from the television.

Coral, bats, fire, spiders – by the end of the summer he was talking more and more about the spider. At the centre of its web it was biding its time. Fate. The great cosmic mother in her most terrifying form. I do not know if it was his own mother he was thinking of. No, hardly, he did not have one.

Large trees of coral, salt-white, like porcelain, meticulously adorned by nature, stood in the windows of the pearl fisher's house, probably smuggled back from his many journeys to Japan. The skeleton of the coral, I read, was attached on the outside, like a protective coating. That is what Lukas should have had. When I stood waiting for him, I heard them arguing, him and his father, each one in his own language. I never understood what it was about, only that it had become worse as Lukas grew older. Before, he never answered back, now he made cautious attempts not to flee, but to stay and take what was coming. Or not take it.

The bruises disappeared and were replaced with new ones. However much love my own family tried to smother me in, what help was it when Lukas' existence was endless prowling around, watching and waiting, trying to escape. Sometimes he stayed the night in our hiding place, waiting for the lights to go out at home. I was setting myself free from the ones I had always belonged to and swimming out to him, what was going on between us never ended, it was just sucked down into a new hole, and then another, and on it went.

The whole time Lukas was scared that we would be discovered. No matter how long the pearl fisher's house had been left abandoned, we were in point of fact intruders. But at any rate no-one could call us vandals, he was very particular that we should keep it neat and tidy, he seemed to think that the pearl fisher *would* come back, though he must have been buried long ago, simple maths, how old could a pearl fisher be? The dust over everything was unquestionably fifty years thick.

One blustery evening in winter Lukas stopped in the middle of the lifeless forest, listening out over the lake. I heard it as well. The pulse. There is a pulse in everything that lives, we stood still and just listened, we no longer felt the cold, we had become part of it. The waves pounded under the ice, rhythmically, like blood between the atrium and the ventricle.

Later that evening I felt it in him too, how it pulsed. We had crept close together in bed to try and keep warm, barely keep warm, as it was hellishly cold. As soon as we started to thaw out, we felt as cold as ice. Lukas was fighting against sleep, unusually for him, but now it was as if he did not want to disappear into it. Sleep was sad, it meant that you had to part.

"People say *sleep together*, but that's wrong. You're alone when you sleep," he said and exhaled the smoke slowly through his lips like Jean-Paul Belmondo. I had learned how to sleep so lightly that I was still aware of his presence.

Lukas' winter belly was the same colour as the soft foam on the water at the power station, his skin as smooth as catkins, flushed cheeks, hands, lips, I felt his heart . . . how it beat resentfully, as if something trapped inside was trying to force its way out. The whole time it crashed against the bars of his rib cage. It will have to give up in the end, some time.

When I was small I had once made a hole in the ice with a shovel, so that the migrant birds could come out. Mamma's mother had told me that they spent the winter at the bottom of the lake, waiting for spring, and I was quite sure that they wanted to come out. But it was just a fairy tale, I knew that. Lukas listened and then shook his head.

"No, Lo," he said, "there's no such thing as fairy tales."

———

I could float. That was my first achievement. Nothing could drag me down, my childhood was happy, and if it was not, I did not realise. I could soon swim almost as well outside my mother's womb as I had inside. She could never really accept that. "We're all born wild," she said, "especially you, Lo." I grew quite tame later, but it was a superficial change.

Surrounded as I was by thirteen adults, I had no need to share their attention with anyone, I had a tough time trying to avoid it. Twenty-six eyes looked round every bend, into every blind spot, through every wall, saw dangers before I detected them myself. After my Aunt Katja was injured by a metal splinter from the circular sawing machine, there were still twenty-five eyes keeping track of me.

If I were to be anyone's accomplice, I would be his. When Lukas was shoplifting he just pulled his stomach in and slipped whatever he wanted into the waistband of his skater jeans, huge, khaki-coloured, drawstrings round the ankles, they accommodated however much we needed, food if we were hungry, drink if we were thirsty. I stood behind the shop waiting for him to come out and empty his haul into a rucksack that we took back to our hide-out.

He experimented with everything he could, cigarettes that he emptied of tobacco and mixed with something, he did not tell me where it came from. On some occasions he tried canisters of laughing gas while he was smoking, to heighten the effect. Sometimes I took him mixed leftovers from cans and bottles, because his own father did not drink. Once he got hold of ketamine, an anaesthetic for horses he had bought at some less than scrupulous farm nearby. He had heard that it gave you a high. It left him utterly beyond reach, he lay on the floor next to the bed and was gone. Like being sucked down into a black hole, he explained afterwards. A well of deliverance that you wanted to return to. I was terrified he would never come back.

Most of it was innocent, but it soon became second nature to associate pleasure with danger. Once when we were talking about the fire along the railway line, he said that he had started it. I did not know what to think. Why? Because otherwise we would never have met?

There was so much we had to fit in, there was no time to go to school, or at least not stay there the whole day. We ran. We passed through our childhood running. Lukas tucked elaborate secrets into me. *You must not tell anyone about this, this is just between you and me, no-one else would understand, can I rely on you?* I do not know, I answered, I had never kept secrets before, we did not do that in our family.

His words touched on everything: secrets, promises, devilry. Apart from the shadow of his father, adults scarcely figured in our world, nor did the other children at school, or the factories, goods trains, cold, hunger, tiredness, mealtimes, bedtimes, seasons. We were fast and focused, as if we had a sixth sense that the future was against us.

*

Of all the secrets that bound us together, the hardest one to keep was the one about the rats. It was Lukas' job to empty the traps his father set. The fat river rats would gnaw at the roof beams if you did not keep a check on them and they would go down into the kitchen at night. His father Gábriel took great care to keep things clean and filled the attic with the worst sort of traps. Then he showed his son how they should be emptied and gave him to understand that from then on it was his job.

When Gábriel was not looking, it was I who brought them down from the attic and stuffed them into the zinc tub behind the house until the cages stopped shaking, while Lukas stood, pressed up against the wall in shame, shame that he had left the worst to me. He looked as though it were he who was about to be drowned. He would rather not have been anywhere in the vicinity, but he was forced to keep watch, so that his father did not see that it was I who saw to the demise of those rats.

The old metal cages were heavy, especially when the rats had been in the water a while, and the next step was to empty their lifeless contents into the barrel in which Gábriel used to burn leaves. Not into the compost, that would just attract more rats. Lukas never got used to it, he could hardly bear the thought that I did it. They had intelligent eyes, he said. He had tried to do it himself, but in the end he just let them go, which made his father furious, as the rats ran through the high grass and shrieked like rubber ducks someone has trampled on. They shrieked when they were drowning as well, a screech like red-hot barbed wire. Despite our attempts to keep the secret, his father found us out. I had never seen him so enraged, never seen Lukas get such a beating, though he was always getting them for nothing.

If ever

It was the penultimate summer of my childhood, the last summer before Lukas became an adult. All those frontiers guarded from all directions. Our days in the pearl fisher's house had changed. He had dropped out of school and started to work at the leather factory with his father. A sabbatical, he called it, but no-one believed that, Lukas and school had never really been a successful combination. Sometimes I cycled up to the factory and waited for him to finish his shift. People poured out of the building, but Lukas was easy to spot in the crowd, always first out.

They tanned a hundred tons of hide a week and it showed on him – as if he tanned them all himself. The youngest invariably looked the most tired, worn out by the unfamiliar. Nonetheless he never refused to come with me to the pearl fisher's house. He just had to go home first to shower away the smell, even though he had showered once at the factory.

We sat in the blazing hot sun against the wall of the house, dozing off and listening to music. When our skin started to blister, we undressed and went out into the water. I do not remember if summer was ahead of us or behind us, we were in an everlasting season of warmth and an intermingling of identical days. I just remember how Lukas lifted me up in the water and hurled me like a grenade that exploded on contact with the quicksilver surface. I quickly swam back to land, though I knew that as soon as I came within reach he would catch me again, throw me far out once more, fling me into my place, make me feel how light I was compared to him.

I wriggled away, dived down and grabbed hold of his slippery penis and pulled as hard as I could. That was the only weapon I had. Under the water his yell sounded like a muffled gurgling. I could feel him catch me and hold me down under the surface, so that I would panic and let go. I did in the end, but as soon as I felt his grip on my head loosen I swam between his legs, where he was standing with his feet apart in the water to keep his balance. Shot up behind him, twisted as I passed from water to air, threw myself onto his back and then we whirled round again under the surface. His lungs could hold twice as much air as mine, I was always the one who had to give in and go up for oxygen first. We carried on like this until we were blue with cold.

It was an entirely normal evening, but in the dusty greenery by the lake disaster lay in wait. I did not notice my father's brother until it was too late, when he had already seen everything he believed he had seen. I had no time to warn Lukas. Rikard was quick, after a couple of strides out into the water, he tore me out of Lukas' arms and pushed me up onto land, ordering me to get dressed. Without waiting for explanation, he hit Lukas. Had not reckoned that he would stay on his feet, that he would have to hit him again. And that Lukas would remain standing. As if it were simply an unusually strong gust of wind between the trees. Rikard had probably not had a chance to think anything at all. He would stop thinking the second he lost his temper and, since he lost the power of speech at the same time, he gave the impression that he was stupid.

Certain things about Lukas were difficult to get used to, how swiftly he switched between bravado and subservience, a dangerous mix of extremes. An unpredictability that would have seemed alarming if I had not grown up with it, but he was like an untrustworthy dog you had known since he was a puppy, did not frighten me, which was not the same thing as me relying on him.

He did not dare hit back but at least he should have defended himself instead of just standing there, uncomfortably resistant to the impact. I screamed at Rikard until my voice shattered his concentration. Only then did the nightmare end and Lukas staggered backwards and sat down on the grass, his face covered in blood. I flew at Rikard, but bounced away like an insect, flew at him again, bounced away. Bent over Lukas at a menacing angle he hissed,

"This is just a little warning. Next time I won't be as careful. I don't know . . . how old you are . . . but my niece here is *eleven*."

When Rikard marched off with me I could see over his shoulder that Lukas tried to stand up but fell down in the grass again. It had never taken much to make him throw up, and now the concussion produced a cascade over the grass. At that moment he did not seem to care where I had gone. Behind me I heard a long string of words in Gábriel's language. It happened sometimes, words Lukas did not even know the meaning of, tirades he had grown up with.

You feel no pain, Mamma used to say. It was not true, seeing Lukas there was unspeakably painful. Rikard carried me to make sure that he got me home and the whole way he blamed Pappa for everything: since David went this and since David went that . . . I had become unmanageable, they could not let me out of their sight for a second . . .

the slightest thing was exaggerated so that Pappa could be held responsible for the way things had gone wrong since he disappeared.

We were scarcely through the door by the time Rikard had reported Lukas and me to the security police back at the house. It always happened this way at home, there was no private life, no integrity, no word of honour.

"I understand why Pappa ran off," I was standing in the corner of the kitchen, howling, "and I intend to report you for assault, Rikard, just so you know!" No-one took any notice of me. Rikard and Mamma wound each other up, they were the most indignant people in the kitchen, on a sliding scale down to Pappa's father, who was sitting at his place by the table looking moderately shaken.

"Lukas isn't a child any more, he's an adult now," Mamma said, in a voice that indicated that this was bad news, and a glance at Grandfather that meant he needed to do something about it.

"You're not going to report anything," was all Grandfather said to me, gently. "If anybody needs to be concerned, it's that lad and his family."

"He has no family," I spat out, "no-one, no-one!"

Rikard stopped me when I tried to slip out of the kitchen.

"Yes, but he has a father, and that's the person we're going to speak to."

"You said yourselves that he's an adult – so don't talk to his father . . . he beats him all the time."

Mamma stopped, mid-step. "You've never said that before." As if she did not believe me. As if it was just a means of diverting attention away from Lukas' crime. A smoke screen.

"Well, that is *not* what all this is about right now," Rikard objected, in a cold voice.

When Mamma went off to speak to Gábriel, to get him to understand that the family's patience with his son had run out, Grandfather accompanied her. Not because she asked him to, perhaps to offer some protection – whether to her or to Lukas' father was not clear.

It did not reflect on me. I was just a child, they said. A name and a reputation, if nothing else at least we have that. That applied to Lukas and his father as well, and they ought to bear that in mind, that was Pappa's mother's opinion.

That night I sneaked out after they had all gone to sleep, down to Lukas' house. He was sleeping in the room behind the kitchen, woke up and let me in through the window. When he switched on the light I got a shock. Which of the injuries were caused by Rikard's outburst by the lake and which were caused by Gábriel, I did not know, but the sight of him . . .

"What does he think I've done with you? That Rikard," Lukas mumbled, "I've never . . . I've just . . ." I laid my hand on his split lips, frightened that Gábriel would wake up. Explained that Rikard believed that he had to play the part of my Pappa now, obviously thought that this was the sort of thing fathers did.

"It's not your fault," Lukas said, but what he was thinking in reality I do not know, his dark eyes were ashen. "Has he hit you as well?" I shook my head, no, no, Rikard would never do that, he just told me off, made threats, imposed restrictions, involved the whole family, raised hell and said that if Lukas and I ever . . .

*

I had collected some toads after the rain, heavy and still from the warmth of the night they had been lying on the gravel track between our houses and let me pick them up. When I was banned from going out they starved to death in the buckets in the pearl fisher's house. A peaceful death, Lukas consoled me, but they did not look peaceful where they had been trying to escape by scrambling over one another and died in a sinking tower of toad flesh. In the place where he buried them the grass stopped growing.

We continued to meet, but took more safety measures. As if nothing had happened and as if no harm could come to us again. But it had, of course, and it could happen again, something had changed and I did not want to see him through the same eyes my family had, but it was hard to stop myself.

"Sex is the only thing grown-ups think about", I said, testing. Lukas stiffened. "They can't stop us from seeing each other," I added.

"I think they can."

"No." He looked doubtful.

"At any rate we have to make them think that they can," he said.

Illusion

If I had just had an inkling it would happen, a hint of a threat brewing, a shift on the horizon, something. Not this: cloudless sky and then lightning that suddenly struck and without a sound set fire to everything. Pappa had been standing in the yard one morning in late winter, his bags packed, his brother Jon behind the wheel of the Volvo to drive him somewhere. Where? The world's end? Mamma's mother was crying, at any rate. Not Pappa's mother, she was not the crying type, nor Mamma, she just stood by the open front door with a face I did not recognise. Rikard, newly awakened, came down from upstairs, Pappa's father was nowhere to be seen, at least afterwards I could not remember him. The rest of the family were scattered here and there in the yard, as if something had flung them apart, a shock wave or simply a feeling of bewilderment, the consternation was still palpable. I was sitting on Pappa's hip, clinging on with all my strength as his hands were full.

"Where are you going, when are you coming home, I want to come too." Not that I wanted to, I had never travelled anywhere and would rather stay at home. But he looked lonely, no-one in the family had gone away alone before, that was not the way we did things.

Around Mamma was an impenetrable air of "leave me alone". The others in the family took turns to keep me occupied so that I would leave her be. No-one explained what had happened or why.

If only I could remember a single time that Mamma and Pappa had argued. Had I forgotten? Or had they lived a secret life that I had not even seen? It is true that they did not sleep together, but it had been like that for as long as I could remember. Pappa slept in the narrow passage above the stairs, Mamma in the north room with his sister Marina.

That very night I had been woken by something, a noise or a dream, sneaked out of bed, discovered that Mamma was not in fact lying in the double bed back to back with Marina as usual. In my drowsy state I thought that maybe she had gone to sleep with Pappa after all. I crept in next to Marina feeling muddled, but contented, and fell asleep as soon as I felt her warm back against mine. Next morning I awoke to a full-blown disaster.

After Pappa disappeared, Mamma did not want to keep any happy pictures of him. She took them out of the albums. I rescued them from the rubbish bin and hid them among the other forbidden things in the dust under her wardrobe. She never gave away their secret, not even in revenge for Pappa leaving. No revelation, apart from what I heard her say to his father – to destroy a man is not difficult, the difficult thing is to get on well with him. The words etched themselves as a permanent enigma.

A cloud perhaps, if I thought hard about it. They were chopping wood in a race against each other once. An unreal atmosphere in the yard with their rhythmic breathing, more and more vehement. Mamma won by a mile. Pappa's talent was not for chopping firewood, I do not know what it was, but not chopping wood, at any rate. He was weak, his father maintained, and I thought that perhaps that was why he could walk on water or at least on ice, something no-one else in our family could do . . . because he weighed nothing. But he was not weak – though I did not tell Grandfather this – how once a long time ago I saw him hit Mamma in the scullery. It was only the one time and she hit back and by dinner time they were pretending nothing had happened. And perhaps Grandfather was right in one way, perhaps it was just because he was weak that he lashed out.

"Don't think about him," Rikard said when he came with me down to the lake to bathe, "and if you don't think about him, he might come back." Since Pappa disappeared his brothers and sisters were even kinder to me than before. But that seemed like a lie all the same.

Rikard's back was warm from the sun when I laid my wet stomach against him and said, "Can't you marry Mamma . . ." Pappa had been away for several weeks and I realised that he was not going to return. Rikard stiffened and then he began to laugh.

"You mean one of those brother-in-law marriages? So that the property won't leave the family?" he said and rolled me off into the grass. I did not know what "brother-in-law marriage" or "property" meant. But I assumed that I was "property" – and I most definitely did not want to leave the family. "If your mother had wanted me I would have married her long ago. Well, supposing I didn't regard her as my big sister, that is. David should have done the same, for that matter. Not messed it up like this." My mouth tasted of water lily, I wrapped myself up in the towel, shivering, and waited for him to continue. Because it felt as though he ought to say something more, something about . . . supposing my parents had not messed it up, I would not have existed. But he said nothing.

*

When Rikard lifted me up I was weightless. He walked out into the water and flung me out over the surface, light as a fishing net, just the way he knew I loved. How could he leave her, I thought, as I sank to the bottom, how could he? For that was what he had done, though no-one said so, wounds just left to heal themselves, conflicts were settled between those affected, you left other people's lives in peace, that was how we did things more often than not.

I let myself sink so that I could be rescued, but Rikard would have to hurry now, what was he doing? The cold water from the bottom of the lake shimmered towards me as I sank deeper and deeper. He did not come to save me, not this time, I had to fight my way up with sludge water in my mouth, blue-lipped. He was sitting in a patch of sun on the grass looking at me.

"When do you intend to learn to swim, Lo?" I could swim, only I dared not show I could as it was Lukas who had taught me. "When are you going to grow up?" I realised that it was time, I was nearly nine and to all intents and purposes fatherless now. No-one was going to rescue me.

————

Our house had never been so quiet, the only thing you could hear were the flies. I did not even hear anything given away when I hid in the stuffy wardrobe in Pappa's brothers' room. Nor under Mamma and Aunt Marina's bed, there were just balls of fluff and silence. Mealtimes were a wordless torture. May I have the butter, pass the salt. Mamma did not even say that. Quietest of all. Go out and play, I saw in her eyes as soon as I happened to fall within her field of vision.

I tried to wear down their patience with questions, but it led nowhere. Grandfather, I thought. Pappa's father had the shortest temper in the family, it should not be impossible to get him to let the cat out of the bag. I started to work on him carefully, at first he paid no attention to my nagging, then he got annoyed. Finally he gave in. Late one evening he came into my room and gave me a picture of an oilrig, high as a skyscraper out in the middle of a blue-black sea with no land in sight. This was where my Pappa was, on this great steel monster which was drilling oil from the seabed far out in the North Sea.

"Stop going on about it now," Grandfather demanded in return. As if Pappa's reappearance was a kitten I was never going to get. I cried myself to sleep that night. Not because he was there, I knew he was not, he had such bad vertigo that he could not even go up into the attic with both Mamma and Grandfather holding the steps. I cried because they lied to me. One lie turns everything into a lie.

The picture of the oilrig where Grandfather alleged Pappa worked hung as a fixture over my bed, even though I was sure that he was not there. It is true he could walk on water, but only when it was frozen, and I found it impossible to imagine my father in the dark with his vertigo drilling oil from the bottom of the sea with storms and albatrosses howling round his ears. Alone amongst men, according to Grandfather. It was only men who worked out there, real men.

I thought that it might have something to do with her – the one who disappeared under the ice, but it was so long ago now and I was not sure what the connection could be. The picture nailed to the wall as a reminder. That adults are not to be trusted. In my dreams the steel monstrosity moved like a giant spider through a desolate sea in a heavy storm. In contrast to me, Lukas was impressed, all that with the oilrig, Alexander Kielland, the whole thing made an impression on him. He did not really care that it was a lie. A lie was at least an answer, he did not even have a lie as explanation for what had happened to his mother.

After Pappa went off I began to see adults in a different light. As bearers of dark secrets, everyone his own. Adults became mere shadows who carried their secrets and lies and lunchboxes and their tension headaches, their hideous hairstyles and tennis elbows through a town that did not even have a tennis court. The elbows they had acquired at the factory. The hairstyles at the Greek's. They carried them between work and the shop, home and the public baths and the lake. Carried their plastic bags and secrets, their tiredness, their hopes, their exaggerated optimism for the future and private despair, and everything in terry towelling, gabardine, denim, corduroy and rib-knits, and the jerry cans, shotguns, snow cannons, bicycle chains, cod for the soup, gossip, holiday plans. Much of it came to nothing. Some things succeeded, but most did not. The adults carried everything around apart from their children, for there was a do-not-indulge mentality that they all made their common cause. All except those who carried me. Long after I could walk they took it in turns to carry me, competed for it. I was big when I discovered by mistake that I could in fact walk by myself. They would rather that I had never discovered it, that I had never noticed the smell of those secrets.

Do-not-indulge. Do-not-disgrace-yourself. It was the unspoken rule that applied to all other children, it was part of the community, but we did not belong to it so we could just as well behave as we liked.

Vertigo

It was Pappa's father who had given him permission to go out. He who said that the ice was safe. Perfect ice to hammer a hole for burbot fishing. It had been an ordinary day at the beginning of winter, Mamma's sister, who was only eight, had gone with him, the thirteen-year-old. He could not save her. The red jacket had slipped from her, just as a petal drops from a rose, without a sound. The red material floated in the hole in the ice long after she had been sucked under and disappeared into the centre of the lake.

The ice-hole where she drowned recurred constantly in Pappa's dreams. The silence. He dreamed of silence – that the disaster was so silent and quick and calm was the most frightening thing of all. It was too late to do anything. To make a sound or even try to save her. He just stood there in the middle of the lake, alone.

There then followed a winter that would never end. They knew that she was there somewhere beneath the ice, her body drifting along the bottom or perhaps it had stuck fast in the ice during the coldest nights. Only when the ice thawed, which happened unusually late that spring, did they find her. Preserved by the cold, naked except for her baptism cross. Identification was a formality but a nightmare nevertheless. Pappa's parents went in place of Mamma's, Pappa went too because his father thought he should. He stood a little apart and was upset that they showed her naked in the cold light of the room at the mortuary. To see her again . . . after all those months. Dead, answered Pappa when I hesitantly asked what she looked like. And yet not dead. He was quite sure that he saw a movement in her pale eyelashes, but perhaps it was just something thawing – not enough to bring her back to life, but enough to cause a movement. It was his fault. No-one needed to say it.

I was afraid of the wind-openings – large open holes where the wind kept the water open, invisible to the eye, the most sinister traps in the ice. Sinkholes, gas holes, erosion holes. Warm currents that made the ice so fragile that it would not even bear the weight of a tiny lynx out hunting. In late winter the sun could be so high that it penetrated the ice and melted the frozen water from below. The ice was a dangerous world that you needed to understand. As a child Pappa had been forced to learn to read the ice: risks, bearing capacity, signs, but there were never any guarantees. Once-only ice could only stand one person walking over it – the next person tumbled through. That was how Mamma's youngest sister had drowned. Pappa had turned round and watched it happen without being able to do anything. The ice that a moment ago had supported him did not support her, even though she was much lighter than him.

I followed close behind Pappa's back. The mist drifted over the frozen water. We were father and daughter out hunting, went right out towards the sun. Every so often I stopped behind him, took aim and shot. When we heard the ice lowing we were right out on the lake, appalled I saw the fracture open up between his legs and mine, convinced that it would widen, separate us, swallow us up. But a glance at Pappa's face told me that the ice would hold. The shots which went off beneath us just meant that the day was exceptionally cold and the ice thicker than usual and it was cracking because of temperature stresses. The warning noise of the thaw was quite different, you had to learn to hear the difference.

There seemed to have been something special about Mamma's sister even before she drowned, perhaps just that she was the youngest.

"As small as you, Lo, and yet she still fell through the ice I'd walked on a moment earlier. If she'd gone first she'd have been fine and I'd have drowned," Pappa said as we were standing right out in the deepest part. Once-only ice, nightmare ice. To be the death of someone else in that way, to want to protect but instead to weaken the ice so that it broke the minute the next person put her foot on it.

Salt ice, sweet ice, blue ice, glass ice, wreck ice, floe ice, diabase ice. Ice that looked like frozen carbon dioxide. Walking along I almost dozed off to his soothing voice, as he was explaining to me how the water was arranged in different layers, coldest uppermost in winter, warmest uppermost in summer. Pappa knew just as much about the ice as Mamma knew about the art of handling an axe. The drowning accident did not make him afraid of ice, it was the depth that frightened him, the vertigo, the feeling of great height, a fear of falling that could strike at any time. But he still went out onto the ice as soon as it froze, set pike traps though there were scarcely any fish here. He never asked me to come with him. Nor did he stop me when I put on my ski boots and followed.

It was mostly for the stories that I went with him. The stories belonged to the ice. About the dogs who were let loose during the polar bear hunt, still leashed together in pairs, two by two they surrounded the quarry, which instinctively reared up in defence. Upright on its back legs the bear became an easy target for the hunters. When Pappa described this to me I thought of his father, who in an upright position was as large as the animal from whom he took his name. He and Pappa did not see eye to eye, it was something you just knew, they were like dog and bear together.

"Were you really all born out of the ice?" I had gone around shaping this question until it had got soft and sweaty – that was the picture I had before me when Pappa's mother said that she and Mamma's mother gave birth to one child every winter, I imagined that they went out and pulled them up from a hole in the ice. But all at once Pappa's desire to tell me things vanished into thin air.

"When we get home tell your mother to explain how children are made. She can give you all the details."

And she did. About the bakehouse that was next door to the house they lived in, and in the bakehouse there was a warm wall, and by the warm wall they had made a bunk bed, and to this bunk bed you could go if you wanted some time to yourself. This is where they had been made, one after the other. In the heat lost from the oven which was often newly lit, in the familiar smell of birch wood and barley flour. If you took a tub of butter with you, you could eat some of the left-over bits of bread if you were hungry afterwards. And you were.

What about me, though? Where was I made? By the warm wall as well? Mamma looked at me as she sat on the chopping-block with the axe and the sharpener and answered that no, the bakehouse belonged to a different time and a different place.

The story of the day I was born had been related to me many times, but never how I was in fact made. Why them? The most ill-matched pair. Pappa was a perfectly normal father, but Mamma . . .

"Not by the warm wall, Lo. You were made under the sloping ceiling."

Under the sloping ceiling? Was that the only answer she could think of? That explained nothing. There was not even a sloping ceiling in our house.

Certain memories are so clear that everything surrounding them seems blurred. It was late one evening several months after Pappa had gone, with the hollow sound of the bittern's cry from down at the lake, a sound like blowing into an empty bottle. An invisible and sinister bird, I had only glimpsed it once, how it flew, heavy at the front, like a bird of prey over the quicksilver water.

I switched on the television to block out the eerie noise. Lying in Rikard's room on a bean bag on the floor and bored. The news. Blah, blah, blah. Lay so that I could watch the screen upside down to make it less boring.

Reporter struggling against the wind, raging storm with gusts of hurricane strength, camera lens so spotted with rain it was almost impossible to see anything, but I saw all the same . . . there in the background . . . I stared – lying upside down until all the blood collected in my head and burst. The ominous words "Alexander Kielland" suspended over everything, the whole disaster. The sea in complete tumult, huge waves, the legs had broken, the platform capsized, tipped over, turned upside down. And sank.

Everything had happened very fast. Most of the crew had fallen in and those who did not fall threw themselves into the ice-cold sea. Why? Because everyone else did? Because there was a risk that the oil would begin to burn? But was the water not also full of leaking oil? Were they not going to drown in the thick black sticky soup like helpless seabirds? Without survival gear they would not last many minutes in the cold, the reporter said, and anyway, what would that matter? When the sea began to burn. A burning sea. I crept nearer to the screen, tried to imagine a burning sea.

They did not yet know how many had been killed, their relatives would be informed before the names of the dead were released. I flung myself forward and switched off in the middle of the broadcast, strained to hear if there was a noise from downstairs, but the television was not on down there. There was only me who had heard what had happened. The appalling event. The oilrig disaster. Horrific words. And all of a sudden I was no longer in any doubt that Pappa was there. I knew he was. Were anyone to have bad luck it would be him. I ran. Down into the kitchen where Pappa's mother and Mamma were standing by the sink, scaling herrings. Buried my face in Grand-mother's fishy apron, refused to tell them what had happened.

The next few days I wandered around in a shocked trance, a bittern in my head, its call foreboding and echoing, day and night. No-one said anything. As if the accident had not happened. As if none of them had heard about it, or they tried to keep me in the dark – how could they act so well? Eat and sleep and work as usual. Laugh as usual.

"If he was one of the ones who drowned, they would've told you," Lukas assured me. If he had been one of the few who survived, they would also have told me. Silence could only mean the worst.

Days of disquieting normality immediately after the disaster. The kitchen in cold sunlight, Mamma chopping wood, Rikard and Katja stacking the wood, Erik and Marina washing the cars, Helena lying on the television sofa with her boyfriend, Jon arguing with his girlfriend on the phone, boyfriends and girlfriends coming and going, they never lasted long in this house, and there was Pappa's mother putting the dishes in to soak, his father had retired to the arboretum, Mamma's mother was wiping down all the surfaces, touching things with light hands. At night I crept down between Mamma and Marina again, as I had when I was small, lay there with eyes wide open, while they appeared to sleep, a sleep as peaceful and deep as ever.

"Girl, you're going round and round like a dog about to have puppies. What is it?" Mamma murmured in the darkness. I tried to say something about Pappa, but I could not get the words out. "Think about something nice. Your birthday. Think about what you'd like. Shall we ask David to come?"

I twisted my head into the pillow: "Stop it! I know he's dead!"

Mamma sat straight up in bed. "Pull yourself together. That wasn't funny."

I buried my face deeper into the foam-rubber pillow. "Ask Grandfather!" I howled.

She grabbed me firmly by the hand and dragged me along the corridor in the cold of the night, down the black staircase to Pappa's parents' room. Went in and fetched out a sleepy Grandfather for interrogation in the kitchen.

"Are you out of your mind? Have you told her that her father's dead? Have you no heart, no shame, are you mad?" she screamed at him. Grandfather looked as though he thought he was still dreaming, pressed up against the sink unit by the sheer force of Mamma's voice. I slipped away to get the picture of the oilrig, the one that was no longer standing out there at sea, but lying on the bottom, collapsed like a house of cards with 123 dead men. That was the final death toll Lukas had heard on the television and passed on to me, more had died than had survived, and Pappa was like Lukas, if anyone was unlucky, it was him.

Before I entered the kitchen I heard Grandfather's voice. ". . . what the hell should I have said then? The child was asking and asking. Should I have told her that her father lives so close and still never comes to visit her because of . . ." Because of us, I thought he said, but just then he caught sight of me and swallowed the last bit.

———

The smell of his night sweat, salty like nettles, he lay on his back with his arms under his head, opened his eyes right next to my face. He had just fallen asleep, but not so deeply that he did not hear my question. His eyes very dark blue with a circle of rust round the pupils.

"Do you love Mamma?" He looked at me, as if my words reached him very slowly.

"I have never loved anyone else."

It was not an answer to my question. It did not reveal whether he still loved her. Not even if he had ever loved her.

Just a few weeks later he packed his bags and left, and I was overwhelmed by the sense that I should not have asked.

"Do you love Pappa?" Mamma was filling the laundry room with white sheets and underclothes. She answered as naturally as if I had asked if the night was dark and the mountain of washing endless. But she never showed it, I tried to remember if I had ever seen her put her arms around him, or he her. I could not recall a single instance.

*

I had been born into the best of worlds, but I no longer lived there. When I was growing up the picture was complete, everyone was there and no-one was going to disappear. Dangers were only things adults spoke about when they thought I had fallen asleep on the television sofa. Oil crisis and Falklands War and embassy bombings, inadequate safety at the factory, the risk of rain during the holiday.

Pappa was the first. When he disappeared the balance was disturbed, then things settled down and we thought that nothing else would happen. Mamma's and Pappa's brothers and sisters had always been my big clumsy playmates, oversized, loud, heavy-handed, spirited, annoying. Better at winding me up than bringing me up. They had all the patience Mamma was lacking, shared the burden of me between themselves. I had taken for granted that they existed just for me, felt hurt if I could not join in, if a door was closed, took it as a personal insult that they had to go to work sometimes, without me. To belong to everyone is to belong to no-one. It was only after the family started to scatter in the wind that I belonged to Mamma.

The chain reaction had started, it was work and love and homesickness and a fish-gutting factory in Iceland that lured. Quick money, you could earn gold at the conveyor belt, if you could just stand the cold and smell and did not need any sleep and could live on a shoestring for a while. The house became more and more empty. The fish-gutting factory, homesickness and finally death. Mamma's father died of chemical pneumonia. He had inhaled a corrosive substance at the factory and his lungs began to burn. He left his shift at the paper mill an hour early on the Friday afternoon and by Monday he was dead.

His boots stood in the hall the whole winter, waiting for his broad feet, were shoved back and forth among the others. Who was going to take them away? There were many of us who could have done it – but no-one who wanted to. I took care of the broken pieces that Grandmother produced in a steady stream in the kitchen when things inexplicably slipped out of her hands. Grandfather's coffee cup, schnapps glass, soured-milk bowl. Buried them at the edge of the field behind the house, they came up every year when they were ploughing, like a memorial.

Mamma's mother died among the currant bushes. Had half filled her plastic tub when her heart gave a double beat in a warning that was altogether too late, and stopped. She had been a little confused for a long time and since Grandfather's death she had been comfort-eating to the extent that her wedding ring disappeared into white flesh, in the end her body so unwieldy that she could no longer climb the stairs in the house. Why she needed to be out in the currant patch on the hottest day of summer with her weak heart, no-one could understand. Least of all her doctor. Her death could have been avoided, he said.

But it cannot be.

The currants flew through the air like a bloodstain onto the layer of manure she had just put under the bushes that morning. Grandmother in her old white dress smeared with berries and blood and earth.

She had told Pappa's mother that she wanted to be buried at home, and this was not home. It cost a fortune to get her there, so much more than if she had been alive. Pappa's parents' last savings.

"A little while ago I was young, wasn't I?" Mamma's face in the bedroom mirror was changed. It was still her face but it was as if an older face had been pulled over it. I wanted her to take off the pale, lifeless mask that was not her. Grandmother stroked her hair, but did not contradict her – she *did* look old, overnight, I did not realise that such a thing could truly happen. When Grandmother did not reply, Mamma turned to me instead, as if I would be able to explain what had happened – where the stranger's face in the mirror came from.

Losing both her parents had happened so fast. As long as one of your parents is still alive your childhood carries on, I heard Grandmother say. When you are no longer anyone's child – that is when you realise what you have lost.

Then Grandmother herself became ill, almost without us noticing. Unlike Mamma's parents, she died slowly. She did not show it, but we knew that she was dying day by day. No visible decline, more as if she were dying from the inside out, her vital organs attacked one after the other. In the end there was nothing left of her, the cancer had eaten everything, though she looked normal from the outside. The doctor had gauged how much time she had and it turned out to be correct, to within a few days.

When Rikard, the last of the brothers and sisters, moved to a hotel job in Stockholm that Marina had fixed up for him . . . it was almost worse than when Pappa left. Now there was just Pappa's father, Mamma and me left. Rumours started to circulate in the village, but Mamma had forbidden me to listen to them. It was something about Mamma and Grandfather, a little domestic war going on, the causes of which only they knew. Love, hate, either or, or both and, just like turning on old taps and the water coming out ice-cold and scalding hot by turns.

"I ought to move out for Lo's sake," I heard Grandfather from inside the woodshed.

"If you move then I'll move."

"But that solves nothing, Karenina."

"Don't call me Karenina!" I could not catch any more through the thick partition wall before Mamma strode away. Soon noises could be heard from the arboretum, Grandfather's black poplar, how she axed it down in a frenzied rage, with the strength and fury of a pig. Smashed it to smithereens, which she crammed into the stove that evening, piece by piece. A few days later she bought electric heaters for all the rooms, despite Grandfather's protests. One thing was certain, she had felt cold for the last time. This is still my house, I am not dead yet, warned Grandfather. Mamma turned in the cold light of late winter and stared at him. There are some people who must not die. He was one of them.

"Dead?" she said, unable to grasp this, as if it had never even crossed her mind that he also . . .

"No, not *yet*," Grandfather said. "It is still me who makes the decisions around here." It never had been him, of course – but it is true that it was still his house and when that was no longer the case, then I would inherit, he said, something he had suddenly just decided. "You brothers and sisters can hardly divide it into nine parts, Katarina. There'd only be a window catch each."

There was a time when we did not know how there would be enough room for all the beds, crisscross throughout the house, now the problem was filling the rooms, stopping the echoes. And then Grandfather started to talk about leaving as well, and that I had to stay behind so that Mamma would not be totally alone.

"Your grandfather," Mamma said coldly, "talks so much. Haven't you noticed? He claims that he's going to die too." The word "die" flew from her mouth with the speed of spit. Grandfather was not even ill yet, but all the others had gone so how could we be sure that he would stay?

However much I missed the rest of the family, what I missed most was Mamma the way she was before the others disappeared. Now she, Grandfather and I were the only ones left. I would soon be fifteen and no-one could be bothered any longer about what I did.

Adolescence

Parted without saying goodbye. Back together again without any particular signs of affection. Just melting into each other, swiftly and soundlessly. What happened between me and Lukas was as unremarkable as the water in a zinc tub slowly warming in the sun.

The only part of me that grew that year as I approached fifteen was my legs, just like a gazelle's. My teenage years did not feel like an inner revolution, but more like constant growing pains. The only interest I had in my own body was as a means to transport my consciousness from one physical place to another. It might just as well have belonged to someone else, I showed so little interest in it, and I was almost as heedless of his. Saw that he had changed since he had started work, become more sinewy, harder, slower – yet there was still something boyish about him, as if the calf in him was lingering on. For sentimental reasons, or to wait for me, let me catch up.

Love makes the one you love complete and faultless. It turns a piece of glass into a shining jewel. I was the hand that held him up to the sun. Eyes as black as spilled oil and everything else that he was, but . . . in love? It was more complicated than that. Our smells began to change, grew stronger, more absorbent and at the same time more different from each other. Together we smelled of burning. Explain love. Explain summer. No-one can explain the summer when childhood suddenly ends. The madhouse filled with water, but Lukas and I scarcely noticed what was happening around us. That time passed. That seasons changed. That the lake was covered with new ice, drift ice, crushed ice. That everyone disappeared, one after the other, until there were so many empty chairs in the kitchen that Mamma organised a bonfire. It was not like her, she used to chop up everything that would burn for firewood, but it was as if she had gone soft.

Childhood trickled away and was gone, leaving only a few sun-bleached fragments of regret. Suddenly I was at an age when I read *Bonjour Tristesse*, read whatever I happened to find in Mamma's bookcase. She must have lost her faith in books at some point in her youth, because everything she had in her bookcase was from that time. In the absence of any revealing diaries that I could read surreptitiously, the novels were the only way I could sneak a look into that period of her life. A glimpse of the outlook she must have had then. There was the scent of pine trees, American suburbs and deserted French cafés when I opened them and let myself be transported away. Lukas was jealous. Books made me unreachable even when I was lying right next to him in bed. He watched me disappear, but did not understand where – still less why. Novels? There was nothing wrong with this world, where *he* existed, where *he* was waiting. He waited for me to finish, whether I wanted him to or not, lit a new cigarette whenever I turned a page, blew the smoke out over the book, looked at me.

I read everything I could lay my hands on. Books made time stand still, while the world was expanding. Everything is beautiful from a distance, like the river delta seen from above, free from the stench of rotting sediment and silt. Made clear and enticing like illustrated maps of inaccessible places where no man can live.

I read about the Chinese method of describing the passage of time, with what logical beauty it elapsed in their eyes. Instead of four clumsily measured seasons they talked about the slight cold, great cold, beginning of spring, rain water, waking of insects, pure brightness, grain rain, beginning of summer, grain fills, grain in ear. Then the summer solstice which led to the slight heat, great heat, beginning of autumn, limit of heat, white dew. And then the autumnal equinox followed by cold dew, the first frosty night when the migrant birds leave Peking and the chrysanthemums are at their most beautiful. And then the descent of frost, beginning of winter, slight snow, great snow, until light's turning point is reached again.

———

September arrived with its long shadows, migrant birds, autumn moon. Virgo's month, my month, virgin, sapphire. We had never been so close together before as we would be when I turned fifteen. When I was a child he was a teenager, and when I was a teenager he was an adult, soon for the first time we would both be on the same side of the crucial line. It would no longer be a case of exploitation of a child, Lukas said as we went down for what was to be the last dip in the lake that year – if something happened. "Happened?" Between us, he said.

There was something in the air, I had felt it for a long time, perhaps just a faint tension, a hint of unrest and change when one season crosses over into the next. Lukas had commented on my fifteenth birthday many times, that it was a dividing line, but between what? I had already been a teenager for two years.

"But at fifteen, Lo, no-one's really a child any longer." The imaginary threshold between the possible and the impossible, as if the border-line itself would make something possible that had not been possible before. He seemed to be imagining this. He had built up a sense of anticipation that made me also believe that in a purely physical way I would feel that I had passed a certain point.

It was as if a sun were scorching him from the inside the whole summer, plaguing him, parched and surly. To live is to wait. At least for Lukas, waiting for the snake to show its real face, it was the year of the snake the year I turned fifteen, which according to the Chinese calendar in Mamma's bookcase meant duplicity and betrayal: sign no contracts, do not change the bedclothes, take care with fire, do not participate in legal proceedings, do not sell your soul to the devil, avoid open water, and washing your hair, eat no peaches, only pay debts if absolutely necessary, avoid distress, and family gatherings, inauspicious time to make new friendships, refrain from disruptive disputes and long journeys.

As the day approached it appeared that Lukas had forgotten all about it. No special plans and no questions about how I wanted to celebrate, even though I was always full of ideas.

"You know what day it is tomorrow, don't you?" I could not stop myself saying in the end.

"The Japanese national day, or no, wait a minute . . . maybe it's the world day for protection of the ozone layer – goodness knows how you're supposed to celebrate that."

"I know you know . . . you're going to give me a surprise."

"Hardly. I've got an extra shift at work to do," he shrugged. We had grown too big for having fun. Could not play games for ever more.

He had begun to work the night shift so that he had the house to himself while his father was at work. Lukas clocked off, rode home and slept for a few hours and got up when Gábriel went off for his afternoon shift, the same time as I came home from school. The house was then ours until late in the evening, unless we went down to the pearl fisher's place. I did my homework at Lukas', if I did it at all, while he sat and rocked on a chair, waiting. No matter how speedily I raced through it, he thought it took too long. That I went to school too often, read too much, not useful at my age, my brain was not fully developed. It was to be hoped that his brain was not either, I said, and how helpful was it to work every night in the chemical fumes of the factory?

I had no idea what I wanted to do with my life, only that factories did not figure in my plans and that being the case, school could not be given up altogether.

"What do you mean, not in the factories? You're not going to move?" Lukas looked utterly nonplussed. As if that thought had never crossed his mind.

———

I wait behind the petrol station as he asked me to do when he rang the evening before. After the night shift he comes past in the car I did not know he had bought, a blue Ford Taunus, far from new but not particularly rusty either. He cannot hide his pride when he swings the car in and opens the passenger door and invites me to climb in with just a nod. Gábriel has neither a car nor a driving licence, this is Lukas' own thing, he has worked a long time to be able to afford the driving lessons and has kept it a secret the whole time.

I have packed some essentials in an old military rucksack, not sure what to expect. Left a note for Mamma on the kitchen table: *Celebrating the day with Lukas. Don't worry.* Regret the last sentence, but it is too late now.

It is oppressive and tense in the car, Lukas has an air of determination rather than expectation. So clean-shaven, as though the hair on his face has not started to grow yet. A white nylon shirt in honour of the day – I recognise it, it is Gábriel's. My neck is itching with sweat, Lukas himself looks completely cool, or rather cold. Coldness as another way of saying I am on fire? The present lies unopened on the dashboard, a minimal package with a curly ribbon that has loosened in the heat. He has forgotten to say happy birthday. It can only be a piece of jewellery, and to receive a piece of jewellery from Lukas seems quite remarkable. I am happy as long as he does not give it to me, just leaves it there.

"Where are we going?" I ask.

"Where have you always wanted to go?"

"The Atlantic?"

He must know that.

"Don't spoil it all now!" he answers, irritated. I should have guessed . . . He asked me to pack for one night, not for a week.

"Tivoli?" I say hurriedly. Now he does not reply, just speeds up along the motorway, looking purposeful.

———

As soon as I climb out of the car I hear music from Tivoli in the distance, shrieks of panic and euphoria, the music of a barrel organ, speeded up. How long has he been planning this? Saving up to take the car over on the ferry and down the coast road to Copenhagen, paying for the entrance, the restaurant and then the hotel. Neither of us has been so far away before, especially not him. Courage and money, where did he get them from? He brings note after note out of his jeans pocket until I dare not point at anything I like, frightened of ruining him.

The only thing in the city we see is Tivoli, but that in itself is almost too much. I love it. Lukas resigns himself to it. Soon has had as much as he can stomach and is content to stand below and watch, the throng of people and level of noise seem to paralyse him.

I ride alone in and out of the demon's mouth, spinning backwards in a terrifying whirligig, a whirlwind at a manic pace. The centrifugal force, the speed of the funfair, the candyfloss kick, I feel as though I am an electrified giant baby with no control over up and down. It does not matter, no-one knows me here, I let go and let my skirt fly, my laughter, my hair, faster, higher, more, climbing, hanging, shrieking. Then to be sucked backwards out of myself, catapulted away from Lukas, open my eyes and see him disappear.

I must have been born for this, to travel at speed and be flung out into a bigger place. Spin around among the deadly sins, ava-rice-arro-gance-lust-ful-ness, how am I ever going to be able to go back down to earth . . . be satisfied with firm ground under my feet again?

At long last I have to, the lights of the amusement park are turned off and it is emptied, we are tossed out into the world beyond, which I have forgotten existed.

Lukas looks resolute as we find our way to the hotel after midnight, until eventually we are sitting on the double bed after what seemed like an eternity of checking-in procedures and suspicious looks from the staff in the lobby.

"Like, what did they think?" I ask and drop, exhausted, full-length

155

onto the bed. Lukas is silent for some time. Then:

"Shall we dance?"

He finds music on the all-night radio, produces two beers from the little cocktail cabinet and plastic glasses that he fills to the brim. Normally he drinks from the bottle, but this is not a normal occasion, he seems to have thought of everything. The beer looks as though it is made for children, with elephants on the label, I am cross-eyed with tiredness and he must be even more tired since he did not have time to sleep after his night shift. But he looks more tense than tired as he sweeps me round in the dance, I feel the music in his hips, Lukas connects with the music in a physical way that I do not. Seems to absorb it through his body, while I listen to it at most. He is good at dancing, but nevertheless it is hard to stop myself . . . I am ready to burst out laughing because he looks so serious. Particularly when the music changes tempo and expression and becomes softer. Soon I lose control, the giggle grows into a fit of laughter, Lukas does not laugh, continues to look very serious and I try to stop but only manage to half-suppress it. He holds me harder. The music is slow, suggestive and sensual. It feels wrong, somehow does not suit us. I cannot relax.

I have had the best birthday of my life, but now I just want to sleep. The beer and tiredness and music and ferry that is still swaying under my feet and the spinning top that I rode on seven times seven times, my ears are ringing, the noise increases every time I take a gulp of beer.

"Don't drink any more," says Lukas. But I am not drunk, I feel horribly sober.

*

I am woken at daybreak by the pigeons making a noise in the gutter outside the window. With the sensation of Tivoli still in my body, like giddiness between a dream and a nightmare. My lips are swollen, my head heavy. The clock radio next to the hotel pillow is showing ten past six, my back is cold, Lukas is no longer lying behind me. When I lift myself onto my elbows to listen for the toilet I see that his trainers and his hoodie have gone from beside the door. He is always tired in the mornings, I cannot for the life of me imagine what could have tempted him out so early. Possibly he had not fallen asleep next to me last night as I has thought, but got up again and went out, and ... what then? He would never leave me alone here.

The presents are on the bedside table, the perfume Eternal Escape and the silver heart with two hands, barbed wire and a burning flame. I am still full of all the strange things I stuffed myself with yesterday. My mouth tastes of last night's candyfloss. My clothes in an untidy heap on the floor, I have no memory of undressing, but I had been so beside myself with tiredness and I still am. Pull the cover over my head, try to sleep while I wait. Let the hours go by.

At some time in the middle of the day I hear ringing, far away in another world, the ringing comes nearer and nearer as I gradually surface from unconsciousness to half-awake and then at last shake off my drowsiness. I grasp for the phone and pull the handset towards me so fast that it hits me on the forehead, a real crack. It is not Lukas but a stranger who asks me in English to come down to reception. A hint of irritation in the voice. I quickly drag on my shorts and T-shirt, throw together my things and grab the giant panda that is leaning against the mini-bar looking at me, and go down. It was checking-out time almost two hours ago, says the young woman in reception, the same one as yesterday but with a different shade of lipstick and she looks stony when she sees me come down alone.

"Where's your brother? Has he sent you to pay?" Pay? I do not have a single penny on me, the only thing I have is a headache and a giant panda that is big enough to carry me. My head is throbbing, I am screwing up my eyes to ease the pain, rapidly need to come up with a lie to get out of here, but I cannot find one.

"He's not here, he's gone," I say truthfully.

"Your brother?"

"No, the one who booked the room – he's not my brother." She looks at me. For so long that I begin to itch all over, there is something in the way she looks at me that stings, little friend, she says, and it is impossible to avoid her eyes.

"Sorry," I mumble, for want of anything else to say.

"No, don't say sorry. I suspected he wasn't your brother. He behaved oddly. I should have realised."

I have no time to pull my head out of the way, she takes hold of my chin and examines my face under the light:

"What's this?" My forehead. No doubt there is an obvious red mark by now. "What a swine," she exclaims, "what else has he done to you?" Now she catches sight of the split in my lip, the spinning-top split, from the first ride when I was not prepared for the force and the speed. Swine? Done? I have no time to reply, my mind is as blank as an icy road. "Has he brought you here from Sweden?" I nod. "How old are you?"

"Fifteen."

"No, no, no. You don't need to lie to me. How old?"

"I was fifteen yesterday."

"You don't need to lie, I said. I don't want to hurt you. I'm going to help you. Is there someone I can ring? Your parents?"

That would be the end. Mamma would report Lukas to the police for kidnapping, if she has not already done so. Then she herself would be charged with retaliation. Something with the axe. To say nothing of Rikard, he has gone off the rails over much less, anything involving Lukas seems to be sufficient. I just have to try to get away from here, and then get home under my own steam without a cent.

Exploitation of a child, he had said it would no longer be called that if he and I . . . if we. But we did not, would I not remember – however out of it I was? The labels on the beer belied its strength and Lukas was horny, I knew he was, but that sort of thing happened, it was not the first time, he just used to hide it better. *This is a man's world*, James Brown sang on the all-night radio, how could you stop yourself being aroused by that, I was as well, but more . . . kind of mentally. Kind of mentally . . . Lukas bit my ear: "*Kind of mentally?* For God's sake, Lo . . ." We were dancing, the elephants were dancing, the froth was dancing, the plastic chandelier in the ceiling was spinning. Lukas pretended I was not stepping on his toes. This is a man's world – but it wouldn't be nothing, nothing . . . without a woman or a girl . . . I remember that, then I do not remember much more.

The day's warning

After the year of the snake comes the year of the rat, the monkey, the dog. Let life run between your fingers like a red thread. Movement holds the promise of arriving one day, perhaps stillness does too, like here on Mamma's doorstep. Home is where nothing smells strange. Pappa's father could distinguish his trees by their smell. The cypress smelled of insecticide, the acacia of boy's sweat, the sequoia of cheap Russian cigarettes after the war. The war was just a strand in time for me, however much Grandfather talked about it.

I peer in between the trees in the arboretum. Mamma is not there. I have waited, searched, called out. She should have been standing here in the door when I came home, when I swung the car in and parked under the white birch, she can usually tell when I am approaching from miles away. The sun is strong but cold, I tuck my hands under my arms, my eye is drawn down to Lukas' house. It looks just the same as usual, at least from a distance. No, do not think about Lukas now. Only good thoughts.

I shut my eyes and let the men in my memory slide along like rosary beads. Hard, smooth, they resemble pearls, without blemish. "Perfect" means complete and by extension dead. Not like Lukas, there was nothing perfect about him. And neither before nor after Copenhagen could we talk about what happened.

*

Have to get up before I am frozen to the spot, the cold makes my back-side as numb as two deep-frozen ham steaks. I walk round the house, looking at Mamma's miniature world from the outside. Seeing her life like a very big girl looking into a very small doll's house and wishing there was room for me inside. But there is no longer space for me here, some things have shrunk and others have grown. All I can do is put my hand inside and touch the little velour sofa, the minute velvet lamp, the tiny radio, the miniature fruit bowl, the fringe on the rug, the hem of her skirt, the doll's house full of objects and habits that have become her life. Long for the past. It seems so strange that the same word, longing, can be used for both wishing yourself away and wishing yourself back home.

When I met Lukas I was still a small child in wellington boots that were far too big, a hippie youngster without hippie parents. The feelings of the person I was when I lived here are aroused as soon as I return. Not exactly unpleasant, but remarkable that this person remains inside me.

I do not like going into the house when Mamma is not at home. It is her life now, not mine. But in the end I can wait no longer, I go and fetch the key from the garden shed. The sound of the wind reverberates in the long corridors, even though all the windows are closed, I am chilled to the marrow, it was never cold like this when the house was full of people. The rooms smell white. Like Mamma's almond soap, a tinge of scorched milk and the faint scent of new-fallen snow, though it is not the time for snow.

The world's smallest film festival. Two women and a guide dog. The hitchhiker I picked up on the way here laughed when I said where I was going.

"So . . . you and your blind mother have a film festival together, and you two are the only audience?"

"Yes, but we don't use that word."

"Film festival?"

"Blind." We behave as if nothing has happened. She wants everything to be as it was, the same routines, that is all she wishes for now.

I cannot say no. Of course I should be able to say no, but I cannot. When Mamma rings to announce that another film festival is coming up, I pack my bag and set off home, wherever I happen to be.

But this time she is not here, I arrive at a dark house, all locked up. Go round looking for a message, the north room, south room, east room, west room, even the attic that she never uses. I can still smell the sickly-sweet scent from before that I did not realise then came from the grass Rikard used to smoke up here. After Mamma's little sister drowned he was the youngest in the family and everyone's eyes were upon him. When I was born he was at last free from the nagging and scolding, perhaps that is why he loved me so unreservedly. Called me his favourite jewel. Mamma called me her favourite worry.

In my memory this house is still full of people, Mamma cannot fill all the rooms with life on her own and I cannot get used to the emptiness. The sound of my own breathing rebounds from the walls like faint sighs. I stiffen when I see the dog lying on the bat chair in the upper lounge. She cannot possibly know that I am the daughter here, daughters and mothers do not share an identical smell, and yet she does not even open her eyes as I pass on my way to Mamma's bedroom.

I lie down on the bed, numb because she should have been here and is not, tired after the long journey, I fall asleep.

I fall asleep hungry and awaken famished. Two headlights sweep over the faded cloudberry wallpaper. I manage to reach the bottom of the stairs and see Mamma close the car door, before the stranger, whose face I do not catch, rolls away in a dilapidated old white Citroën.

Mamma feels her way towards the house, up the outside steps, starts when she realises someone is standing in the door.

"It's only me, Mamma."

"Lo! You frightened me!" A kiss on the cheek. An unusual greeting for her. In the hall she stumbles on my bags, pulls a face as she picks herself up but waves away my offer of help. "Why have you got so much stuff with you? Everything's here. Clothes as well, if you need to borrow anything."

"I have to move on soon, Mamma. I told you on the phone. Can't stay long."

She is not listening. Her thoughts are elsewhere. Goes in with her boots still on, right up to the stove she uses.

"You could have lit it, couldn't you, it's freezing in here." The temperature must mean that she has been away for quite a while. An explanation would be in order, but no . . . she seems to be preoccupied. Who was he, the man in the white car? That she, after all these lonely years of "beware of men", might have met someone, is inconceivable.

Maybe I will be forced to get used to the inconceivable. Just have to let it sink in before I can ask her about it.

"That dog you've got," I say instead, "isn't it the idea that you should take her with you when you go out?"

"She's a guard dog," Mamma says. No, she is not, actually. God knows how long the waiting list is for such a . . .

". . . specially trained guide dog for the blind, Mamma," I risk saying it, she detests the word.

"I don't want her, I've asked them to come and take her away. I'm not *that* blind."

That is what she wants everyone to believe, but she cannot fool me. I can tell that she does not see me. She always used to have a special expression when she looked at me, like watching a favourite problem, with a sort of affection, however hopeless it might be.

———

For a long time she kept it a secret from me, or at any rate hidden. When I eventually realised, it was because of certain particular details. A coolness that was not like her. As if she were not happy to see me. Introverted. Irritable. Things that had not been important before suddenly took on such meaning: "Shoes," she said sharply, when I kicked them off by the door as I had always done – nothing was allowed to lie in the way on her secretly practised routes throughout the house.

Tales of blindness are just romantic stories about wisdom and a noble spiritual life. In reality it is bruises and spilled milk, burned flesh, windows not cleaned, a constant searching for missing items and stumbling over everyday obstacles. Seeing her walk into chairs and doors hurts me as much as it hurts her. Especially when she does not complain, just tries to conceal her loss of dignity.

When I have made an effort to prepare some food, I receive a mild telling-off for not putting everything back in the right place afterwards.

"Knives, for goodness' sake, Lo, knives – go in the side drawer." I have the urge to go up and put my arm around her and say, what's the matter, Mamma? She does not normally go on like that . . . as if she were trying to stem a much greater chaos. Knives. Spice jars. Shoes. Death. In the side drawer, Lo, the side drawer.

"I don't understand how you can look after your own home," she sighs and sorts through everything that has been done wrong. But I do not, I have no home, or none that I feel at home in. It is me and the dogs.

Dogs? Mamma turns her empty gaze towards me. Yes, dogs. I cannot explain.

Immortal, despite a life of hunger, despite the dog catchers' nets and traps, zigzagging through the traffic. In all the unfamiliar towns I come to, the wild dogs are the least alien. They roam where they want, do as they wish, crap where they like, do not care a jot about anything they dislike. A free and perilous life. If I had been one of them, I would have died long ago, and yet it still attracts me. A dog's only task is to be a dog, sleep in the sun, be four-legged. Just to be a human, however, is not sufficient, life has to be lived inside the lines.

All those years I avoided my mother's eye:

"Where are you going?"

"Out."

"When are you coming back?"

"Some time."

"You're coming home for summer, aren't you?"

"Maybe."

All the long journeys and secret men, unanswered telephone calls, vague addresses, poste restante so-and-so. Those eyes that I avoided for so long, I miss them now. It is a desperately bleak feeling, being the only sighted person in the house, it makes me feel alone. And unprotected. Now I am the one who has to keep watch over her. If an atomic cloud started to grow on the horizon, she would not notice. But at least she would die without being afraid.

I sense a pattern. Of love. Want to see her eating and sleeping to make herself strong, enjoy the sun on the steps, comb her hair, keep her safe. When she goes out alone she gets lost and has to be driven home by strange people in strange cars. Can scarcely see her way about now, but that does not prevent her from chopping wood and cycling and last summer she went down to bathe in the lake, lost all idea of where the shore was, swam round and round in circles until she almost could not carry on. At the last moment she felt the bottom beneath her feet and managed to find her way on to land.

"Close to the eye," she pulls a wry smile.

The feeling between us is changing. A new mixture of tenderness and irritation. I want to nourish and feed her, like a little child or a sensitive love. As she cannot see I pour extra oil into the coleslaw and cream into the egg sauce. In my nightmares I see myself slowly being transformed into Nurse Ratched in *One Flew Over the Cuckoo's Nest*, the little white hat over the stiff hair, zealously conscientious, a witch in a starched collar who means well but does harm. Must be careful not to be like that.

I do not like the thinness around her hips and neck. Her jeans are loose. Sad to eat alone . . . but Mamma never complains about loneliness, even though she stopped eating for a time when she was first on her own in the house, when Pappa's father was no longer there. Later on she seemed to have made the decision that she had to survive that as well. To lose yourself is the most dangerous of all, she tried to teach me that when I was younger. If you lose something else you can always get it back – but if you lose yourself, who is going to search? While other mothers warned their daughters about rapists, unwanted pregnancies and venereal diseases, she was always warning me about losing myself to someone.

The demon's mouth

Don't drink any more, Lukas had whispered in my ear, but I was already beyond that point. So sober that I fell asleep as soon as I felt his body against mine.

Afterwards I just recall single moments, like flickering rays. Memories that cannot be pinned down because they are too fuzzy, like the light in Copenhagen that day, swiftly changing September light over everything. Lukas and me. I remembered his body, his weight, the smell of bleach in the hotel pillow, but not the scent of him.

I had drunk as I had seen him drink on other occasions: quickly and with the deliberate intention of getting drunk. But that evening I do not recall him drinking anything at all, at least not as long as I was awake. The memory . . . too much bleach, too little oxygen, too much weight, too much flickering. Remember only a feeling of being alone, greater than any I had experienced before, like rubbish blowing along deserted streets in the morning. My loneliness or his? I did not know, we were so close that I could not see him properly, could not separate us.

His weight was enough, he did not need to move a muscle. A ton of flickers, a ton of light, a ton of candy floss, a ton of Lukas. I could not move. A ton of loneliness. I only saw the marks afterwards. Long afterwards. On either side of the artery in my neck. Still open and tender. It had been going on so long, perhaps forever, as if he needed what I had, something he was lacking, sucked it from me until I had almost nothing left.

Under the swaying plastic chandelier we had moved towards the bed. With beer in every limb and hundreds of swirling merry-go-rounds and Lukas' hips against my ribs, *danse macabre*, equally strong, equally weak, his hand on the curve of my back. A place it had not been before, not like this, when it had no reason to be. His eyes turned away, but his hand remained.

I do not know why I did not start to cry. He was crying, or something else was happening on his face. I do not know if he had lifted me off the floor or if I had lost the feeling in my feet. The dance of the devil until you drop, until your feet go numb and you have danced a hole in the floor, all the way down into the underworld, the unknown.

The whole of my childhood I had danced on his feet, believing that I was leading. Now I was fifteen, no longer a child, I had to dance by myself and now it was he who was leading and I did not know how to follow or how to resist.

Too much alcohol, exhaustion and excitement straight into the bloodstream. Overcome by candy floss and Elephant beer, I disappeared into the mouth of the demon again and again. *This is a man's world*, even in my sleep, when I woke up he was gone and the first thing I felt was relief.

I was allowed to leave the hotel despite not being able to pay for the room. It was not my fault, the staff said. They seemed to assume the worst. They would trace him through the number on his driving licence and make sure they got their money, these things had happened before. Clearly relieved to be rid of me as if they were watching a problem walk out of the door. A problem that could have been difficult for the hotel, a failure of responsibility . . . I was nowhere near fifteen, they were agreed on that, and he was so much older.

If the whole thing had not been about Lukas, I would have rung Mamma and asked her to come and fetch me. That was the last thing I could do now, but I had no other ideas as I stepped out on to the street, not even any notion of where I was in the city. No money, no map, no memory of the day before other than a vague feeling of soreness in my body. There seemed to be no solution, but none was needed – when I surveyed the street I saw the Ford in the spot where Lukas had parked it the day before. He was sitting in the front seat watching me, as if he had woken up at the very moment I came out on to the street, or maybe he had not slept at all that night. I slid on to the passenger seat without a word. He said nothing either. First he had to wake up properly, pull on his top, and smoke a morning cigarette leaning against the car. Then he had to find a toilet and a cup of coffee and a piece of bread and some tobacco and go and pay for the room. I debated whether to warn him about going into the hotel. He might face a problem with the staff, but I said nothing and when it came to it they seemed to wash their hands of the whole thing, just wanted their money.

After that he had to drive round to find his way out of the centre and north to the ferry. He had still said nothing. And I had said nothing. The silence became harder to break the longer it went on. We just drove.

"I didn't want to hurt you," he said finally, his eyes fixed on the queue of cars as we drove up the ramp and into the gaping mouth of the ferry.

He stayed on the car deck for the entire crossing, while I went up and bought far too many sweets, but I really just wanted to stand by the rail and watch the shoals of jellyfish under the oily-black surface. Feel the strength of the wind sweep everything away as I leant far out over the water.

Only when the ferry had docked and I heard the irritated sound of horns from the car deck, did I go down. Got into the Ford that was holding up the others behind. Lukas started the engine and moved off, saying nothing, but his last words hung in the air. And I replied that he had not. Hurt me. He never would, would he? But he just looked at me oddly, as if it were not something I had the power to decide.

———

On the road here I had thought about him. My eye was caught by the hitchhiker's hands, the lad I had picked up by the slip road on to the motorway, I had glimpsed his hands and could not stop staring at them. How they rested on the thighs of his jeans with the fingers spread out, in a way that reminded me of a game we used to play at school. A knife plunged faster and faster between someone's fingers, the bravest one or someone who could not say no, while the others watched, egging them on. I still had a scar on my left ring finger. It was Lukas who was holding the knife that time. Since then I have had a habit of looking at people's hands. My memory is full of them: first a quick look at the face, then the hands to find out what the face is holding back, hands never lie. A woman I met on a train to Berlin claimed to remember every penis she had ever touched, and one could well imagine that that was quite a few. I can only remember fingers, nails, knuckles, palms, backs of hands. A unique ability to remember hands and forget the rest. The hands of sleeping men with the smell of seawater, garlic, hash, perfume, lubricant, dog's fur, chlorine. I cup them over my face, watch the blood flowing, twisting in the blue veins just beneath the skin. Remember all the hands that ever touched me. Remember the ones I wished would touch me. The hands, the men, the towns.

The woman kept me awake the whole night talking about herself, it was that kind of night, caught in a trap, confined to a sleeping compartment on a slow train with a stranger who had taken life to heart. She was no longer afraid. Everything she had feared had already happened. Now she lived in a *fait accompli*. There was no point to her fear. Fear of what might happen is always the worst, that must be what it was the time that Lukas stabbed me in the finger, it happened not because he was trembling, but because I was, fear provokes danger.

Nothing happened the night in the hotel room in Copenhagen, and nothing was ever really the same again. I have never believed the myth about the butterfly beating its wings on one side of the earth and causing a hurricane on the other. But perhaps after all there is such a moment in everyone's life, a moment that spreads and grows until it changes reality. And for me it was a few seconds of that evening.

———

I wake up late to a day of unexpected warmth and the day's first warning from Mamma: do not forget to hold your breath when you fetch wood and wash your hands thoroughly afterwards, vole fever is spread through fresh and old droppings.

She starts to prepare the meal, no surprises, the national food: sausages and potatoes, a beer, does not want any help, *just sit there at the table, Lo … sit in your usual place, as normal.* Everything has to be as normal, though nothing is. It looks dangerous when she handles the knife as if she could see it, cuts the potatoes rapidly in her hand like her mother used to do, fumbles when she lights the gas stove, what if the flame gets hold of her sleeve … I want to help set the table, but she waves me back to my place. Instead I look through a pile of books that are gathering dust on the window sill, she must have forgotten a long time ago that they are there. Pull out the one at the bottom, a well-thumbed *Anna Karenina*, the abridged version with stills from the film with Greta Garbo. Cannot imagine the loneliness in store when you can no longer see to read. I started to read because I saw her doing it. Wanted some of whatever it was that made her disappear into herself. When we had crawled into bed and I was warming my feet between her thighs, I shut my eyes and listened half-asleep to her turning the pages.

The sound of white birch being cut is like glasses clinking. Mamma does not chop wood as effectively as she did, but she is just as obstinate. Then she puts the heavy axe on the chopping block and helps me to stack. The trimming axe swings from a strap on her work trousers with every movement she makes, the daughter axe, I always used to think that I would inherit it. We have soon finished piling the wood, as long as she does not take it into her head to chop some more, there is always a risk. This is the best time. To sit chatting after a job well done.

She takes off her gloves and the padded lumberjack shirt. Not much left of her when she takes off her unattractive protective layer. She is a walking pair of collar bones, Pappa's father used to say. Her hair has become thinner too, but still has its colour, fair like the fields in the days before the crops are gathered. Clumsily she strokes the guide dog's head. Not used to patting dogs. Not used to patting anyone any more.

"Do you remember the day of the fire, Mamma?"

"In the field? Of course I do." She dries the perspiration on her neck, still looks good, just older. She has the sort of face whose lines are not rubbed out by age and fatty tissue, if anything the features become sharper. If only she would stop going round in Grandfather's old cast-offs, his various sizes of large work trousers with the belt tied round her waist twice, the lumber jacket that is her second home. A waste of beauty. When I point it out she looks at me, amused.

"You've made so much more use of it."

"Your beauty?"

"No, your own." It is not true, I have never been beautiful like her, my eyes are my only asset. Seductive, I sometimes hear. My mouth as well, of course, it tends towards the generous, but generous with what? What does it promise and what does it hold?

"I haven't seen that Lukas for a long time," Mamma says.

"Must you call him that?"

"What's his name then?"

"His name's just Lukas. Not *that* Lukas."

"You always were oversensitive about him. I thought you had got over it." Got over it? It would be like getting over a brother or sister.

"It wasn't me who was oversensitive, it was you lot who were completely insensitive." It was not an easy situation, she reminds me.

"Whatever anyone said you got angry, Lo."

I do not want to spoil this precious moment, we have them so seldom, and yet I hear myself say: "You detested him."

"We didn't detest him, we loved you – there's a difference. We were scared of . . . It's not hard to understand, is it? The relationship was so lopsided, when you were at middle school discos he was at high school parties."

"He never went to high school parties, Mamma."

"No, and you never went to middle school discos either. I know. That's the point." I really do not want to fall out with her, have to be quiet, otherwise I know exactly what will happen.

This woodshed was one of our hiding places, a dark realm of spiders' webs and light filtering through the thin boards, the smell of newly cut wood drying out. The pearl fisher's house was our best place, but if we did not have time to go there, we could come here. I had only the well-meaning concerns of the adults to escape from, Lukas had his Pappa, as unpredictable as a fox-trap.

"I really don't understand why you're still so sensitive about him. If anyone was inconsiderate towards him, Lo, it was you. He became so odd afterwards," Mamma mutters.

"Odd?"

"Odder."

We have never spoken properly about what happened. I had hoped that she had wrapped up what I did in some sort of all-forgiving mother love that can break down any sin at all into soft hair-balls of the type that mothers, with a little good will, can swallow, as long as they come from their own children.

"Inconsiderate?" She nods. I know. Only I did not think she saw me that way.

"Actually you have no idea at all about what happened," I say, shifting uneasily against the stack of logs. For certain conversations there is no good time, I just want to get out in the sun.

"Does he still live in the house?" She does not know, but no-one else seems to be living there at any rate.

"It would've been easiest if he'd just disappeared after what happened," she says to herself. Where? Where would he have disappeared to? If ever anyone had nowhere to go, it was him.

"He didn't ask about you once, Lo. Not once. That's how I knew something was wrong. Then I saw him less and less. But why don't you go down and see if he's there?"

How can she ask? She knows that I never go down there. That I do not want to. Cannot. It is impossible. Certain things are simply impossible. Perhaps for him as well. If he has been aware that I am at home, he has always managed to keep out of sight.

"All this wood-cutting business, Mamma," I say as a diversionary tactic.

"Yes?"

"Do you really think you should be doing it?"

"Why not?"

The word.

Full of shame.

A word I hesitate to voice. Her unseeing face is unreadable, she pushes the tin of mink fat into her pocket and fumbles for the axe again, tests its sharpness on her thumb and takes the sharpening steel out of the other pocket of her padded lumberjack shirt. She has always cut wood, all the wood that was ever needed to keep this house warm, she has cut wood since the day we arrived here.

"Why not? Who else would do it? You?" You might as well stick the axe straight into me, she looks as though she is thinking. But make sure it is a death blow . . . She hands me the axe, lingers a moment. "Why don't you go down there?" Turns her back on me and leaves.

———

Whenever I enter Mamma's room I have to resist the feeling that it is out of bounds. Listen for her step in the corridor as I go round looking at her things. Sometimes I hope that she does the same, goes into my room and pokes about in my luggage, but I know that she would never do such a thing, never write "Your mother who knows you", like Jean Seberg did to her son.

I take a few books down with me. She has lit the stove in the draughty living room, I fan the books out and let her fingers choose. Begin to read as I once read aloud for Lukas.

I buy him cheese and yoghourt and butter in Trouville, because when he comes in late at night he devours that sort of thing. And he buys me the things I like best – buns and fruit. He buys them not so much to give me pleasure as to feed me up. He has this childlike idea of making me eat so I don't die. He doesn't want me to die. But he doesn't want me to get fat either. It's hard to reconcile the two. I don't want to die, either. That's what our affection is like; our love. In the evening and at night, we sometimes throw caution to the winds. In these conversations we tell the truth however terrible, and we laugh as we used to do when we still drank and could only talk to one another in the afternoon.

The impossible balance of love. Do not become fat, overfed, blasé, too sure of yourself. But do not starve or fade away either, so that satisfaction is sought elsewhere. How do you feed one another just the right amount? I have not a clue. Remember hearing about a pair of lovers who arranged to walk two thousand kilometres along the Great Wall of China and meet up somewhere in the Gobi desert, a fantastic idea. But it did not work out as they had planned, love ran out along the way. They went there to cement their relationship, but when they eventually met, they decided to divorce, having been a couple for more than twenty years.

Mamma asks to pick another, not happy with her choice. This is not a night for love. I set out the fan of stories again. Her fingers stroke them gently and she chooses a new one. I open it and begin to read.

It was a queer, sultry summer, the summer they electrocuted the Rosenbergs, and I didn't know what I was doing in New York. I'm stupid about executions . . . I knew something was wrong with me that summer, because all I could think about was the Rosenbergs.

I walk round the room while I am reading. Mamma is developing the hearing of a bat, tells me to leave the Venetian blinds alone.

"What are you looking for? You're making me stressed, your footsteps are echoing. You can't keep still for a minute . . . Must you walk round indoors in your shoes, as if you're on your way somewhere?" I am always on my way somewhere, Mamma. And I do not take off my boots for anybody. Perhaps by arrangement, but definitely not to order. These boots have walked many miles through foreign towns, boots that know what they want, even when I do not.

"Shoes," Mamma says as I make an extra circuit round the room. "Is it a full moon? I've never understood what a full moon does to women. The rabbits in the field are on edge as well."

"Can you feel that?"

"Yes. The vibrations," she says.

She keeps the Venetian blinds closed most of the time nowadays, she has become more sensitive to the light, strange to be light-sensitive when you cannot even see. I check Lukas' house, but there is no sign of life.

"Actually I don't think he lives there anymore," Mamma says, as if sensing where my attention is directed.

"Are you sure?"

"No, but it feels empty down there." A vague impression of absence – I can feel it too now.

"And the house?" Who would be interested in that, she sighs. Difficult to sell now that the factories have closed, everyone is moving away, no-one is moving in. Always the same old story, foreign companies buy them out and shut them down, ignite hopes and blow them out again, until people give up and clear out, leaving their houses even if they cannot sell them. Especially noticeable here on the outskirts, empty houses and overgrown gardens everywhere. The paradise my mother once migrated to has packed up and moved on.

"Perhaps he's waiting for better times," she says hesitantly. Yes, if I know Lukas, that is exactly what he is doing.

I cannot imagine where he could have gone. He may not have belonged here, but he belonged still less anywhere else.

"Just try and think when you last saw him," I say. It must have been a long time ago, it was a long time since Mamma could see her own reflection in the mirror. If Lukas had moved away, she would hardly have noticed. Nor would anyone else. Did anyone round here know him? Apart from me. And his Pappa. She rubs a wood-cutter's muscle in her neck.

"Never asked about you, Lo, when I happened to meet him anywhere in the village, isn't that strange?" She half turns, her silhouette as slender as a boy's. "What does it matter anyway if he's still there? In all these years you've never been down to see him, it makes a person suspect the worst."

"The worst?"

"Yes. That something went very wrong at the end."

The last chore of the day, I tackle the piles that are growing in the laundry room. Feel a warm breeze through the window while we fold the sheets. An acrid waft from the mink farm. The furs do not sell here any longer, they are sent to Russia and China where they sell like hot cakes, if Mamma is to be believed. It is not appropriate for wild animals to be kept in captivity, the humiliation makes them smell bad. I recall how they used to climb up the mesh, chattering hysterically, when Lukas and I passed the low pens. One male or several females in every coop. Reminded me of the rat traps in Lukas' attic.

Help her to roll up the dusty rugs that I will take to the dry cleaner's. She can no longer manage to wash them by hand and under no circumstances wants to let me do it.

"Unnecessary."

"I'll pay, Mamma."

"Absolutely not." Only once does she cast her eyes straight at me, squinting like someone looking at the sun through grimy glass. "Lo, just think . . ."

"That I've grown so much?"

"That you're my daughter."

Mamma was the woman who cut wood faster that her own shadow.

Collapsed into bed at night, exhausted after the day's work. Now she needs to take a long bath each evening and listen to all the repeats on the radio, ritualise going to bed in order to cast out its demons. I go into the bathroom to ask her what films she would like to see tomorrow, I have brought a few with me that I think she will like. "Repulsion"? She shakes her head deprecatingly.

"Something with Marlene Dietrich?"

"Oh, no . . ." she says as she lets the hot water run.

"'Breathless'?" Not that either. She has not watched that since Jean Seberg died, she says.

With the years she has become less sensitive to horror but more easily moved by sadness. You need to lay yourself open when you are young and shield yourself when you are older, says the person who warned me against everything when I was a child.

"You tolerate less. That's all I mean," she adds, as if sensing my objection. Because you realise how unfair life really is. What havoc it causes for certain people. Lukas, for example . . . I always bristle when she mentions him. She has thought about him from time to time, she admits. And about not being able to see, about being so worried about me, about him having a bad time. She rinses her face with the shower without shutting her eyes, and says no more.

The one cloud in my sky for a long time had been the cloud that hovered constantly over him. The pools of blood beneath his skin that subsided, only to be replaced by new. His problems were my problems, just not apparent in my skin. And the jealousy, I was frightened of catching it, the melancholy, as if he were filled with darkness, but there was something shining under all the mire, was I the only one who could see it? The way he saw the river rats was different from the way I did and he could not bear to see them trapped and helpless – delivered up to me, a human kindness that did not include their sort. Gábriel nearly wrecked his face the time he found Lukas leaving the disposal of the rat cages to me. Lukas never recovered from the shame. Nor did his face.

My old bedroom is cold, I dream about the bottomless blue water again, how I sink and cannot reach the other side, in a bathing suit that shrinks in the water instead of stretching. There is a burning pain, I wake up with my hands between my legs, perhaps it is just nocturia, get up to go to the toilet half asleep, am I not far too young for this? Ageing is an impersonal disintegration, according to Mamma, but I do not want to know anything about that yet, my life has not even begun. The acid taste in the mouth in the morning, fingers stiff with cold and bad sleep. Worst of all love. And time. You cannot claim them back, irretrievable like fallen rain, ripped-up letters, virtue, innocence, everything that has been lost.

Period of rain

After Copenhagen nothing felt straightforward and we could not talk about it. I looked at him. He looked back. In that new way he had of looking at me since we had come home. Black jewels nestling in their case behind bullet-proof glass, those sorts of eyes. We were attached to each other without touching, on a fixed path, like the planets, we could not draw nearer or further away, could not be together or apart, burned each other. Silence was his weapon, the only thing I have never coped with, the face turned away. Like Mamma when I was younger, how she sometimes withdrew her love, to get me where she wanted me.

Childhood is a reverse telescope that keeps the world at a distance, but I was no longer a child, the railway was an enticing stream of silver that I wanted to float away on every time I saw it from my bedroom window.

The year from fifteen to sixteen was the most troubled between Lukas and me. To fill the emptiness that had developed between us, I devoted myself for the first time to school. A little late in the day, according to the teachers, but Mamma was relieved that, thankfully, I appeared at last to have realised that there was life after being a child. I was at the age when it irritated me to do what she wanted, but it was so much more satisfying to shock the teachers. I improved my grades, raised them above shame and ruin. "You can do it, you see, that was what we thought. If you carry on like this, then . . ." Then what? The bright future would soon be mine? The reward for doing well in your studies was more studying, so much I understood.

It was the autumn I turned sixteen. The rainy period had just started, the windows misted up again, the road was transformed into a deluge and all the trees in the arboretum stood up to their ankles in water. The ground was saturated, nothing drained away, everything stood still, going rotten, tempers as well. The rains were worse for the trees than the summer drought and the winter cold. The parasites had a whale of a time all through this endless period of wet, Grandfather was powerless. The arboretum was his harem, that poor collection of trees was supposed to fulfil all his desires, Mamma said. He spent several hours a day out there, we could see no reason why – what could there possibly be to do, surely trees looked after themselves?

Almost imperceptibly I was drawn back to Lukas and he began to look me in the eye once more, as he had not done for many months. Time did something for us that we could not do ourselves. Nothing was as before, but we had to take what remained or lose each other completely.

After Copenhagen Mamma had let go of me as if I were no longer hers, a young runaway animal who came home smelling unfamiliar. She stopped asking me where I was going and where I had been. There was a sad feeling of freedom that should have been intoxicating. Something had happened, there was no denying it. Whatever Mamma thought we were up to before, at least it was no longer illegal. Even if she did not approve, she could hardly stop us.

"I see how you look at him and it makes me worried," she said one evening. That afternoon Lukas and I had been sitting at home in the kitchen in full daylight for the first time – Mamma came past and happened to see us, stopped abruptly, regained her composure, came in and took a drink out of the fridge and went out again without a word. "And that is nothing compared to how worried I am when I see how he looks at you," she added. There was something about him that was weak and weak people are the most dangerous, they drag you down, strong people you can fight free from, but the weak get under your skin. After having warned me about Lukas' strength, now she was warning me about the reverse, as if it were the same thing. But weak was the wrong word, he was not weak, there was no word for what he was. When he slept, when he laughed, emptied the buckets of rainwater, ate bananas, when he said that ordinary happy moments are the best, I could see the pain in his face.

There is no such thing as fairy tales, he had said, but perhaps it was just happy endings there was a shortage of.

———

Lukas' Pappa, Gábriel, kept himself to himself. In all the years he lived in the village he spoke to no-one, mixed with no-one. If he has not learnt Swedish yet it must be because he is either stupid or stuck-up, people said, and they did not know which was worse ... He was a steppe wolf at any rate, a recluse, odd, a rum one, as they said in my family. He went his own way in the community. It was alleged that he could not ride a bicycle, people alleged so many things, they were so good at gossip. It was alleged that he had answered a personal advertisement. That was what brought him here, if you believe the rumour, and most people did. Things went well with the woman for a while, a very short while, and then they started to go wrong, so he took his suitcase and his son and moved to the wooden house by the lake that he bought for next to nothing. According to some, he had not bought it all. Just moved in because it was standing empty and no-one laid claim to it. He made it decent, cleared the garden, fixed everything that was hanging off and chased away the vermin. Soon it was one of the best maintained houses in the district, even if it was jerry-built. He painted it in a colour like no other house in the area and it was difficult to know what to call it, when you spoke about it. Hungarian green, said my mother's sisters, who could not help spying on it every now and again. A colour that was hardly going to melt into the surrounding greenery. At least Gábriel was particular about keeping things neat and tidy. And a good worker. Could have worked his way up, become a foreman, if he had had the language, but he did not – or did not want to – there were different views on that.

Gábriel was most often seen walking beside the bicycle, which it was said he could not ride, on the road between his home and the factory. Like a dog walking alongside. What would a steppe wolf need a dog for, company or protection? He was good-looking, at least that was what my mother's sisters said, and it seemed to guard him from a worse fate. Despite everything, people were not as suspicious of him as they might have been. They talked about him. But they let him be.

My fear of Gábriel was not logical, it was Lukas' legacy. I always felt awkward in his presence and it was made no better that he was always kind towards me when we met. If my family treated Lukas like something the cat had dragged in, his Pappa seemed to view me as something unknown that you offered a chair to and treated with reserved respect. The unpredictable bouts of anger he directed at Lukas were never shown to me.

One afternoon when Gábriel was at work the telephone rang. Lukas was trying to do some repairs on the Taunus in the yard, though jobs requiring an adjustable spanner were not his forte. It was raining as well. It had been raining the whole day, for weeks. The only progress Lukas was making was to become more and more oily, more and more wet. He had got it into his head that he could change the drive belt himself, since he could not afford to take the car into the garage and he could not stand being unable to drive around in it. I had been sitting perched with my feet on the bumper, watching his endeavours for a whole hour. I realised that he was not going to manage it, I had seen both Rikard and Katja do it on our cars and Lukas was doing everything wrong. And he refused to listen to me.

He did not bother about the telephone either, though I urged him to answer it. It must be something important, the telephone never rang in their house.

"You might have come into a big fat inheritance there and you've missed it," I said when the ringing had stopped.

"There aren't any relatives, you know that," he hissed, and knocked me so hard that I fell off. "Go and do something useful, rustle together a few leftovers or find something else you can do . . . answer the phone, for example, if it rings again."

That might happen in another year, I thought. But I was wrong. I had gone in even though I really wanted to go home, because when Lukas was in this mood it was like waiting for a time bomb to go off. When I heard the telephone again, I followed the sound through the house, until I found it in Gábriel's bedroom. A man's voice that did not introduce itself asked to speak to Gábriel Puskás. Since Lukas'

Pappa still did not speak any Swedish, I went out to fetch Lukas instead. Reluctantly he left his fruitless repair work, went inside in his wet boots and pushed me away to a safe distance, before going into his father's room and taking the receiver.

It was immediately obvious that something was not right. Monosyllabic, hesitant answers as his face stiffened. In the end he turned his back on me and stood silently with the telephone in his hand. I was rooted to the spot by the door, trying hard to catch what was being said at the other end. But the conversation seemed to be over already, at least for Lukas, he stood with the receiver in one hand, propping himself up against the wall with the other.

"Bloody hell," he whispered.

I went up to him. Did not dare to touch him.

"Lukas?"

"Go home," he said softly, but I did not.

This is the sort of thing that happens when people are stressed and fail to pay attention, "a breach of confidentiality", and this is how we learned – even before Gábriel himself – that he was dying. Bone cancer. Very advanced. Incurable.

We had not noticed that the illness had taken up residence in the house a long time before. Like an uncomfortably discreet uninvited guest. It had been very unobtrusive so far, none of us had been aware that Gábriel was ill, doomed, in fact.

Lukas' soundless and at the same time violent reaction surprised me, I understood and yet I did not understand. He and his Pappa had lived side by side for so many years in a strange silence, an absence of words and feelings, even their body language was mute. When Lukas had grown too big for Gábriel to beat him, the last remnant of bodily contact between them ceased.

Gábriel was the only family Lukas had, and there was a sort of love between them, even if I had never seen any warmth. Coldness, distance and violent arguments were the only things their co-existence appeared to consist of. And in a way, it was the "almost" nature of it that was the most painful. Because every now and again there was a moment's contact, a smile, a glance between them that gave just a hint that under other circumstances, in a completely different life, they might have been close.

A stranger in the village

Winter passed and so did spring. Lukas worked the night shift at the factory, Gábriel went down to half time and then was forced to give up altogether. The treatment he received was like sugar-coated pills in the face of death. April passed, its promises broken time after time. May the same. June – no more promises. We heard the nightingales, the area around the river was typical nightingale territory and however alluring their song was, it still made me uneasy. The early summer slipped past in warmth, morphine sulphate, waiting, while the illness spread through Gábriel's bones.

We put a bed outside his room to be able to hear if he woke up in the night and needed something. I dreamt that a violent storm was tossing us apart and when I woke up Lukas was holding me so hard I could hardly breathe. Sometimes he murmured his own name in his sleep, as if he were already alone, the only one left.

Rice and cigarettes for breakfast. While he was waiting for the rice cooker, Lukas washed in the homemade shower that turned into an electric current in stormy weather. I followed his movements behind the nylon curtain. Suddenly he stopped, he was motionless for a long time, stood quite still in the jet of water until I was afraid and went up and pulled down the shower curtain. He was just standing there, as if he had forgotten that he was supposed to wash his hair.

"Fetch my cigarettes."

"Are you going to smoke in the shower, Lukas?" He had gone mad, forgotten where he was, what he was doing. Lack of sleep and worry had eaten away at him and made his body sharper, more chiselled, as if death were attacking it as well. When I reached my hand forward to touch his chest, he fended me off quickly.

"Fetch them." I did not intend to. If we started to do more than one thing at a time, how would we make the time pass? If I were to go and fetch things for him whilst I had the sheets in soak, and he were to smoke whilst he was showering . . . then the days would be endless. The time we spent in the house to be there for Gábriel crept forward so slowly, even when we only did one thing at once. But he said: "The days won't last. The nights." And it was true, the endless days were numbered. For Gábriel and perhaps for us as well. We were on a narrow strip of ice, alone. There might be a thin band of ice that would bear your weight in a large area of weak ice, Pappa had taught me that. We were standing on it now. If you walked out on a narrow strip and it broke, no-one could help you.

It was clear that death was not going to take Gábriel quickly and mercifully, it was going to take its time. Bone cancer . . . the worst sort, Lukas had heard. His Pappa's body would soon be as hollow as the coral in the pearl fisher's house.

Did Mamma guess what was happening, when one afternoon I said I was going to Lukas' and then did not come home again? Or did she think that we were in the claws of love, that we spent all those days in bed, wrapped round each other, irresponsible, lazy, defiant, shirking school and work?

The first time she came and knocked on the door was twenty-four hours later. Lukas said that I was asleep, which made her suspicious as it was afternoon.

"Have you been *drinking*?"

"No." He had. I had not.

"Why is Lo asleep at this time of the day, then?"

"Because she's been awake all night, we . . ."

"I don't want to know any more," Mamma interrupted. Though of course she did, even though she thought she already knew.

I was sitting measuring out Gábriel's afternoon dose, following the instructions left by the district nurse. Through the door I could smell the sweet scent of ripened corn and heard Mamma point out that even if I was not under age in one way, I certainly was in another. If Lukas was giving me alcohol . . . he made a sign to me that I should stay where I was, he could handle this, he was on his own ground now.

"It's cool, trust me," he said and shifted a millimetre in the doorway. Mamma could not even peep round him.

"Trust you?" she said coldly. As if she ever had . . . ever would . . . "When she wakes up, send her straight home," she ordered, as if I were the common property of two foes and it was her turn to have me now.

"She'll do as she wishes."

"No, she'll do as *you* wish, that's the problem!" I heard Mamma say, before she turned and left.

Whatever you do, do not lie to her, that never works, I whispered when Lukas came back in. He pulled me out of Gábriel's room so that we could speak undisturbed.

"Listen, it makes absolutely no difference what I say to your Mamma, you know, she's never liked me." I wanted to contradict him, but that would have been ridiculous. I caught sight of the two of us in the hall mirror. We looked wrong. Especially together. It was impossible not to think that our eyes should change places, he with his summer-bleached hair and almost black eyes, I dark and green-eyed. He held me a little too close, a little too hard, I wriggled away. Since Copenhagen he had kept his distance, but now it was as if he could no longer maintain that restraint. There was something insensitive about everything he did, he let both his irritation and his randiness spill over on to me and I was afraid of provoking in him what had become so easily provoked since Gábriel's illness. Sex and sadness in a desperate mixture. I moved out of the way with a no. You always say that, I saw in his eyes. Love, love not, love, but what sort of love? Sex had always been the thing that could not happen between us. Mamma would have detected it in me straightaway and then we would never have been able to be alone together, that feeling was still there.

"Must you go around semi-naked? Can't you show my Pappa a little respect?" Lukas said, out of the blue. Semi-naked? Skirt, pants, top, worn-out sandals, was that not enough? What did he expect? It was thirty degrees.

"What about you then . . ." See-through, threadbare black shorts, that was all. Not that there were any secrets hidden under there, but at least he should not complain about me.

"It's not a problem for you," he said vehemently, "if I go around like this." I shrugged. "No, well. Go and get dressed."

We had entered a time of constant fatigue, nights broken into small meaningless pieces by Gábriel's restless sleep. When Mamma returned it was Lukas who opened the door again. He looked as if he had been living hard for days, his hair had started to form natural dreadlocks and his only article of clothing was hanging yet further down his hips.

"I want to speak to my daughter." I was on the point of going out into the hall.

"Where's your Pappa?"

"Asleep," Lukas said.

"You know – I don't like this at all." She insisted on speaking to Gábriel, but Lukas said it was not the time to wake him. "Fetch Lo," she demanded.

"If she wants to go home, she knows the way. Calm down!" I stepped in just before it got out of control. Mamma looked so alone standing out in the porch, we had never been apart as long as this. As soon as she saw me she started telling me off.

"What do you think you *look* like? Have you been in bed all weekend, has he turned your head completely, when are you coming home?"

"Soon," I lied. It was best that she did not know. She was afraid of dead people and dying was so much more frightening and Mamma had never been good at dealing with anything to do with death. "Mamma, I just need to . . ."

"What?" she asked, looking out over the scorched sloping fields as if she were searching for storm clouds on the horizon.

"Stay with Lukas for a little while . . ." I did not expect her to understand, and she did not. She just said that she hoped I knew what I was letting myself in for. Looked at me as if convinced that I did not have the faintest idea.

———

You know when a newcomer has arrived in town if he steps down from the train in slow motion, the last passenger, his eyes sweep along the platform, probing, squinting into the peculiar light that platforms like this are always bathed in, before he puts his bags down on the ground and suddenly he looks exhausted. He has not arrived yet, he does not even know that he is on his way to our village – first we have to place an advert. It is just a question of persuading Lukas.

"Everything's so easy for you, Lo."

"And you make everything so hard."

Always the same, waiting and hesitating. It is only an advert . . . A gamble.

"What do you have to lose, Lukas? Nothing." I slip away when he tries to keep hold of me. We have discussed it all morning, I have run out of arguments. Thrashed out. I am tired, it feels as if we have been talking about this for half the summer and soon it will be too late.

He thinks it is a bad idea. Full stop. Mostly because it is an idea at all. Ideas imply change and Lukas' immediate response to anything that deviates from our normal routine is: no. When did he become like this? I do not remember him this way.

"You're going to regret it."

"Why the hell do you always think you know best, Lo? Especially things you haven't got the foggiest about." The questions he has . . . it is time to ask them now. *Now* – not later. There will not be a later, Gábriel will not live many more weeks.

It is not intended to be a truth commission, just a conversation. The last chance, the last conversation he will be able to have with his Pappa – and the first as well, for that matter. Interpreter required, for private case, that is all that needs to be in the advert.

195

"Private case?" He looks at me, distrustful. "Sounds like something dodgy."

"Oh Lukas, stop it . . ."

They have argued over everything, without understanding one another. Never spoken. There are so many things the two of them have never talked about, the short and yet insuperable distance of language. They have shared the same life, the same kitchen table, over which they could see but not reach each other, just enough vocabulary in common for everyday life, simple commands and sometimes not even that. When Gábriel turned on Lukas it often seemed to be caused by some misunderstanding. Something Lukas neglected to do, simply because he had not understood that he had been told to do it.

This unwillingness to speak as well. Gábriel surrounded himself in silence as if it were a natural condition, small wonder that Lukas soon forgot the language that was his when he arrived here. He quickly began to speak better Swedish than Hungarian, the new language became his only one, since that was the only one he heard.

Only when I have given up the idea, stopped believing in it myself, does Lukas unexpectedly give in. Before he has a chance to change his mind, I make the call. Half a minute, that is all the time it takes to dictate the advert over the telephone. Then it is just a question of waiting. We sit on their wooden porch, listening for the ringing of the telephone, scratching at mosquito bites, watching the kites soaring with predatory elegance high over the late-summer sky. Bide our time, or maybe it is Gábriel's time we are biding, it is at any rate his time that is running out.

Every day he grows worse. Before it was every week, and before that it was every month. The irrevocable process of distraint and seizure has begun. Death's henchmen, some kind of execution squad, come and, bit by bit, remove his life and carry it away, and we cannot stop them. As if it is no longer his, as if he has lost his right to it. All of a sudden they come and take away his ability to climb out of bed by himself. He could do it a moment ago, and we did not even think about it – now he can no longer do it and we have to think about it all the time. For him it means immense frustration, for us it means that we can no longer leave the house together for more than a very short time. He can still manage to get to the toilet, but first we have to help him out of the bloody bed and support him against the wall through the hall.

He is in pain when he walks. But he is also in pain when he is sitting and lying down. He seems to have reached the stage where he suffers with most things, it is merely a matter of how much.

A week passes without a single response. I had imagined that the telephone would start ringing immediately, at least not this humiliating silence. Another one of your bad ideas, Lo, Lukas appears to be thinking. Gábriel himself is luckily unaware of the whole thing. It is the only luck he has at the moment, so we let him remain that way.

Lukas seems relieved that there is no call, after all it is not he who has been the driving force in this, he acts as if he would rather be spared the trouble. But one day he will thank me, even if it just ends up as a failed attempt.

Sometimes it rains at night, but where does all the water go? A parched summer, as if the illness within the house were spreading out into the garden and the countryside beyond. Rustling brown vegetation, the trees around the house no longer cast shadows, they have rolled up their leaves until they look like cigar trees that you want to stretch a hand out to and pick from. We are careful about only doing one thing at a time – while Lukas rolls cigarettes, we are sparing with conversation – so we do not squander a pastime. He smokes instead of eating and I have also lost my appetite, but that does not matter, we do not need any energy, we hardly move, we are in power-reduction mode, do not even argue, lay all feelings aside. It is arduous enough to sit here on the wooden porch that has been our fixed point this summer, with the door open so that we can hear if Gábriel needs anything. It is almost too much to sit here watching the kites lazily glide over the field in quest of the characteristic movement of prey. We are the prey. They have not discovered us yet, but soon the farmers will start to reap the crops and then there will be nowhere to hide.

Lukas needs to be held together and it is I who must do it. I sit right behind him on the step with my chin on his shoulder and hold him hard. And still I can feel how he is falling apart.

He murmurs strange things between sleeping and waking: "I know you can't forgive me."

"Forgive?" I say.

He wakes up: "What?" Draws back from my touch, falls asleep again with his face in the pillow, begins to mumble: "I didn't want to . . ."

"Alright," I whisper, though I do not know what he is talking about.

The constantly gnawing worry has given Lukas' body a boyish frailty, as if he is regressing, like the lake – it has withdrawn too, dried up like a dead eye in the summer heat and left a circle of slippery grey-violet slime that you have to walk over barefoot to reach the water and cool down. But we do not do that any longer. There is an invisible line by the steps that we cannot go beyond. We are anchored here now.

Life is like a fairy tale, cruel and cautionary, weee-oo ee ee ee ee ee-oo, sounds the hunting cry of the kites. I follow the steep drop as one of the huge birds of prey angles his forked tail and dives. Where did all the kites suddenly come from? I do not recall them as a child. They would have been etched in my memory with their long dark shadows. Lukas says that they were almost wiped out for a while. They stopped breeding, too much pesticide in their natural diet, then people started to put out scraps from the abattoirs on to the fields and the species fought back from the brink of extinction.

The vertical dive of a bird of prey is like a falling star, you should wish for something the instant you see it. I shut my eyes and murmur my hope into the sweaty curls on Lukas' neck.

"What?"

"Nothing. A secret."

Death rocks the chair in the darkness. And on the porch steps we sit and wait. The ad was cheap at any rate and we have at least tried, no harm done, Lukas says.

By the afternoon the mercury has risen to thirty-two degrees and all we can speak about is water. Lukas talks about the coolness of the Danube, something he is not likely to remember, while I spin refreshing fantasies for us of mountain streams, fjords, waterfalls, rivers, clear and ice-cold. We have to go down to the lake and have a dip. Gábriel has just fallen asleep and for the first half hour he usually sleeps without anxiety and sweating, so peacefully that he looks as though he will never wake up, and sometimes I almost wish he would not, for his sake. We do not have time to look for bathing suits or even make our way to our sheltered bathing place, just rush straight down near the house and plunge in, naked, and forget for a little while.

I try to keep the sensation of cold as we hurry back, but we are already perspiring when we reach the house. In one way, leaving the house was not in vain. The first thing we see as we enter the kitchen is the flashing red light on the answering machine. I have a sudden feeling of unease. As if the message were bringing news of his death, as if someone had rung to say that now it is over – the fight – Gábriel is dead in the next room and here is a very favourable offer covering all your death-related requirements.

Twice I listen to the message before handing the receiver to Lukas. The voice easy-going to the point of distracted.

"Hi, Yoel Farkas here, saw your ad and . . . yeah, if you still need someone . . . give me a buzz and we'll have a chat." There then follows a message of about the same length that according to Lukas is in Hungarian.

One bite in a whole week, so your hand must not shake when you reel it in. Afraid that Lukas will start to hesitate and make a fuss, I make the crucial call myself. The guy's voice is as smooth as it is on the answering machine and he says yes without asking me to explain the almost inexplicable. He does not even hesitate when I am honest and say that we have no money.

"I'm not doing it for the money," he says, as if he has already realised that this is a particularly deserving case that he can enter on the credit side of his karmic account. "I haven't done any interpreting for a while, so it'll be good practice. And besides I can't wait to get out into the country, it's like walking on a hot tin roof in Stockholm."

When should he come? The sooner the better, I say. The doctors have said that Gábriel only has a few weeks left. They must be able to see that kind of thing. There is a risk that he will lose consciousness at the end, we cannot afford to waste any time at all. He has grown so thin that his bones are rubbing at his skin from the inside.

Lukas is circling round me as I speak, makes a sign that I do not know the meaning of, something about being careful, or maybe something about money. I explain the unconventional remuneration we have thought of. Not sure that he understands at the other end, he is not listening very carefully, just says yes, seems pleased to be getting away from the city, just has one or two things to finish off, then he will pack and take the train down from Stockholm.

Mamma has told me that the last few weeks before I came into the world, she was obsessed with the thought of a baby being like porcelain, the cranium of the finest bone. The delicate fontanelle, how could it withstand the pressure of the whole universe? She could not stop thinking how soft a baby's skull is, how small its lungs, fingers as easily broken as matches, the fragility of life, that I would stop breathing, be born with a rattlesnake inside my head or some incurable disease. On the ultrasound pictures my skeleton was so thin it was almost invisible. I will have to be careful bearing this child, she thought. But when I actually arrived . . . Well, then it was just a matter of getting used to me. She sensed that suddenly she knew exactly what she had to do – and did it – the fear of making mistakes disappeared. A feeling that this was natural, when I was hanging there at her shoulder with my needs. I try to think of Gábriel in this way.

While the heat rises as if it is oozing out of a white-hot hell just beneath the earth's surface, he is growing weaker and we try to play at grown-ups: sick buckets, morphine, fear, sick buckets, morphine, fear. Sweaty sheets, district nurses, communication problems, pain, oxygen mask, nightmares, long agitated nights of sleeplessness. This is serious playing, I think. There comes a time when you have to play this game, but it will not be forever even if it feels like it. We do the best we can, but sense that it is not nearly enough. Gábriel sometimes temperamental, sometimes apathetic, sometimes brave, his condition constantly worsening, with a strength that leads inexorably to nothing. It drains me and Lukas of energy too. The undertow of death. At least we know what we have to do – that is positive, the only positive thing. Feeling that we are in fact *doing* it. Staying. No-one deserves to die alone.

———

You know a newcomer has arrived in town when he steps down from the train in slow motion and suddenly has that look of exhaustion in his eyes. Him over there. No doubt. White shirt and kind of . . . optimistically large bags. What does he have with him? No-one has asked him to stay for long. Have I got this right? What am I doing here? He appears to be thinking: should I really have come, am I going to regret this, when is the next train back? He has come to the end of the line and alighted there, no, it is not even the end of the line, the end of the line *is* something – this is a few stations before. An insignificant place where most trains do not even stop.

He is dressed as if he expected to land in another climate zone. The mercury is certainly as high here as in Stockholm, the asphalt is just as hot, he will probably soon discover that. Yes, look, he is already undoing a button at his neck. And another one. Rolls up the white shirtsleeves, wipes the palms of his hands helplessly over his face, as if the blazing heat is a bad dream he is trying to wake himself out of. At least it is the same for everyone. Except animals, it is worse for them. Two cats have already been caught like nightmare fish in the valves at the power station dam. No-one has ever heard of cats drowning before. Desperate to quench their thirst in the devastating heat.

"Bloody hell," he says, as I go to meet him and stretch out my hand, "I mean . . . sorry . . . hi . . . Yoel. How many degrees is it here? Forty-five?" Lukas does not take his hand, as if he did not understand what the gesture meant.

"We have stopped wondering," he answers tersely. It is true, we have. This is a heat that has to be ignored, like any other evil. In the hope that it might disappear. It will be better next week, the stranger says he has heard.

"They said that last week too, but it just got worse," Lukas says. But now it has reached the limit, it has to change, the stranger thinks.

"What limit? There is no limit," says Lukas. He has neither shaken his hand nor introduced himself.

"Of course. If you say so. Here in the country you forecast your own weather." The one who says he is called Yoel smiles.

I am relieved that Lukas does not hear the last remark, because he is clearly not in the right mood. Begins to fasten the luggage on to the old Yamaha that is his only vehicle now that the car is in for repair. Once he has secured the bags and kicked-started it he turns to hand it over to me.

"Are you riding with me?" I hiss. I am usually always nagging about driving the old monster, without ever being allowed. It is not me he is worried about, he always assures me, but the motorbike. Now he sneaks a glance at the stranger and I immediately guess what is going on. He wants to change our plan so that I drive the heavy luggage back to the house while he acts as guide. He had not reckoned on the interpreter who answered our advert being young and handsome with a captivating smile. I refuse to take the motorbike when he passes it to me. A little while ago I had fallen off and nearly injured myself and that was just in testing the seat. Now we are going to stick to our plan, that is all we have. Without it everything will get out of hand.

He gives in, but makes his point by behaving like a lout and not picking up on the polite small talk on the platform. Just takes care of the luggage as if he were the anonymous footman. Half-heartedly he steps on the accelerator and sets off home.

"And that was . . . ?" asks our interpreter, who by now if not before must be regretting his decision to come here at all.

"Lukas. It's for his sake that you're here." I have no desire to apologise for him, I never do normally, but now I ought to – Yoel is someone we really need, nothing should ruin that, not even Lukas.

All that Lukas and I used to need to believe in the impossible was each other. That we now had a plan too gave us a sense that what we were doing was feasible. "A long stay in a charming lakeside cottage," was what I offered the guy on the telephone in exchange for his services. Lukas had stood in front of me and rolled his eyes. We'll cross that bridge when we come to it, was my thinking. Now I almost feel sorry for him as he walks beside me, full of expectation, as if he is really looking forward to it all. He does not yet know that the person he will be interpreting for is high on morphine most of the time and for the last few days has been more dead than alive.

"I didn't know he was *so* ill," is the first thing Yoel says when we arrive at the house and he grasps the situation. "I thought he was on a visit from Hungary. Have you really lived together your whole life without being able to speak to each other . . . I've never heard anything like it." If he had not broken off at that point, I would have been obliged to interrupt. Lukas has not asked for a sweeping analysis of his childhood and adolescence.

"You'd better go in now, while you have the chance. Gábriel sleeps more than he's awake," I inform him, this is deadly serious, if he has not realised that yet.

"O.K., so what do you want to know?" I fall silent and Lukas does not seem to know what to say either. We have not actually talked about what the important questions are that he has to ask. This is Lukas' business now, I imply with a gesture.

"I want to know where I come from," his answer is almost inaudible, "and why we moved here." Yoel raises his eyebrows.

"Is that all?"

"And about your Mamma," I add. I see the effort Lukas is making, somewhere deep inside.

"As much as possible about her. I know nothing."

"And if you have any relatives left anywhere," I fill in.

"Yes. I don't want . . . don't want to be left alone," he murmurs. Alone? You are not alone, Lukas, I want to say. I am here.

If Yoel thinks the whole thing is extremely strange, he does not show it. Lukas sucks in the last of the cigarette and stubs it out in a juice glass, listening to Yoel's quiet voice.

"Let me sit alone with him for a while. We'll try to take the most important questions first. But you'll have to reduce the morphine if we're going to get anything sensible out of him, he's delirious."

Merely by making an appearance and being present, Yoel is like soothing water washing over all the clammy anxiety. Not that he displays a great deal of empathy, but an ease, a sense that this whole thing need not be as impossible as it appeared to Lukas and me. I stand beside him and just breathe in the smell of clean shirt. It smells alive, I think. Fresh. And grown-up.

Lukas has been in the same clothes all summer, worn nylon shorts and a threadbare Bob Marley top. He does not even smell of sweat any more, he just smells of "that long hot summer when Gábriel was dying". Presumably I smell the same. In my not-so-white top and denim skirt that hangs like a sloughed snakeskin and itches round my hips day and night. I have tried taking it off, but it still itches, phantom itching, it is the heat.

Now and again I have had a shower, washed and changed the bedclothes in the vain hope that some things can still be clean. A machine-load with Gábriel's sheets that have to be changed often. And so off with Lukas' T-shirt in passing and toss it in the drum with my snake-skirt and a few underclothes, watch it all go round for an hour and then into the tumble drier. Sit there watching it as if it were a little child that had to be supervised. The laundry room has been my only refuge this summer, the coolest room in the house, the only place death does not reach. All is as it should be in there, all that has gone wrong outside is still as usual there, an exceptional state of normality. I sit on the concrete floor until Lukas comes to fetch me with just a look from the door, a silent glance that says: come on, I need you. And I reply:

"Soon . . . just have to do the tumble drier too." And so I switch the drier on one more time. Steal twenty minutes more of liberating, irresponsible solitude.

When I remove the washing it smells just the same as when I shoved it in. Perspiration and lingering panic.

Sometimes when we doze for a time on the mattress by the porch door, I slip my hand into Lukas' limp T-shirt, bury my face between his shoulder blades until I am nearly knocked out by his body's strong secretions. He is too tired to protest about my sticky presence, we are both too tired to protest about this summer.

We keep hold of each other while we sleep. Not with force, but hard all the same, not open for negotiation. As soon as one of us shows signs of waking up, the other drags the traitor back down to sleep again. We have to keep together here. It is the only thing that can save us now. Keep together. Sleep. Wake only when you must and do only what you have to. It has been like this for weeks.

Sometimes he presses against me as if he thought that a bit of listless sex would be a comfort, quell the anxiety, even keep death at bay for a while. But it has never felt as wrong as it does now. Not here, not now, Lukas, it does not feel right . . . I push him away, careful but unyielding. He does not try again, at least not that night. Just holds my breast over my top and his hand is so cold it is refreshing.

*

To flies we are just another surface area. Salty humid dried flat curved bare fields of flesh. Open to invasion. So tired. No, much more than tired – spent.

When Yoel arrives it is like a window flung open in a room that has been shut up for too long. A cold blast of oxygen rushes in and wakes us out of the torpor that has filled the house. He smells of summer, not damp and musty like us, no, he smells of bonfire and dry grass, brackish water, fresh air, aftershave. The house becomes more bearable when he is in it.

The outcome from the first session is meagre, but it is at least a start. According to Yoel most of the time was spent explaining why he was there at all. You could have prepared this better, he gives us to understand. But how? That is precisely the problem, an almost insurmountable obstacle to communication. Otherwise we would not have needed him to come.

"Do you think that we're . . . strange?" I ask when Lukas has gone out, indicating clearly that he wants to be left alone.

"Do *you* think that you're strange?"

"Yes. Or no. Maybe . . . but we're only doing what we've got to do."

"Well," Yoel says, "it's not that strange – to do what you've got to do I would say is quite normal."

Gábriel is not in fact as reluctant as I had feared. But it is a strain to speak and even more of a strain to remember. He answers in one or two words the questions Yoel puts to him from Lukas. I have the feeling that what Lukas gains from it is not worth the battle. Stop torturing him, I want to say. But what right have I to interfere?

They begin with what is important but not dangerous: places, names, family details. Gábriel comes from a village outside Kecskemét. In the middle of the Puszta, in the Great Hungarian Plain. From an area with many fruit farms and the apricot brandy they are famous for, Yoel relates between rounds, he seems to put twice as much into Gábriel's short replies each time. There is a special shine in Gábriel's eyes when he hears Yoel say Barack Pálinka. Yoel cannot help but laugh.

"It's really awful, Barack Pálinka . . . you need to have grown up with it to like it," he whispers to us. There is a moment's levity in the room, the pressure suddenly drops and everyone becomes a little giddy, Gábriel smiles, Yoel laughs, Lukas and I laugh as well even though we have no idea what about.

Yoel seems to know most things. Has studied history at university, travelled all over. Gives us complimentary mini-lectures between Gábriel's brief and hesitating answers. About the Puszta, how the people were driven out under Turkish rule, how the ground, when no-one was cultivating it, was reduced to a wilderness and for centuries was just pasture land for cattle. From Gábriel he has learned that his older brothers, Lukas' uncles, worked as *czikós*, cattle drivers, when they were young. Gábriel was the only one in the family they could afford to do without so that he could continue with his education, he had a head for books and got as far as studying medicine, even though his studies were extended for financial reasons. He was obliged to work at the same time, married and had children and then . . . Yoel pauses, searching for the best way to say it, the gentlest way. But there is no such way.

Then – before he had passed his final exams – Lukas' Mamma died. That was what happened.

A few years later Gábriel left the country with his son.

*

The conversation ends there. Gábriel indicates that he needs to rest. It is frustrating for Lukas to break off, but there is no choice.

Lukas has always imagined that his Mamma died shortly after he was born. That has been his explanation for having no memories of her, not the slightest little tone in her voice, no blurred snapshot. That he was five years old and still cannot remember her affects him deeply. He raises objections. Yoel must be wrong . . . But the next time Yoel asks, he receives the same answer from Gábriel, so Lukas has to concede.

Stop tormenting him, I want to beg him. But Lukas has a look in his eye that says "You owe me this". I have to hold him back now, instead of urging him on. And his Pappa is no longer capable of defending himself. If he speaks he knows that he will be left in peace afterwards – so he speaks. What life gives with one hand, it soon takes back with the other. We learn that Gábriel finally succeeds in catching his teenage love, Lukas' Mamma, after several years of waiting while she was married to someone else. Mara worked as a nurse in a Budapest suburb and one day a week as a volunteer in a prison. Gábriel's greatest fear was that she would catch tuberculosis, as the infection often spread between inmates. But it was not tuberculosis that took her, but fire. In a summer cottage they had borrowed from some friends, the last day of their holiday there, the fire that took hold in a pile of clothes on the bed, it happened so quickly. Gábriel had gone out into the wood to empty some partridge traps. He had actually gone off because they had fallen out, they who argued so seldom had disagreed about some small thing, something to do with the children, the two sons. She, Mara, thought that he was too easy on them, would always smooth things over when she had reprimanded them. That meant it had all been to no avail and she was made to feel ashamed that she had been too hard. They started to argue. After a short quarrel he went out. As he was returning he could see from far away that the little wooden house was engulfed in flames.

After a long silence Gábriel tells them about the other son, that there was another boy, Lukas' older brother. As the cottage was burning, as Gábriel was coming along the dirt road and saw the flames, Lukas had managed to get out. In spite of being the smallest. Or perhaps for that reason, because, unlike the others, he thought of no-one other than himself and he ran. His Mamma and his brother were still inside. Lukas' burns indicated that he had been in the flames, but the only thing he could say was something about a candle in the bed. Afterwards, when the burned-out house was examined, it was established that the fire had started in the bedroom. His Mamma and his brother, András, were found on the floor in the kitchen, presumably trapped in the noxious smoke.

Lukas is suddenly stricken with a splitting headache and goes out. A sudden flash of memory, like migraine? Perhaps his brother, the memory of someone he shared a bed with, a name or a smell . . . He just pushes me aside and disappears. Yoel persuades me to leave him alone.

Gábriel has spoken about the brother as if he were certain that Lukas remembered him, Yoel tells us later.

"Are you sure that you don't . . ."

"No!" says Lukas. "I don't remember him. Maybe I knew about him, but if I did, I'd forgotten him. No-one has ever said a word to me about a brother."

I had noticed something in Lukas and his Pappa many times – without really understanding what it was – the remoteness in their way of looking at each other when one of them came into the room. A hint of disappointment in their eyes. As if they thought: *Oh yes, of course, you're the one who survived. It was you and me. Not the other two. They were left in the flames. It happened to be us* . . . So many years after the fire in the summer house, they still had that look in their eyes.

Scars

I hear the music before I can make Yoel out through the tangled greenery, he merges in so well there on the veranda. As if he has already made the pearl fisher's house his own. He is sitting with his eyes closed, drinking a beer, in the last hazy light of evening, in Lukas' cane rocking chair, wrapped in our blanket with our cassette player on his knee, reggae disco. Lukas would hate this if he saw it, this picture of Yoel in front of our house. How handsome, how laidback, how natural. How he squints into the sun and smiles at the fact that I am standing there – and the thought of what that might mean and might lead to.

"I was just going to leave this," I splutter, handing him the bicycle pump, which he accepts in a reflex action without taking his eyes off me. I have to brace myself against that look. Take a step back. That is not why I have come, if that is what he is thinking. He calls himself an interpreter, but I could see ages ago that he is not.

He is an amateur who likes playing at being a man. What's a girl like you doing in a dump like this . . . he waits for my next move.

"What's this for?"

"Didn't you say you had a flat tyre?"

"I haven't even got a bike," he smiles. I hope that my flushed cheeks cannot be seen in the red evening light.

"So what shall I do with this?" he asks again and swirls the pump round in one hand. "Bring a bike with you next time," he says. I go down one more step. "No, wait, don't go . . ." Yoel gently catches hold of my arm, stops me when I just want to slink away, mortified. "This is the nicest bike pump I've ever had. Truthfully."

"It's just an ordinary pump," I mumble, as the redness burns like wildfire from my cheeks to my neck, down between my breasts and further on.

"I'll keep it as a reminder of you. Come and sit down for a minute," he says and sweeps his arm over all that he is offering: a leaky wooden veranda, a tattered cane rocking chair and his own irresistible com-pany. He is inviting me in as if this princely residence were his and not Lukas' and mine. "You're not in a hurry to go anywhere. You need to get out of the house for a while. A beer? No? O.K., I'll just have to switch to wine . . . no-oh . . . what about tea? That's what you'd like, I can see."

As a reminder of you . . . does that mean he is about to leave? That was what I was afraid of. The job is not finished yet.

"You're not leaving already?"

"Tomorrow."

"No!" I say, far too desperate. Yes. He has to go back to Stockholm, this is his last evening.

"Have you ever been to Stockholm?"

"Of course. I've been to Stockholm," I lie, as he shows me into the house, as if it really were his now. Hugely messy in the three rooms already. When he arrived it was spotlessly clean to hide the shabbiness. On the table by the window Mamma's typewriter was sitting in state, waiting for his arrival. On the telephone he had said something about a dissertation, thought that he might stay here a while to finish it.

The typewriter looked like a trophy, and it was too, but when Yoel saw it he just said:

"What an old monster, cool! But I've brought my own with me, a new portable typewriter." If only he knew . . . what effort was required to bring it here – heavy as a small nuclear power station as I balanced it on the pannier rack and carried it the last bit in my outstretched arms. If he only knew what risks I had taken to get it here. Mamma would disinherit me when she discovered it had gone. Pappa's mother had given it to her. She often repeated the story:

"When my father was seventeen he stopped working in the mine, when I was seventeen I was given a typewriter. When you're seventeen . . . what would you like, Lo?" I did not know yet. But there were only a few days to go.

———

Scars are sexy, Yoel says, they mean that you have made a mistake, that you have crossed a line. He runs his finger over the thin white streak above my lip. He has a birthmark himself, a blue spot at the bottom of his back – would I like to see? I shake my head quickly, afraid that he will take off his top and that it will not stop there.

"Is it supposed to taste like this?" I ask to distract him and take a gulp of the hot drink. Dust. I take another sip. Yes, dust. The tea he has brewed must be several decades old, something the pearl fisher brought home from one of his many journeys in the East. Yoel assumes the air of a connoisseur.

"Of course. This is green tea, Japanese, have you ever tasted it?" I take the bowl with the strange-smelling chicken soup instead, a mouthful, quite unprepared for the heat that explodes in my mouth, green curry, red curry, I think I am going to die, my gums feel like open wounds.

We do it. And before I have time to take in what we have done, we do it again.

This secret will die with me, I am thinking. Feel his birthmark against my hand, rough like the devil's teeth marks in the curve of his back. Think about Lukas the whole time.

I pulled up my skirt, he pulled down his jeans, it was over quickly. It was a bit awkward, but it did not hurt, no worse than being scratched by hawthorn bushes on the way here. The whole time I am thinking about Lukas – not that it is him I am with, I am only afraid that he will appear, that I will catch a glimpse of his face at the window, see him open the door and suddenly be standing there.

"Is it alright if I come inside you?" Yoel breathes in my ear. I do not have a chance to reply. He takes that as a yes. He fills me and it really smells of seed, exactly like grain ripe for harvesting in the fields around the house. I will have to . . . wash the sheets before Lukas comes here, I will have to rinse myself in the lake before I go home. Become pregnant, that does not even cross my mind. The least of my problems. A considerably bigger problem is that Lukas will die when he finds out about this.

I try to concentrate on how good it feels when Yoel caresses me. Fluctuate between enjoyment and fear at two-second intervals. I dare not take my eyes off the window. Yoel kisses my neck and round my breast, armpits, stops:

"Don't you shave yourself?"

"What?"

"Under your arms?" I feel his foot along my shin. "Not your legs either?"

"No. Do you?"

He laughs. "I like you. You're feistier than you look."

In the pearl fisher's house of all places, on the pearl fisher's bed. If Lukas saw me now, I am thinking in the midst of it all, with Yoel on top of me in bed. Afterwards I take off my top and wipe away his semen, as naturally as if I had done it many times before.

"How long have you been together?"

"Who?" I ask absently, heavy with heat and tiredness.

"You and that Lukas, of course. You're safe with me, baby, I don't intend to tell him about this, it's best for both of us." We are not together, I assure him. We have never been. Why does he think that? Because you act as if you are, he replies.

It seems that the only thirst Yoel focuses on satisfying is his own. He has been thinking about this since he got off the train and saw me – he claims. I am not accustomed to compliments, if it is a compliment, I squirm under his weight. Was that maybe what Lukas could feel, the scent of another man's lust over the platform? He lowered his horns at Yoel instantly. Is it really so simple? Laugh or cry . . . I cannot decide. Marsupials. That is what Mamma calls them when she is in the mood. Yoel lifts aside the quilt, pulls out of me, it hurts a little. He rolls off me, grimacing as he pulls his foreskin back into place, and with great vigour he leaps out of bed.

"Tell you what, we'll go down to the sea and have a dip," he says with a smile that turns into a laugh.

The sea? Just like that?

217

Laugh? Just like that?

I have not laughed since last spring.

And the sea I have only been to a few times in my life. It was a whole-day affair for my family, who so seldom went anywhere.

"Just for a dip, Lo. It won't take more than an hour or so there and back. How far is it?"

"A long way."

"For God's sake, this is Skåne – how far can it be? Nowhere's more than a few miles from the coast? The water's going to be lovely this time of the evening. Come on."

Yoel just sort of . . . is. Just sort of does. Just takes. For granted. And me? I drift along.

"Can we borrow Lukas' bike, do you think?" Yoel pulls on his underpants and throws me mine. "I'm sure we can," he answers his own question.

Do you have to be so compulsively nice to him, Lukas had remarked sulkily the very first evening. As if he had guessed what was going to happen. Now I am sitting next to Yoel in Mamma's white Volvo and praying to the gods that Lukas will not see us backing out of our house and driving off goodness knows where.

I explained to him that borrowing Lukas' motorcycle was out of the question, not a chance.

"What do you mean? Are you together or what? But your Mamma's car then? Can we take that?" Yoel had already taken enough . . . or that is what Lukas would have thought at any rate. My virginity, my virtue, whatever you want to call it – my innocence, that word, what was it you were guilty of afterwards that you were not guilty of before? Yoel took me in passing like a chocolate in a dish he could not help snatching for himself as he walked past. And soon I was sitting by Mamma's bed telling her a sickening little lie, the car, we really need it, Mamma – while Yoel stood outside in the darkness, leaning against the garage wall, waiting.

"I should really say no," Mamma said as she gave me the keys, "but obviously, if Gábriel's so ill and needs to get to hospital quickly, and Lukas promises to drive carefully." I could not bring myself to look her in the eye. Took the keys without so much as a thank you.

The worst deceit towards Lukas was not that I slept with Yoel, but that I slept beside him. Close, still – so much more intimate than lying under or on top of someone. I lay on his sweaty arm and tried to distinguish constellations in the microscopic fly specks on the alcove's damp-brown wallpaper. My own, the Lynx, should be there somewhere in the swarm of dots, but I could not find it. My eyes darted round among the flecks until they started to sting and I had to shut them. Yoel began to caress me again, but soon stopped, already satiated.

Now we are driving to the sea, perhaps this is also a form of treachery. I have never been to the sea with Lukas. Yoel drives in the middle of the road, as if he owns it. Mamma's Volvo usually causes trouble, but it obeys him. Obliging his every whim, fast for once and like putty in his hands.

"Isn't he a bit too old for you? Lukas. Bit too old, huh? How old are you?"

"I'll soon be seventeen."

"Seventeen," he says, surprised, "I thought you were younger." A hundred and eighty degrees of violet sky, curving above us. Yoel drives as if he owns both the road and the sky.

"We're not together. I told you."

"So you don't sleep together. What do you do then? There's not much to do around here. Tell me. Catch grasshoppers? Count goods wagons? Smoke? That Lukas seems a bit . . ." We should not be talking about him, but Yoel does not notice when I try to interrupt him. ". . . seems a bit stoned. Not just because he goes around in a rasta top wrapped up in his own world, but because he doesn't sleep with you, the sweetest chick in the village – it's obvious you like him. You seem to be prepared to do anything at all for him, at least. What kind of hold has he got over you anyway?"

Lukas is the last thing I want to talk to Yoel about. I have mixed blood with Lukas, with Yoel all the other body fluids, so much more transparent and easily combined.

"Why do you ask so many questions about him? I'm with you and all the time you talk about Lukas."

"O.K., O.K.," he whispers, smiling, "to hell with him."

I like Yoel because he is everything Lukas is not. I like him because I do not love him. Everything happens so easily with Yoel. Screw, chat, bathe. All at the same time, on the same day, and before the evening is over, he says:

"What do you say, babe, are you going to come with me to Stockholm? Life's just begun. For you at any rate." He is the same age as Lukas and is already beginning to feel old, perhaps because he has lived life at such speed, been everywhere, done everything. Stockholm is so far away in my world, he might just as well have asked me to go with him to Ittoqqortoormiit.

That night I hear Yoel's words, this is no place for you, girl, while the river rats scuttle along the floorboards. Nocturnal animals, the most intelligent and sensitive of creatures. For as long as Gábriel was well, they did not last long here. Why did they not come down to the pearl fisher's house instead? We would have left them in peace there, like the Indian temple Lukas had seen on the television where rats were holy – free, quiet, well fed, unafraid. Rats are not just rats, he tried to convince me, they run with the wind in their fur when they are free, scream like red-hot barbed wire when you drown them, hiss and splutter steam like green wood when they burn, have feelings like you and me. And the separation between body and soul does not exist. In the womb the skin grows out from the brain, Lukas explained, opening his hand and letting a drip fall, that is why it is so sensitive. It fell right on my back and my skin was so hot that one single drop gave me goose pimples.

The afternoon Yoel arrived on the train in the blazing heat was a day when everything smelled strong and burned and acrid and carnal, as if all the hay were flesh. An oppressive smell in the house was the first thing he pointed out to us. I thought it was the illness, but he said it was an animal smell. We had lived in the odour for so long we did not notice it, but Yoel said that it stank. He was sure it was coming from the attic.

"The rats," Lukas said bleakly. When his Pappa stopped forcing him to empty the cages, he had forgotten them, suppressed the thought of them . . . the cages his father loved when he was well.

"I'll take care of them," I said quickly, since Lukas looked as though he would pass out at the mere thought of what it looked like up there.

However disgusting I thought it was, I did not harbour the same feelings for the animals as he did. I put on rubber boots, tied a kitchen towel over my nose and mouth and fetched the hook for the hatch to the attic, before Yoel blocked my path:

"Are you mad, girl – we'll ring for Anticimex!" Stared at me as if he really was asking himself what loony bin he had ended up in. A few minutes later he had had a telephone conversation, explained the situation and persuaded them that they had to make an urgent call-out.

You know what people say – that girls who sleep with everyone don't want to sleep with the only one who loves them. It was only a line from a film, Lukas . . . from "Breathless". I feel his eyes on me as we sit in Gábriel's bedroom. Yoel next to me. It is a strange way of getting to know your first lover, as an observer at Lukas' Pappa's deathbed. On the last day Yoel is sitting quietly by the wall, prepared to be there but not to be seen. A stranger in their home, in the bedroom amongst the most intimate secrets of their life. Sitting in the darkest corner interpreting at a distance to show respect, or perhaps keeping a distance for his own sake. Because the situation upsets him.

He is not a trained interpreter, but his mother works at the embassy in Budapest and has found a few assignments for him. And the job is like this sometimes, he says: headlong into the life of strangers, vitally important events, sensitive conflicts, delicate situations. How do you make that alright? He explains that when he leaves he forgets everything that has been said. At the time he is concentrating so hard on the words, that the content and context almost escape him.

Yoel sits with us until the end, ready to catch any last crucial words, but there are none.

Too late. Too late for me and Lukas too – something has happened this summer and it is not Yoel's fault. It would have happened anyway.

Lukas and Yoel. An incompatible chemistry. They even smell as though they have a totally different composition. Lukas slightly metallic, like water in storms at high altitude, he even looks as though he is suffering from altitude sickness some days, something going out of control. Yoel smells of expensive perfume, even if he is broke, he does not want to smell broke, he reveals. But he is not poor in the way Lukas is, a wealthy family always provides protection against the wolves. That way he can buy expensive eau de cologne with his last few cents.

I know that I have fallen for him. And I almost hate him for it.

Morte

Should the eyes be open or closed? They are half-open now, how do you close them without touching him? You should not touch a dead person, should you? As a child I was not supposed to touch the dead birds in the garden, but I did. Always carried them in and laid them on a bed of cotton wool in clean butter dishes. Should we put a coin under his tongue? And his hands. What should we do with his hands? They are lying so haphazardly, one clenched, the other open, bent at a strange angle, as if he were trying to hold on to this life with one hand, though there is nothing to hold on to. Oedipus stabs out his own eyes with pins from a brooch, only I do not remember why. A desperate gesture from a grieving man because he cannot weep? I have seen Lukas cry before, but not the way he is now, without tears, much more frightening. I feel like I am only a hired mourner. I did not have any strong feelings for Gábriel, at least not positive ones. Lukas' feelings were not positive either, but despite everything there was a bond between them, and the line between bond and love, where does it lie? I look at Gábriel's hands. He was skilled with them, but I cannot see them without thinking of all the times they hurt Lukas. Had Gábriel really deserved this summer of patient watchfulness, deserved Lukas' . . . kindness?

"Kindness is something people seldom deserve. That's why it's called kindness," Yoel says, when we have gone out to leave Lukas alone with his father for a while. We sit down under the roof of the porch in the rain and each eat a bowl of soured milk, famished, have not eaten all day. To think about your own hunger in the midst of it all felt so wrong, I let my stomach grumble while we sat by Gábriel's bed.

His last sentences were incoherent. On one occasion he opened his eyes and looked at me, I felt like an angel of death, sitting there in my white T-shirt, pale after a summer indoors. I did not know that dying was such a struggle, thought it happened by itself, without opposition. But when I looked at Gábriel it seemed anything other than simple, he was fighting and I could not decide whether it was to die or to live. At first I thought he was trying to cling on – you know it is the last thing you will ever hold on to, this bloody little life, the last wrung-out remnants of it – but perhaps he was trying to let go?

When he finally died I did not even notice. It took some time before I realised that he was no longer breathing.

Failed miracles, the wisteria sways as if charged with electricity in the evening wind. It has been a still day, but now the wind is blowing up from all directions. The wind through Gábriel's hair gives me a start. Without me noticing, Yoel has opened the window and Gábriel's hair rustles like dry winter grass in the draught. As if he were coming back to life for a little while, but it is a false alarm. What did Lukas whisper in his ear before he died?

"Whispered? Don't remember," he answers, absently. "I don't actually remember. Did I whisper something?"

The last thing that Gábriel told us was that Lukas was the cause of his mother's death. I thought it was so unnecessary to say it here and now, it was so harsh. I wished that Yoel had chosen not to translate it. What would Lukas do with this knowledge? Other than bear it for the rest of his life. Possibly it could explain Gábriel's antipathy to him as he was growing up, the constant coldness. But did it bring any comfort to know the cause? What Lukas had now learned could never be retracted – that the fire he happened to start had robbed him of his Mamma. And the Pappa he loved. If it were a relief for Gábriel to unburden himself in his last conscious hours, it was now Lukas who would carry the load instead.

When I looked at Gábriel's hands, before they became slack and the blood stopped flowing through them, I thought of all the experiences they had in them. All the blows they had dealt and all the caresses, albeit long ago. All the thousands of hours at the factory, hand grips, muscle memory, everything you had to learn, only to die.

When he closed his eyes for the last time he had less than twenty-four hours to live. Something loosened inside me and was cast out when I realised that it was the end. A fear, a doubt. Now it was over. We had done what we could. It was not much, but we had done it. Now we could begin to live once more. Sleep and eat and laugh and touch each other as usual.

But for Lukas it was different. He had become less and less approachable and now something in his eyes had withdrawn completely. His face was so haggard, it looked as though the whole summer had been one long all-night party. I stayed with him that evening, but when he refused to ring the hospital and ask them to come and fetch Gábriel's body, I left. Could not cope with one more sleepless night. Something had come to an end inside me too. For Lukas perhaps the body was still Gábriel, but for me it was dead.

"I'm going now," I said. He could have stopped me. He did not, he could have said: "I love you" or "Do you love me?" or "Hold me for a bit" or "Come here and I'll hold you for a bit". Whatever he had said, I would have said yes.

"Go," he said.

"Yes," I said.

"Well go then!"

"Yes."

I went. Home to Mamma, showered and changed my clothes and answered her questions as well as I could. Then I went down to the pearl fisher's house and spent the night there with Yoel. It was the last night before he returned to Stockholm. He was already late, had stayed longer than he had planned.

"For your sake," he said.

"You mean for Lukas' sake?"

"For all your sakes . . . You're the most remarkable constellation I've ever come across." Constellation? Like stars that form something together even though they are so far apart.

That night I dreamt of electric machines and legs of lactic acid that desperately resisted. Morphine injections, stained sheets over a dead body. Empty lungs, empty words of comfort. Don't comfort me, help me to shout, Lukas asked me in my dream, but in reality he did not reach out to me, and I did not dare approach him either.

I thought the whole time that he would knock on the door. I had told him that when he had rung for the ambulance, he should come

227

and fetch me. When he had arranged for them to come and collect the body, he should tell me. But he did not come.

When Yoel entered me it was the first time for a long time that I felt anything at all. It was painful. And good.

Pain, good, pain. In and out and in.

Simple.

I wanted us to do it again. And again. It was so long since anything had been simple.

On the morning before he was due to take the train back to Stockholm he said:

"I want you to come with me. You owe me that."

"I don't owe you anything."

"No, I know. But all the same."

"O.K."

"O.K.?"

"Yes. Now. Before I regret it." I already regretted it. Mamma would kill me if I suddenly just took off like this. And when I was dead Lukas would dance on my grave.

"Go home and pack then." It was maybe meant as a joke, but I took it seriously. And Yoel thought . . . well, why not? Sure, if she wants to come along, as long as she takes responsibility for herself. After a summer with Lukas, Gábriel and death, it would be sheer relief to take responsibility just for myself. And in contrast to Lukas, Yoel seemed to give more energy than he took.

It was as easy as that. Just to leave. I was not going to live and die in this village after all? In Mamma's house, in Pappa's absence, in Grandfather's arboretum, in Lukas' shadow. When you start thinking about childhood you know it is already over. Perhaps it is the same with love.

"We'll see how it works out. Not that it's ever worked before, as soon as anyone's moved in with me, it's gone wrong," Yoel warned, "but you're different." What do you mean, different? I did not want to be different, I wanted to be the same as all the others.

"Well, you don't seem to have such high demands of life, I mean, and you're so bloody sexy when you look at me like that – but be careful – I'm the sort that strikes back." So strange that it has gone wrong then . . . with the girls. I began to suspect that maybe it was not such a good idea after all. Reminded him that I did not have a ticket for the train.

"Haven't you got a ticket? That means we'll have to nick a car."

". . . no . . ."

"Well, that depends on you. How much you want to come."

As if it were a game, a film, a "Bonnie and Clyde" remake. He sat by one of the open windows looking handsome, had packed but not cleaned, obviously intended to leave the house in the chaos he had achieved in such a short time.

"Besides, didn't Lukas say that he had a car in for repair and he couldn't afford to get it back?" The apple of Lukas' eye, the blue Ford, he will never let that go, I thought. "I've always wanted a cool old jalopy like that."

"Do you always . . ."

"What?"

"Well – do you always, sort of, get what you want?" I asked, provoked.

"Get? It's not a question of getting, Lo, it's a question of fixing."

O.K. But you will never get the Ford. It was Lukas' pride and joy, the only dream he had managed to realise. Gábriel did not even have a driving licence, so the car really was Lukas' own affair. When he was forced to put it in the garage at the beginning of summer to have the front axle changed, it was as if he had lost an arm. The garage had immediately found five other faults that they had taken care of, without asking him first, and now he had an unpaid bill there of several thousand, more than he had paid for the bloody Ford. If he did not come and fetch it soon, they threatened to sell it. He could not pay, I knew that. I wished that I could help him, had turned over in my mind ways that I might wheedle the money out of Mamma. And now Lukas had to pay for the funeral too, thousand-krona notes would just flutter away, even if the undertakers agreed to an instalment plan. He had no idea dying was so expensive. He had thought that Gábriel had money in an account somewhere, since they always lived so frugally, but there did not appear to be a cent anywhere. He must have sent money back home out of his pay all these years. Lukas just did not know to whom.

"Maybe he won't think of it as selling the car to me, but as me paying it off for him," Yoel was calculating.

"Sure."

"Do you think?"

"No. Never! He would never do that."

"We'll see," said Yoel, as if he already considered the car his own.

Lukas looked as though he had fallen asleep in the sun on the wooden porch. Lay outstretched on our blanket, but rose hastily as if he heard our footsteps reverberate through the ground. I felt uncomfortable as soon as I saw him. As in the past, when I saw that he had been beaten but he wanted to pretend he had not. It always gave me a bad conscience, as if it were my fault, which most often it was in one way or another.

I should not have gone with Yoel to ask about the car. I was not his accomplice and the invitation to Lukas to be released from the car problem was completely Yoel's idea. It was like extortion. I knew how hard-pressed Lukas was and when I explained that to Yoel he had seen his chance – even if he did quickly turn it into us helping him out of a tight spot . . . it could mean debt collection, action for non-payment of debt and God knows what that would keep you in debt for ever.

I wondered whether Gábriel was still lying inside or whether an ambulance had driven through the village and I had not heard it. With sirens switched off, as always on that mission. I wondered if Lukas could see that I was holding my breath as we approached. That I had just been screwed and was ready to clear off. But how would he be able to see that? He did not even look at me. Not one single time.

He just waited to hear what Yoel had to say and listened, expression-less. With every moment that Lukas did not look at me, I felt more and more transparent. Soon he would not be able to see me even if he wanted to. I could still feel the sensation of Yoel's penis inside me, if I became invisible it would be the only thing to be seen, floating in the air like a raised finger at Lukas. I crossed my legs even though that would scarcely help. It was aching slightly and the rest of me was so numb that I could not help but focus on it. Lukas looked the worse for wear and worn out through lack of sleep, but at least he was standing up. Had he slept at all? He usually slept so lightly that he woke up if

I was not holding him. Had he eaten? Spent the night out here? Was he cold? Had he drunk? Did he have a hangover? He was wearing my red socks. They looked out of place, the rest of his clothes were black for the occasion.

He was silent, as if he had not grasped what Yoel had just suggested. Yoel went through it all one more time, a deal where he paid the garage bill and a few thousand more into the bargain and took charge of the car. He did not mention anything about "we", otherwise the chance of Lukas agreeing would of course have been zero.

"You're joking?" after an eternity I heard Lukas' voice.

"It's actually a good deal," Yoel persevered, "you'll get rid of a problem. And haven't you got enough problems just now?" Lukas gazed at him as though looking at a cheat and a traitor and trying to decide what category of swindler he was dealing with. "You should always ask for an estimate when you leave your car at a garage or call in a workman," Yoel admonished, as if Lukas had not understood that. Now there will be a fight, I thought. Now Lukas will take out all his frustration on him, wallop him.

"Take it," was all Lukas said. Yoel was caught off-balance. An arsenal of arguments that he now would not have use for. He had not reckoned on getting off so lightly.

"Take it."

"O.K. . . . I don't have that much cash on me at the moment, but I'll send it as soon as I get to Stockholm. O.K.? And we'll have to sign all the registration papers over to me, to avoid any hassle."

"Do what the hell you want," Lukas said and walked into the house. He knew. We had always been so close to each other that one look was all he needed to see that I had been with Yoel. It was not hatred in his eyes, it was a kind of inverted love.

Yoel and I went off and recovered the car at the Loan Shark Garage, as Lukas called it. The dark blue Taunus that I had been in so many times with him – Yoel just pulled out a credit card and paid the bill and the car was his. The debt, which for Lukas was insurmountable, was settled in a quarter of an hour.

I travelled without luggage, did not want to go home and pack, just to leave, ring home when I was out of reach. If my things were still at home perhaps Mamma would think that I had only gone away for a while rather than moved for good. I did not know how long this was going to last. Yoel had warned me that he was an unreliable, fickle type. It did not scare me, quite the reverse, with Lukas everything had been in earnest and forever.

———

I rose to my feet and shook everything off. Went with him. Left a gaping hole behind me. Did not look back.

Left with Yoel's seed still inside me. The one who sows, he shall reap, Lukas. God helps those who help themselves – it could have been you . . .

I left without saying goodbye. How could I? Impossible. Like saying goodbye to yourself, dividing yourself in two.

Went away with a feeling of relief, so great that it outweighed the shame. Saw Lukas in the rear-view mirror, he was carrying Gábriel's things out into the yard, the petrol can on the steps, working gloves, the flames leapt up behind his body, stripped to the waist. He had grown so thin. The body I had always had so close to me that I never really regarded it as a separate part of reality, more an extension or duplication of myself.

Do not play with fire, Lo, Mamma said all the time. It was Lukas who was the fire. The first one, when we met, was an accident. It must have been. A spark in the grass where it was extra dry along the railway embankment, a gust of wind that made it flare up. That spark was like a first meeting – you need to keep it alive or it will soon burn out. The one that was burning now, outside Gábriel and Lukas' house . . . even if it was his Pappa's belongings he was setting fire to, I knew it was to do with me. He was burning what we had and what we did not have. He was burning everything. Mattresses, bedclothes, blankets, chairs, shoes, books, piles of Népszabadság newspapers. Started a fire and walked right into it. I saw his frenzied movements in the mirror, it was a scene I had witnessed before, a circle that was closing.

Had Lukas not always had a dangerous combination of fire and mad-ness to some degree? Throwing things into the blaze, everything he did not know what to do with. A relief that things can go up in flames, it is possible to burn them and carry on. The same relief that you feel in the face of any catastrophe – anything that is greater than you – the relief in being powerless.

I saw that he could see that I was looking at him. And yet he did not even lift his hand. Nor did I, paralysed by a mixture of relief and shame. Neither of us lifted a hand in any sort of sign to each other, a salute or a blessing or even a finger in the air, go all the way to hell, it is where you are going anyway, bloody deserter.

Lukas' hands were busy carrying out the last of Gábriel's things, all that had been his life, throwing it on to the fire and pouring petrol over the lot. And in my hands there was only lead, they weighed on my thighs while Yoel's fingers found their way up there in such a natural caress I could not stop him. With one hand on the wheel and the other in pursuit of pleasure, he pulled out on to the motorway and put his foot down. It went like clockwork now, Lukas' car, money lavished on it and oiled. To me it would always be Lukas' car, whether Yoel had bought it or not.

It is the strong who remain behind, the weak who leave. I deserted, forced to go away to become myself. Something inside me dried up that summer. Lukas was so ravaged by sorrow and misery. In the end I could not bear to be near him, could not cope with him, look at him, breathe the air around him. Just wanted to be alive, see something different, anything at all, the Atlantic. Had I not always said I wanted to see the Atlantic, Lukas? You could have taken me there, we could have gone there together, everything could have been different. I will never leave you, I am leaving you now.

You never lose the one you loved.

It takes two to tango, but only one to let go.

Words, words, words.

"See you in hell, Lo."

His last line, never uttered.

Played, laid, betrayed

Yoel is in the sun, cooling himself down with a beer, looking at the view and from time to time at me. Now and again he shouts out something that must be an instruction, but I do not hear, his voice is drowned by the music from the car radio. It is going well all the same, I must have a natural talent. Round and round over the tacky late-summer asphalt, wider, hotter, faster circles. You need to be able to drive a car to feel truly free. Halfway up to Stockholm he had thought it was time to stop and practise, at a service area with a fantastic view over the motorway and a sparkling stretch of water.

I want to slip out of the parking place without him. It is not Yoel's car, it will always be Lukas' car, and the two of us never distinguished between yours and mine. When Yoel thinks my circles look perfect, he asks if I want to drive properly, nods in the direction of the motorway – there are three hundred kilometres left and he is tired of sitting behind the wheel, he wants to sleep the last stretch.

I focus on the road. When thoughts of Lukas intrude, I accelerate.

"You're a natural."

"I know." I put my foot down.

"Just take it easy. Stay in the inside lane until I say." Reluctantly I ease up on the accelerator. "You've got my life in your hands now, how does it feel?" It feels good. Better than it has in a long time, in fact.

I want to overtake. He laughs: "Not yet. When I say. You couldn't wait to get away, it's obvious."

He lets me drive until we arrive at the outskirts of town. We must not tempt fate, if anything were to happen he is the one who would be held to blame, he has both an American and a Hungarian driving licence. I have had a taste of driving and would prefer not to hand back the wheel, but the fun is over now.

"You're not even old enough, you're underage, aren't you? Not that you look as though you're not smart, but . . . inexperienced. Inevitable, growing up like that." In the shadow of the factories. That is what he calls it. He grew up in Stockholm, Berlin and Budapest, studied in New York. He is the same age as Lukas, but so much more sophisticated and confident and that adds years to his age. He has been everywhere, done everything. He looks good in neon and looks good without. We glide into a tunnel, I have never been in a car underground before, but I read *Alice in Wonderland* from cover to cover and this is a darker version of the same thing.

When we have emerged above ground I wind down the window, the smell of the city is the smell of exhaust fumes, new asphalt, frying from the restaurants. This is the best present I could have had, I say, with my hair streaming in the wind and my eyes watering with the cold night air.

"What? Is it your birthday?" he asks, surprised, as he zigzags through the traffic. Yes. Seventeen.

His flat is in the Kasernberget district. A concrete block built in the seventies with windows the size of portholes. As we carry in his luggage I think that the ugliest house is the best location – that way you do not have to look at it. The street sign. I stare at it. Too much . . .

"What?" he asks.

"Strindbergsgatan? Did Strindberg live here? Really?" He must have done. At some time. He lived in loads of different places in the city, but it would hardly have been in this Berlin bunker, Yoel says, displeased. In his presence you are always reminded that the English word spoiled has two meanings.

Good-looking when he smokes and when he laughs, sexy in a good-looking way, he is even rich in a good-looking way and looks good drunk, he likes drinking but it does not put him in a bad mood like Lukas. The almost provocative levity around Yoel, everything is just a game. Not like a game with Lukas, over in a flash – no, with Yoel the game carries on and one of the rules is that I forget Lukas.

If he could see us now, thank the good lord that he cannot . . . He would have been beside himself.

"Don't think about him now," Yoel whispers. His stomach smells of ylang-ylang, sandalwood, a drop of semen, he slows the pace, to lead and to follow is a simple logic. Sex is about not thinking, he says, as if he knew it is the only thing I long for now.

It is so easy for him, not just in bed. Everything was so easy from the moment he opened the passenger door of the car, which a little while ago had been Lukas' prize possession, and asked me to jump in. Took my virginity in passing, then he took it again and again, before we had time to unload the car, unpack his things, before I even had time to draw back the curtains and look at the view.

Afterwards: "Don't tell me that I was the first? But for God's sake, Lo, how could I have known? You should have said something, then I would have taken it a bit more . . ."

"What? Steady?"

"Maybe. At least I would like to have known. It's a . . ."

"Big responsibility?"

"No, but cool, like. Special." He looks at me doubtfully. "Do you mean to say that you and that Lukas never, not once, he didn't even try?" Now we are talking about him again and I do not want to.

Lukas would soon be twenty-four and I had thought that obviously he must do it sometimes. I could not imagine him with anyone else, but there must have been someone, some time, but who could it have been? Someone at the factory? He never spoke about work when he was off, as if it did not exist, other than a slight ache in his shoulders and hands. Perhaps that was why he was so secretive? Because he had someone there? I knew well enough that this was not so, but it was too sad to think that he had never had anything more than he had with me.

Stockholm the first morning: I release myself from Yoel's hold and launch myself at the window, tear the heavy white curtains apart. There it is. Sparkling like a glass of water in the sun. The city. Stunningly clean and water everywhere with a perfect silhouette against the cyanide-blue late-summer sky.

Whilst I slept I really must have landed on my backside in another world, strangely similar and yet utterly different. The city is a forest of light and sound and motion, I cannot remember when I last felt so small, perhaps the time Pappa carried me in his arms over the field in the worst thunderstorm of the summer. He did not dare to carry me on his shoulders in case a flash of sheet lightning were to seek out the top of my wet head. I had been scared and bolted, with my eyes shut I had rushed straight out into the field of corn – too small to be seen as I raced round in a vicious circle of panic. The movement in the corn revealed where I was. Pappa caught me, comforted, scolded, saved and carried me in a rough grip through the nightmarish thundering light.

Whether it is the world that has grown while I slept or I who has shrunk in my sleep – it has all taken my breath away. He laughs and kisses me between the eyes, a typical Yoel gesture. My fascination for Stockholm is clearly very moving, like a mole who sticks her head up for the first time and sees the light. He shows me the view from Söders Höjder. Just that I call it "Söders Höjder" makes him kiss me again between the eyes.

"It's just the most fantastic thing I've ever seen," I whisper.

"But you've never seen anything, honey: railway, lake, same old countryside, same old . . . what's his name now? Lukas?" I lay my fingers on his lips – do not want to talk about him – especially not with Yoel. Think about him all the time and that is painful enough. Left him without saying goodbye, is there any forgiveness for that? Not even Yoel would have done something like that. If only I had waited until after the funeral or softened the blow by ringing and speaking to him. No, I try to silence my conscience instead with everything that is new, but I cannot rid myself of the feeling that I am a deserter, a heartless, heartless traitor.

I like going out after a storm to have the streets to myself before anyone else has realised the cloudburst is over. The empty city, mine for a short time.

240

"You know we live in the ugliest building in the whole city," he says, to bring me back down to earth.

"But I like it." That, according to Yoel, is because I was born between two factories. Four factories, to be precise. To be exact: four factories, a railway, an industrial estate and a hydropower station.

I do not know if he was a child who had too much love, but he must at any rate have had too much of everything else. Nothing is really good enough for him, the flat is way beneath his dignity. At the moment he is too broke to live the sort of life he thinks he deserves. If only he had not made himself impossible with his Pappa – that is the risk with fine families, it is easy to be banished from them, he says. Monthly maintenance withdrawn. His father has taken his support away.

"What would've become of you if I hadn't come and rescued you?" I hear him say one day when we are eating breakfast in bed, so late in the afternoon that it is beginning to get dark again. The mud-king's daughter? A factory moth spinning an endless thread in the darkness of the wool factory? Eternal virginity? Shrivelled up. The croissant in my mouth swells up like a ball of cotton wool the more I chew. I know that he is joking. But all the same.

"I don't come from the country. I come from the outskirts." It was not true countryside, because we had street lights, but it was not true village either, because the road was not made up. It had something of a bad reputation, along with those of us who lived there. The houses were not so well cared for, the gardens not so well tended, like the children. If only the railway had not cut through the view of the rolling landscape, if only the sound of the long goods trains had not shattered the conversations at the kitchen table. In late winter the lake always overflowed and the fields lay under water and the local flowers had ugly names like bog asphodel, frogbit, waterweed, water plantain, pod grass. The smallness of everything made it more noticeable that we did not belong there, Lukas and I. If only we had had normal family circumstances that might have given the illusion that we fitted in. But not even that.

"Factory moth," Yoel says, or do I just read it in his eyes? He himself is of a nobler species, without necessarily being more sensitive: a spinner of silk and satin, sharp and alluring features. Self-assured, unequivocal. The sophisticated sort who has lived and travelled and knows his culinary French. In a restaurant he sends food back if it is not to his taste, and expects to be compensated for his disappointment. Loves everything ending in *confit*, which I eventually gather just means that it is cooked in its own fat. It sounds unappealing, but he maintains that duck confit is as near as you can get to heaven. And *coeur de filet*, the heart of the fillet, is the thickest and best bit. It is the part of me he will never have, but he does not want it anyway.

A playful and relaxed prelude, is that all we are for each other? If we make love early in the evening, he goes out afterwards, seems to be hungry for something that is not available at home. I am too young to go with him, too young for the only places it is worth going to – he gets in everywhere, people know that he is no pauper, at least not in the pub.

———

Lukas and I shared our lives, shared days and nights, dark and light. We had no secrets from one another. Secrets are the devil's tools, if you keep them for too long you become an extension of the devil's arm. "Trust me", Lukas said. I did. It was almost too easy. There was only he and I and the trust that had to be directed towards someone – and there he was in the window of the pearl fisher's house in the pale greenish light from the lake. Alert and preoccupied at the same time, as if on guard, but against what, no-one knew that we were there. And the risk that someone would walk this far along the thorny path and discover us was minimal.

Each day finally became evening, we had to part, a moment Lukas never grew accustomed to. Mamma stood on the veranda as if she were calling in her animals from the pasture lands, on the lookout for me, saw me coming up from the lake alone. Lukas always told me to run on ahead.

"Where have you been?"

"Out." Mamma sniffed at me before she let me slip into the house to the others.

"You smell of smoke," she said. Every time.

"They're lighting fires on the fields," I replied, always. And slunk into the kitchen, starving.

It was not a graceful exit that I made and the last months with Lukas are not a time I wish to remember. An evil sun had shone upon us our last summer together. I could scarcely breathe in the sticky heat, waiting for Gábriel's days to end, the valley of the shadow of death infinitely long, it took an entire spring and summer to walk through it.

Every time I try to imagine what Lukas is doing just now, I see him by Gábriel's coffin in his black mourning shorts, the only thing he wore at the end. Funeral for close family and friends, what do you do if the close family and friends consist of one person? A very simple ceremony?

It takes some time before I understand what the smell is. Only sense it at night, when I try to sleep and there is nothing to distract me. It is the smell of the summer in the house with Gábriel that has clung to me. Showering and washing my clothes does not help, it is embedded far up in my nostrils, inaccessible, until in the end it subsides, like a sorrow you can no longer bear.

The harsh light of summer has changed when I arrive in Stockholm. Gentler and softer, like Yoel's laugh. *Mañana*, he says, and I try to learn from him, we will do it tomorrow, everything can wait, everything but the moment that must be enjoyed whilst it lasts. Now, only now.

Playing and caressing and deceiving. I straddle him in the Hiroshima four-poster bed. Promise him eternal fidelity under a cloud of creamy white tulle. We make love. We laugh. Make love a bit more in the pale light from the Sodom bedside lamp. Order Chinese food in small white cartons delivered to the door. I have never eaten Chinese food before, never had food delivered to the door, only seen it in films. Yoel opens the door naked, the Chinese man does not let his mask slip, it is called losing face in Chinese, Yoel explains, and he gives him a generous tip, "keep the change" . . . money burns a hole in Yoel's pocket . . . we are on fire and make love and fuck behind the Gomorrah silk curtain. Love is like lighting a cigarette on a burning curtain, an exaggerated gesture, an excessive risk, be careful, Lo, I hear Mamma say . . . I like the kissing afterwards with the taste of sweet and sour sauce, even when I take him in my mouth he tastes of sweet and sour sauce. I have started to write down in my oilcloth-covered book the words you need to know when you are with Yoel. Sweet and sour. Fellatio. *Mañana*.

I am making love to a moth, he weighs nothing, lifts me off the sheet, we levitate, revolve, transpire. I give him an erection, he gives me goose pimples, I give him . . . well, what? He has everything already. I can only give him the one thing he does not have – myself.

"People like you don't grow on trees, Lo. Or maybe you do, a very rare sort," he whispers, thrusting so deep inside me it hurts.

A man's penis is enlarged during dream sleep and on physical contact. I look at him to check and yes, that is correct. On the other hand, if impotence can be cured with the smell of cinnamon, as they say on the radio, a scent from childhood, a mother's baking, that cannot be proved with Yoel, he is not at risk. Sometimes he has an erection while he is frying eggs or when he is shaving or talking to a friend on the telephone, even when he is sitting staring at his dissertation.

"I want to have you, can't you see?"

"Put a bag of ice on it." I have promised to say no to him next time I distract him while he is studying. But I do not say no. If it is not me, it will be some other craving that disturbs him. This thesis will never be finished, and it is not my fault. *Coitus a mammilla*. The urge to play.

"Slowly," he whimpers, when I try to swallow him too fast. It is so powerful that we can hardly move, a blackout of pleasure, *la petite mort*, Yoel is fluent in the language of love.

"I love you," I say and do not mean it. It is so easy to say.

"I love you too," he whispers and does not mean it either. Storms and accidents do not touch us. I am naked apart from some black pieces of jewellery around my wrists and neck. Some cheap trash he has bought me for fun, magnetite, jewels for those on the way down –

245

and I go right to the bottom with him, not deep, because he has no depth. He says that himself, and laughs with all his crooked white teeth.

He requires nothing of me. Not like Lukas. There are things Yoel wants, but it is not a need, not dependency, just desire. He fills me up and at the same time he makes me feel lighter than ever before. But when I want to dance on his feet, he complains that I am too heavy and when I want to go out with him, he says that I am too young. At least for the places he wants to go to. Kisses me between the eyes and goes.

When we are drunk we are useless in bed, but the day after we can keep going for hours. There is no greater aphrodisiac than a moderate hangover, I soon learn. The ease with which Yoel moves through his life, I am waiting for it all to be overturned. Is there really no cloud on his horizon?

One of his former girlfriends seems to have the same unequivocal attitude to life as he does. She comes past sometimes and has a glass of wine on her way somewhere else. Treats me as if I were a home-help who is having a break between cleaning the toilet and ironing shirts and quite possibly sexual services that in her world are clearly part of that sort of job. She has always bought something incredibly expensive that she wants to try on and show off, after Yoel like a fool has helped her with the zip. It is the only time he ever appears to be an idiot, we all have someone who is more than a match for us, and she is his.

I start to feel very ill at ease when I see her through the peephole.

"You're such a loser still living here," she says and gives him an air kiss without touching his cheek. She never touches anyone, he says, except possibly when she has to lie with someone to . . . well. At least once every six months so that her boyfriend does not tire of her, and now and then with someone who can give her something she wants. The one-night stands seem to be selected for what they can give her outside the bed rather than in it.

I listen, my ears like cupped batwings. She is not bothered that I am listening, perhaps that is the intention – just as the whole time she can obviously see me, though she never looks directly at me. She spreads disquiet with her mere presence in Yoel's kitchen, has the ability to use up all the oxygen in the room. Always the same pattern: she sweeps in, asks him to open a bottle of wine, takes three sips and leaves the rest, rapidly sums up everything that has happened to her since the last time. Her life is a triumphal procession and we have the honour of being the audience. I glance at Yoel while she is talking. Have the feeling that he is actually dazzled by her successes and that the apparently self-inflicted disasters awake his sympathy. Then she relates her human conquests – man or woman, it is not all that important, however it is never a question of sex. Sex is just the means, tried and tested, a win every time.

Several times a day I lace up my gym shoes and stuff a little money into my pocket, coins and small notes that I find all over in the flat.

"Where are you going?"

"Out." Kiss him as I go past and take the steps in long strides, eager to be moving. It is like having a dog, according to Yoel, a dog that takes itself out. I have nothing against being a dog. Adaptable, independent, always on the move.

"I miss you when you're not here . . . but you'll come home when you're hungry, won't you?" Yes. I will come home when I am hungry, but first I have to sniff around the whole town.

Stockholm is a dream from which I do not want to wake. I find my way to the water, drawn there. It does not smell at all like the lake at home, not fermenting sludge, if anything an acrid chemical smell of diesel and oil. Stockholm, surrounded by water. To begin with I managed to ignore everything that was ugly. In Yoel too.

Wallpaper with ominous eczema-coloured flamingos in the bedroom, kitchen chairs in poison-yellow plastic that make me lose my appetite, on the wall above the bed Warhol's "Car Crash" in shocking pink. *The monotone repetition and the garish colours express a moral and an aesthetic emptiness that is a goal in pop art*, he recites. The monotone repetition and moral emptiness swim above us every time we make love, the cars crash at the same moment he twists my head backwards.

The days with him float by like music in a piano bar, you hardly notice them. Neither of us goes out to work, he has money so we manage and if he has none then he sorts it out one way or another. Yoel the fixer, trickster. Money is something to be handled with discretion, not something you talk about. If you have it, you spend generously on yourself and others. If you do not, you lie low for a while and do not grumble about it. Behave as if nothing has happened, it is just a downswing.

Lukas talked about money all the time, for him the downswing was perpetual, mental, or even in the blood. He was oppressed by it. Often talked about what he would do if he ever became rich, though we both knew it would take a miracle for him to become rich, and miracles never happen, that is why they are called miracles.

For Yoel the crises are never serious. He can afford to have a cavalier attitude to everything, can always ring and bow and scrape a little and get his Mamma to write a blank cheque for him when the bills are piling up, or he has found something expensive he wants for himself. Yoel the *bon vivant*, the dandy, with his from-one-day-to-the-next lifestyle in which he does not need to bore himself or anyone else with thoughts about money.

If there is a single cloud in his sky it is his parents, though it is more of a light cloud that at regular intervals passes by and is gone. The family meets twice a year, dispassionately. Gathers together in a large apartment on Riddargatan that is empty the rest of the time. His Mamma travels from Budapest, his Pappa from Berlin. To play at being married. The whole thing is topped off in a weekend, punctually and dutifully.

"Come home and sneak the wedding ring on again, just often enough to keep up appearances. They don't believe that we know they're separated, isn't that touching?"

He is the last sprig on some noble old tree, as high-class as he is poor. There is money in the family even if he does not think he has an adequate share of it. He has grown up in his brothers' cast-off clothes, and when he was a teenager his father was so stingy that Yoel was obliged to seduce his mother's friends for pocket money. He did not tell me that, but he told his ex-girlfriend, who passed it on to me on one of her night-time get-togethers in his kitchen. A middle-class objection to spoiling their children, you have to have a certain hunger to get anywhere in this world. Yoel's Mamma wants her sons to get as far as possible. So that she does not have to look at them, is his guess.

My Mamma did not want me to get anywhere at all. All the others had gone. I try not to think about it – the reason – it is like a thousand-piece jigsaw puzzle, where most of the pieces are missing, you will go mad if you try to do it. The only thing I know for certain is that it all began when Pappa left. That piece of the puzzle was in the middle, and even though the family was large, it only needed one person to disappear for it no longer to be whole.

I do not ring her. Do not even open her letters. Reply to them unread. I miss you too, I write. But I cannot go home, I cannot cope with the feeling I would have standing in front of Lukas, even in my head. We met and parted against a backdrop of fire, perhaps it meant nothing, but behind my eyes when I am asleep it is still burning and in my dreams Mamma rings and tells me that Lukas walked straight into the fire when I went. He left me a farewell letter, she says, but when she tried to read it the ink was smeared, completely illegible.

"But you'll definitely know what it said, Lo." I slam down the receiver as if it has burned me. Then I wake up.

I have begun to think like Yoel, *mañana*, I will do it tomorrow, anything less important than sex can wait until tomorrow. But tomorrow never comes. With every day that passes it becomes more and more impossible to contact Lukas. Likewise to ring home and the letters Mamma sends I leave unopened in a pile.

"Isn't it better just to throw them straight out?" Yoel asks. He thinks it is reproach I am afraid of, but it is not that.

———

In Mexico there is a volcanic mountain that has not erupted for three hundred years, and yet clouds of smoke can still be seen over the snow-clad peak. When I heard about that I thought of him, sometimes time is of no consequence, I'd like to live in Mexico I hear it's so lovely, if you don't love too much you don't love enough – words, so easy to say.

What happened when I left with Yoel must have felt to Lukas like being overtaken in the last metres of a marathon. He had always expected me to race him at growing, his way of looking at me. He was an adult, but he could not live as an adult, must have felt castrated, seen the change in my face, sensed the teenage smell. To be starving and recognise the smell of something you want to have.

I know it is only words, but perhaps you have to stop trying to forget, so that it has a chance to wear off by itself. So that one day you notice that it has happened, the cloud of smoke is no longer hovering above the volcano.

If I ever imagined that life is fair, that illusion is shattered when I meet Yoel, and still more his former girlfriend. They share the enviable ability of not allowing anything to drag them down below the surface. But she is more ruthless. No core, it seems, whilst Lukas was only core with no protective covering.

It is hard to say what ruthlessness is, what insensitivity is and what just pure thoughtlessness is. She will never get away with it, I think, as she tells me how she does what she will with people to get what she wants. But the world around her seems infinitely forgiving. She does alright every time and Yoel too, life's natural injustice.

When she looks at me her eye moves straight on, as if my face bores her. "Don't take it so seriously. Look on it as entertainment," Yoel tells me, when she has finally gone. Entertainment? Is that really all she is for him? "You're just jealous," he teases me. Jealous? Never. Me? What is there to be jealous of? Well, yes, for that matter I am jealous of the way she gets him to look at her – it is the only time he shows a hint of vulnerability. At some time she has hurt him deeply and he knows that she can do it again.

While she leans against him and laughs at something only they understand, from the corner of one eye she looks at me: *I could seduce him ... if only you were worth the effort, if only it did not mean I would have to touch him ...*

Why does she never touch anyone, I ask Yoel when at length she has gone. "Yes, why?" He hesitates.

"I don't know, because she thinks it's a waste of herself, probably."

When Yoel thinks I have gone to sleep he satisfies himself.

"Masturbation ..." he says at breakfast.

"Yes?" I ask and hand him the deli liver pâté flecked with truffles like black demon eyes.

". . . comes from the word *manus*, meaning hand and *stuprare*, meaning violate or defile."

"Mm, I know." Have started answering like this when he tries to enlighten me about the big world, it is starting to be tiresome, I have natural talent, all tuition is superfluous. And sex is not as revolutionary as I thought it would be – certainly not more than staying awake all night with Lukas or swimming underwater with him the length of the lake. It is pleasant, it keeps your mind off other matters, you want to do it again, but that is the case with so many things. Perhaps because it is not quite as satisfying as you would like it to be.

Yoel is free throughout the daytime apart from a few hours in the late afternoon, when at last he overcomes his reluctance to grapple with his dissertation. Hungarian migration from the turn of the century to the Velvet Revolution. It is difficult not to be fascinated by his family's chequered past, twisting its way like a red thread though European and American history. My own family's history has looked the same generation after generation. If you know where you come from, perhaps it is easier to know where you are going, was that why Lukas always seemed so lost? If you have no memory of a past you cannot imagine a future either.

Leaving everything behind you, emigrating like Yoel's relatives, the feeling of freedom imbued with guilt. A black vein running right through the relief – that you can actually leave . . . just go. Yet at the same time you have to live, perhaps forever, with the sense that you are a deserter.

He stays long enough to teach me how to handle the remote control for all the unnecessary electrical appliances, to make love to me until even that becomes a part of the everyday, and then he goes. The first trip is to Berlin and Budapest, he has a parent in each city and an acute financial interest in a reconciliation with them. I do not know what I am going to do in the flat. At home there were always jobs to be done, but here in the apartment there is nothing to occupy me.

The whole of the first night I spend in front of the television. The picture changes with the level of my intoxication, I have opened one of Yoel's expensive bottles and empty it slowly. Marsupials. Tasmanian devils. Completely normal kangaroos. Remarkable creatures with a highly unusual reproductive pattern . . . While other mammals carry their young until they are fully developed, the marsupial's babies are born soon after fertilization. I sit on the floor in front of the sofa with my glass of wine, Yoel has taught me to sit on the floor, it was unthinkable at home, the floor was something you touched only with your feet.

I edge nearer to the television screen and watch the embryonic little baby crawl out of its mother's womb, creep blindly through her fur to reach the pouch. This particular female kangaroo is strangely like my own Mamma, more and more like her the more I stare at her. When the baby is born it is so small it consists of only a mouth and a pair of front legs. Under its own power it moves from the vagina to the nipple, latches on and starts to suck. The nipple expands to become firmly clamped inside the mouth and hanging there the baby accompanies the mother wherever she goes, the deep voice-over explains. Only after a few months have its jaws developed sufficiently for it to open its mouth and let go.

Sooner or later you have to crawl away from the great mother animal with her enfolding oxygen-deficient love-pouch. That is when you meet the other sort, the ones like Yoel.

My life is entering a new phase. For the first time I am alone, all by myself, solo. One brief jaunt is followed by another: Yoel has been to see a friend in New York, Yoel has been to see a brother in Paris, a girl-friend in Copenhagen, a cousin in Zakopane. The flat is full of cases that have not been unpacked, he does not like to dig around in the past. Instead of being reminded of old journeys, he wants to plan new ones.

I stop missing him, and he does not seem to miss me very much either, as the date of his homecoming is always being postponed, without further explanation, until I begin to feel quite used to the solitude. *The most beautiful place on earth is your collarbone*, he said not so long ago. As if he had been in every place, in every woman. *The skin under your arm . . . if I had to choose something to take with me to a desert island.* Silky smooth words about chiselled collarbones and soft skin.

Slid inside me as if I were a icy street, as if it were never his intention, a pleasing mistake, that is all. And slid out just as easily.

However much I may dislike his former girlfriend and her way of marching right through his life as if she owned it, I find that I have taken one piece of advice from her for getting on in all situations: high heels. The higher the better. I want to know how it feels to be as high up as her. Buy a pair of sky-high calf-skin boots second-hand and walk around in them all day in the flat until Yoel comes out with:

"You look different. Have you had your hair cut? No . . . wait – have you lost weight? You have, haven't you?" He studies me as he sits fiddling with his newly purchased stereo. "It suits you. Not that you needed it, but you look bloody great."

"What about you then?" I ask coolly, I have a sudden desire to deflate his self-adoration: "Shouldn't you do something too . . ." It does not work. His belief in himself is not shaken so easily. He stands up, slowly moves in and then goes for the attack.

Make love. With a hungry Yoel on top of me. With the sky-high boots on. Afterwards I try to watch "Breathless" with him, but he falls asleep in the middle of the long bedroom scene that is my favourite. You know that they have sex, but you never see it. They make love in French, with their mouths, speaking, almost without touching each other at all. Jean Seberg, cool and playful, intense and unapproachable, a mystery, like cats who allow themselves to be patted and tormented at the same time. I sit there with Yoel beside me, knocked out, and I know all the lines by heart without having anyone to play opposite:

"You don't even know how to apply your lipstick. It looks terrible," he would say.

"Say what you like, I don't care. I'll put all this in my book."

"What book?"

"I'm writing a novel."

"You?"

"Yes, why not me? Stop it – what are you doing . . . ?"

"Taking off your top."

"Not now."

"You're a bloody pain."

"Do you know William Faulkner?"

"No, who's he? Someone you slept with?"

"No way, José. . ."

"To hell with him then. Take off your top."

"He's one of my favourite writers. Have you read *Wild Palms*?"

"Take off your top, I said."

"Listen. The last sentence is beautiful . . . 'Between grief and nothing, I will take grief.' Which would you choose?"

"Let me see your toes. Toes are important in a woman. Don't laugh."

"Which would you choose?"

"Grief's stupid. I'd choose nothing. It's not better, but grief's a com-promise. I want all or nothing."

I keep my boots on until I tire of them and of Yoel's compliments. Take them back to the same second-hand shop and go to the hairdresser's, ask for a super-short Jean Seberg-style. The hairdresser does not know what that is, but I have a picture from the scene where Jean Seberg is sitting on the bed and has just taken off the gangster hat.

"Are you sure?" he asks, looking at my hair that reaches almost all the way down my back. I think so. At any rate, I have never been more sure.

"It's a great sixties' look, but it needs a film star charisma for this style to really work," the hairdresser guy says. I have that. "It needs the eyes," he says. I have them as well. All that is missing is a single dimple. I would really like to go blond . . . but I do not have enough money, that will have to wait.

"What the hell have you done?" Yoel bursts out when I come home. "Your hair!"

"Exactly – *my* hair," I reply and stride past him on my way to the bathroom.

He looks at me as if I am a stranger, as if he cannot trust me with this hairstyle. Something in him cools down markedly when he is deprived of my hair. Was that all it was? The long dark childlike hair, was it so paltry that that was all it was?

Incognito

Lukas' unattainable dream is just one of the many places Yoel has been to. Out of the blue one evening he asks me if I would like to go there with him for the weekend. Budapest. Just like that? For years it had been like a mirage for Lukas, a distorted reflection of something he only vaguely remembered. How many times had we talked about going there together? It would feel like a betrayal of Lukas to go there with Yoel.

I say I do not have a passport. Yoel the fixer can usually pick up the telephone and arrange anything at all with just one call, but this time he says absently what a pity, perhaps he will ask her instead. At first I do not understand. Who? Her? His ex? He does not even like her. How can she behave as she does, be like she is, and still have his . . . whatever it is – love? Most people do not last long in her presence, only the very strong and the very weak, he had once suggested, without revealing which category he counted himself in.

Yoel draws back the curtain and looks out at the rain, one of many showers that have become one continuous downpour the last few weeks.

"We've got something going again. I don't know what. I, kind of, can't be free of her," he says, preoccupied.

As if he had tried.

He fancied girls like her. Leggy felines. With a squint, dangerous.

So what was he doing with me . . . no idea. I was not going to cause multiple collisions when I went over a crossing. Not even if I walked very slowly with everything hanging out, that was clear enough to see.

I left him. Or he left me. When he returned from his trip I was to be gone. It was unspoken.

He had not specifically said that I could take the car, but I knew where the keys were, I knew where it was parked and which tricks were needed to start it, I had seen Lukas coax it into life so many times. Yoel had not used it once since we arrived. Lukas' old Ford was not a car you wanted to be seen in when you were in town. It did not look as cool here as he had thought, more of a sunken wreck with circles of rust round the wheels and the watered-down lacquer that seemed to have lost its colour on the way here. He thought it smelled of fermentation from the bottom of the old lake, would probably miss it as little as he would miss me, no deep void when we both disappeared along with a few bottles of wine, bedclothes and a mattress from the attic. And a bit of cash. I knew where his hiding places were and took what I could find, a mixture of crowns, dollars, marks and forints. He had never lifted a finger himself to earn that money.

Either he would be furious, or he would understand. In any case I would not be here, so it really did not matter to me. It is not a question of getting, it is a question of fixing, he had said himself. People with principles rarely like to be treated according to those principles themselves, but his money would go towards something important. I would use it to forget about him.

A permanent loan. Exactly like the life-long credit he had from his parents. It was not a small amount that he had put away in his secret places that he thought I knew nothing about. His parents must have been more generous than he acknowledged.

While I was searching I discovered an envelope in my own handwriting, the letter I had addressed for him so that he could send the payment for the car to Lukas. It had never happened. Even though I reminded him several times and even though he said he had sent it. It was only a few thousand, Lukas' life did not depend upon it, but it was the principle. The envelope was empty, I put in some of the notes I had found but then changed my mind. Could not send them after such a long time, it would be an insult. As if it were all about the money, when in fact it was about everything but the money.

Later that evening I went out, wandered up and down all the streets in all parts of town, over all the bridges, through all the parks. It was like stepping down into a purifying bath, it was still raining and I picked up all the "Flat for rent" notices I could find. Rang round until I got lucky with a third-hand rental in a district I had never heard of but sounded pretty, like the countryside, Hjorthagen.

At midnight I stopped at a little bar, just to see what would happen. Almost immediately a man came up and sat down on the bar stool next to me, ordered me a drink without even asking what I would like.

"I'm thirty-three, the same age as Jesus when he was crucified. How old are you, honey?" he asked.

———

Lukas' old car was my only fixed point, in it I moved what little I had from one temporary address to another. Most often in the small hours when the streets were deserted, I ought to use Yoel's money to take my driving test, until then I had to be careful.

The smell of the lake that Yoel had complained about still lingered in there and made me feel at home. The smell of the fields, the factories, the familiar wildness. Sometimes I would sit in the driver's seat in a car park and let my thoughts wander from my house to Lukas' house to the pearl fisher's, out over the sloping fields, along the motorway, further, the Atlantic next. If I was between rentals I could sit there the whole night. As long as I had the car I was never really homeless. In the glove compartment and pockets I found things I had left there long ago, Everyday Escape perfume, my Lee shorts, a packet of my favourite chewing gum, the ugly yellow scarf that Rikard took a great deal of trouble to send me, an earring I had lost and searched for everywhere except in his car. I found nothing of Lukas'. Not so much as a cigarette paper, he never left any visible traces behind him.

I changed my job at the same rate as I changed my abode. Cafeteria, dry cleaner's, hospital cleaner, taxi switchboard. Delivering papers was the worst paid, but it appealed to me. The routine and movement, rhythm, monotony, the turns in the stairs so easy hour after hour. The freedom to think in peace. The freedom not to have to smile at someone for money. The load that gradually lightened as I did my job was so simple and genuine. The good feeling after a day's work, although I did it at night. I mostly saw the dark side of town, did not really have a plan, more like an undercurrent, an expectation of something.

"You can be whatever you want," Mamma had said.

"I want to be someone else."

"No, you can only be yourself." Myself? Why would I want to be that, that is what I was already.

261

I used to come home from my newspaper rounds just as the morning traffic started up. The exhaust fumes seeping in through the window sent me to sleep. Yoel showed me how to find pleasure, but through him I also learned that I needed no-one. First I had a taste of sex, then of solitude, relished it like a thirst that I had suppressed and now could not quench. Began to guard it like stolen goods.

I lived incognito in different third-hand rentals, moved in a wide curve through the outskirts back in towards the city. With every new place I unpacked my few belongings in, I felt less at home and more free.

One day at a time, that was what counted for the temporary contract I managed to get, on the corner of Vulcanusgatan. The rent was negligible as the house was waiting to be blown out like an egg and refurbished. Thirties' standards with communal showers in a cellar so full of cross spiders that I kept hygiene to a minimum.

"View over the water," I wrote to Mamma, though I lived where the Barnhusviken channel of water was at its narrowest, obscured by the massive concrete pillars of the bridge. Sleep was shattered by the sirens from the Sabbatsberg hospital and the noise of the trains that never seemed to cease.

I was not afraid of the dark, shadows in the light frightened me more. And the throng of strangers on the underground was worse than loneliness. Lukas had been scared of quick movements, a caress could give him a start and a whisper could wake him up. As if he never really slept. Cooped-up birds, fluttering, panic, the sound of wings against a pane of glass, that sort of thing frightened him. That someone might find our hiding place, that we should be discovered and exposed. Do not worry, I said to him. It is easy for you to say, Lo . . . He responded to sounds I could not even hear, he had the acute hearing of a blind person, could hear snakes swimming in the water. The snakes were the only things that made me feel safe with Lukas, he caught them with such lightning speed and flung them far away from me.

No snakes in town, just the underground dragon that rattled in and out from beneath the earth. And I let my memories of Lukas slip into a fragile neglect, repressed just enough to be bearable.

Time weighs light

At first I did not understand what Mamma was talking about at all when she mentioned on the telephone something about a letter – by the way, in the middle of a conversation about something else entirely – that Lukas was supposed to have written to me. I was quite sure I had not received it. Oh yes, Mamma insisted, a long time ago, a blue envelope, do you not remember?

She fell silent on the telephone as if she thought I was lying to her. The letter, she said again – she had acted as intermediary, folded it in two and put it in with one of hers that she sent at regular intervals.

She had never referred to it before and now she wondered suddenly what Lukas had on his mind. As if conceding there may have been something.

For him to write to me must have been an almost impossible thing to do after what had happened. And besides . . . I could not remember ever seeing Lukas write anything, except possibly his name. It was one of the last things I saw him do before we parted, when he signed the devil's contract, leaning against the bonnet of the car that last summer. As far as I knew he could not write, he just hid it well. To go through school without being able to read or write, that calls for a lot of intelligence and skill. A letter from him must have required an almost insurmountable effort, not to mention the shame he had to overcome to go to Mamma and ask her to send it to me. Without even being sure that I could decipher it. And the reply he received was silence.

The letters from Mamma were never opened, I placed them in a growing pile under Yoel's bed and thought "later", when everything is less contaminated – that day never came. In the end, after all the moving and travelling, trips and years, I no longer knew where the bundle of letters was. Just knew that I had not thrown it away. Gradually Mamma and I started to talk to each other again, short conversations at long intervals about absolutely nothing, everything that might hurt carefully avoided. All the same it was better than nothing. And since we had started to ring each other, I had forgotten all about her old letters.

It took forever searching among my unsorted belongings before I found the bundle with the unopened bad-conscience letters, carelessly tied together, hidden and forgotten at the back of the boot of Lukas' car. That is always the way, at the back, the last box, you know it will be, and yet you go through all the rest first, as if preparing yourself for the moment when you will find it. I quickly ripped open Mamma's envelopes with my fingers, one after the other without reading them, until I found the folded blue one from Lukas. She had not imagined it, it was there. There was nothing on the outside, but it still smelled of him.

I did not open it immediately. Thought: this evening. And when evening came: I will wait until tomorrow. And in the morning ... tear it open quickly with my finger, skim through – a few seconds of temporary discomfort – how dangerous can that be? How difficult, how unpleasant? I already knew what must be in it.

To make it easier I tried to read it whilst I was doing something else. In the queue for the car wash, by the freezer cabinet at the grocer's, in the bathroom while the water was running. Sat on the edge of the bath, brushing my teeth, brought out the envelope without opening it.

Every so often I have to check that it is still in my pocket, as if a draught might suddenly whip it out like a chewing-gum wrapper right up into the hot sun, it would burn like magnesium and be gone. That things can burn up, come to an end, is a relief as well as a dread. Each time I am about to insert my finger, slippery with sweat, to slit open the envelope, I cannot do it. For as long as I have not read the words, they have not reached me. I let it slip back into my pocket, it has been unopened for so long, it can stay that way a little longer. There is no rush. It is all too late.

I recall a story I heard on the radio a long time ago, a man and a woman, an extremely strong love between them, how circumstances forced them to part. The man had to travel to the other side of the world, but as soon as he had settled down there, sorted out the practicalities and found somewhere for them to live together, he would write to her. That was what would have been agreed. She waited. And waited. No letter. Waited until her love had changed to bitterness, convinced that he had met another woman and did not have the guts to tell her. The rest of her life she lived alone. After the woman's death some of her relatives were going to renovate the house to sell it. They pulled up the linoleum in the hall. There was the letter. Wedged underneath by some careless postman. Fifty years had passed and now, with her death, it was all irrevocably too late. If only she had swallowed her pride, written to him, tried to find him. If only he had swallowed his pride when he did not receive a reply to the letter that never reached her, and written one more time. If only.

*

To have a weakness for someone is an expression I would rather not use, but sometimes there is no other way of saying it. To Yoel I was attracted, for Lukas I had a weakness. I remember his laugh, not because he laughed often but because he laughed so seldom. Time weighs so light in comparison, the letter in my back pocket is as heavy as if it were sealed with lead. Certain things just become impossible. I already know what the letter must contain. Words I actually do not want to read.

I cannot imagine Lukas asking for help with anything at all, especially not from my Mamma. When I ask her how it happened, she says that a few weeks after I had gone he came up to our house. She saw him coming from far away, immensely slowly, he stopped for a smoke twice on the way up. She had scarcely seen him after I left, now he was there asking for my telephone number. When Mamma opened the door he had already gone down the steps, prepared to be sent away.

She told him the truth, that she did not have my number, all she had was a poste restante address in Stockholm. He did not believe her. But it was the case, I had not sent her my address at Yoel's, afraid that she might suddenly be standing outside the door. Or even worse: that Lukas might be standing there.

The day I disappeared it was Mamma who got Lukas down from the blazing porch. A moment later the beams gave way and the burning roof fell in. She had probably saved his life, but at the time it was not something he was capable of feeling gratitude for.

First, without understanding what was happening, Mamma had been standing in the bedroom when she saw Yoel and me driving from the garage in Lukas' car, stop at Lukas' house for a few minutes to have some papers signed, concluded quickly against the bonnet of the car. She wondered what was going on. Whether she ought to go out. But at least at the window she had a general view of the situation, if indeed it was a situation, it certainly looked like some sort of situation, only she had no idea what it was about. She wondered even more when she saw Lukas begin to carry things out of the house, throw them in a big pile until they formed a pyre, and set fire to it.

Far too close, she was thinking. Far too close to the wooden house, dry in every nook and cranny after so many weeks without rain. The lighting of fires was prohibited after a summer so hot and long that the days burned by themselves. When the fire had taken hold he went inside and fetched more things that he threw on to the flames. At the same time I came back along the path by the lake with Yoel and the baggage we had collected. Mamma had no idea who Yoel was, as he sat behind the wheel in Lukas' car with me beside him. And then we drove off. She had assumed that we would stop when we saw Lukas, try to persuade him to listen to reason, but we just drove past. The fire took hold on the steps. Mamma had no time to think about me and where I was going. She saw Lukas get up on the porch, not to try to put out the flames, he just stood there as if he . . . had lost . . . she raced down to the kitchen, rang the fire brigade and ran.

Lukas was no slender thirteen-year-old now, as he was when she had used mild force to drag him out of the flames in the field fire along the railway line. She could only use words now to try to persuade him to save himself. She knew that there was a risk of lack of oxygen near large fires and that lack of oxygen led to confusion, she needed to act quickly to bring him down from the flames. She does not remember exactly what she said, something about me.

"After that? For God's sake, Mamma, what happened after that?" No-one has ever told me about this.

"You disappeared, Lo, and since then you've never asked about any of it," she answers, as if I have thereby forfeited my right to know. Then she tells me anyway: at the last moment Lukas came down from the burning porch, disaster averted, the emergency part of the disaster at any rate. The help Mamma had sent for arrived and she let them take over. After that she did not see him until he came and knocked on her kitchen door a few weeks later. He looked tired and black as if he had been rooting around in the charred remains in search of anything that had escaped the flames. Should she ask him to come in? He really looked as though he were in need of a bowl of broth and she had cooked enough for a whole army, she had still not got used to the minimal size of her reduced family. He looked so lean around the eyes. He looked like someone who could easily become emaciated, as if he only had his body on loan, like everything else that had just been taken away from him. But she could not bring herself to.

"He didn't ask about you and what would I have said? I had no idea," she says, ". . . about why you, from one day to the next, had decided to leave everything behind. I knew even less than him – but it must have had something to do with the two of you. He didn't ask for any answers, either. Just the telephone number. He wasn't satisfied with the address."

"He couldn't write, Mamma," I interrupt.

"What?"

"No, he couldn't."

"But he wrote to you in the end. I sent that letter on myself . . . what did he want?"

When I do not reply she continues. Lukas had looked so dejected she was afraid he would throw himself in the lake, so she tried to inspire some hope in him. Of what, I ask.

"Of you coming back eventually – if that was what he wanted." *Give her a little time*, Mamma had said, when Lukas came back two days later with an unaddressed blue envelope that he asked her to send to me. And perhaps it was that hope that made him start to demolish what had been burned and decide to rebuild Gábriel's house. He set about the house construction in a sorrowful frenzy, as if he was trying to make something rise up out of the ashes. Mamma could see how the work was progressing from our house. When the first cold spell came, she saw him buy two Calor gas heaters for the derelict house where he had moved in, for want of anywhere else. It must have been cold and damp, so near the lake. Bit by bit, when he had the time and the money, he rebuilt Gábriel's house. The same house that he had allowed to catch fire – as if all he had wanted was to be free of it.

All his spare time he spent building, single-handed, apart from the roof trusses that a joiner in the village helped him with. As soon as the outside was finished the building work stopped. Lukas never set foot in there after it was finished, as far as Mamma knew. An empty mausoleum at the end of the gravel road. Became a refuge for the river rats then, the ones his Pappa had forced him to catch and drown. It was just a facade of a house. At the point when he gave up hope of me returning, he also gave up building, Mamma says. After that he left it standing empty, one of many houses in the area since the redundancies and dismissals at the factories. I never understood why he did not move as soon as he dropped out of school and started work. Away from his Pappa, as soon as he could. There were cheap flats near to the leather factory. But maybe he could not imagine waking up every morning to any other view than the one over the lake, the motorway and our house up on the hill.

"Were you happy with that guy you left everything for?"

"Yoel? I didn't leave everything *for* him, I left everything *with* him. And yes, I was happy. For a while. What more can you want? Were you happy with Pappa?" She does not answer, just says something about how it could have been anyone at all, that guy, couldn't it? No, not anyone at all, but certainly someone else, I was forced to go away to become the person I am. There had been a relentless breaking-up atmosphere for a long time. Pappa and the other brothers and sisters who moved away, Mamma's father with his burning lungs and her mother with her heart embedded in the fat of grief and Pappa's mother with her cancer and Gábriel with his crumbling bones. Death, death, death that summer, good God, I was only seventeen and it felt as if life was over.

Just in time Yoel came gliding in over the disaster area and winched me up. I am not lying when I say that I have thought of Lukas every day, but going away from here is the best thing I did. You shall leave your father and your mother, that is the way it is, it is not something I thought up. But maybe you could say goodbye first and clean up your messy room, Mamma thinks. I do not know, there is nothing about that in the bible.

*

It had been a summer to remember, water sprinklers going all night in the district.

Fire ban and watering ban, but this was a village for the quietly lawless so everyone watered anyway, though no-one got it into his head to start a fire, apart from Lukas. Born under a falling star. He could have been prosecuted. If you start a fire in a house it is always considered arson, and what was worse . . . Gábriel was still lying inside, in the innermost room. Admittedly in a part of the house that escaped the flames, but there still had to be an enquiry and a post-mortem to establish the cause of death and to rule out the possibility of him being killed by the smoke or the heat.

Even Mamma had to make a statement about what she knew.

"But I wrote about that in my letters. I can't understand why you didn't come when I asked, you could definitely have given information that would have exonerated him, you were there when Gábriel died, weren't you? I assumed that you would want to help Lukas, but suddenly you seemed to be deadly enemies."

Mamma put in a good word for him with the police, more than she really should have done – she did not know how much he was to blame in all of this. Only that he must have been in despair that afternoon the fire started. For some people hell seems to have more than nine circles: Lukas lost his Pappa and me and his home and all his possessions and his car and not long after that his job at the leather factory too. At that point, if not before, he should have left.

If it was anyone's fault, it was mine, but my crime carried no penalty, the worst seldom do. In the end he was cleared of suspicion, he must have denied it successfully or he was not considered responsible for his actions when he let the fire burn. But the fine for negligence was still a minor disaster, destitute as he was. The only asset Gábriel left behind him was a house that had now burned down, without insurance. Lukas owned nothing. All he had was a hire-purchase debt for the funeral, and his life, but who could call it a life? There was no collateral.

River of oblivion

I planned to leave, never to return. I have not told anyone that. I was going to take what was left of Yoel's money and buy a ticket to somewhere. Where was less important. The main thing was that it should be far away. Mexico, perhaps. I'd heard it's so lovely.

I had a passport, Yoel must just have forgotten he had helped me to fix that. As if all he did was fix passports for girls he thought had not seen enough of the world. You have to have a passport or you are not free. Passport, money, car. Once I had set off the rest would sort itself out, it always had before. I had the sense that I could do anything at all as long as I was alone. As long as I did not have to fulfil someone else's needs. I could manage my own, they were simple – just to live, that was the only thing I wanted. With no other weight to bear than my own.

I bought New York boots and a New York cap. Played "Porgy and Bess". Took Yoel's money and went with the hope that the skyscrapers, dollars and smell of frying would heal me. Heal me? That was not what I hoped for, New York is just a city. But if forgetfulness would not come to me, I had to search for it, cross the river of oblivion, whatever it was called, I was not fully conversant with the geography of hell, just knew that I was right in the middle of it.

The city of dreams must also be the city of forgetfulness, how could you ever dream about something again if you have not first forgotten what was there? I had always dreamt of flying, dreamt of the Atlantic, of flying over the Atlantic . . . it was almost too much, it was perfect, it was overwhelming, I sat wide awake the whole way as we soared through the darkness.

I had heard about the underworld river that formed the boundary between the world of the living and the world of the dead and I had a vague idea that you had to be able to cross the other way round, against the flow, back to the living – it had to be possible – it could not be like this. I was in limbo, between life and death, the remarkable state you end up in if you deserve neither heaven nor hell.

I got on the plane and crossed the river of oblivion with a case full of clean clothes and unread books. Nothing that smelled of him, or him, nothing they had even come into contact with or that in any way reminded me of someone I knew. On the way in from the airport it was snowing. A reluctant, frightening, provocative defiance, this was the city that would make me forget and I might as well start now.

It is only a town. The leap to New York cannot be any greater than the leap to Stockholm from the village where I grew up, and yet the first glimpse of the city takes my breath away. It is not particularly beautiful at the spot where I come up out of the ground, but it is New York. Exactly as you imagine it, even the street is belching out smoke and the dark facades push the sky so high up that you can hardly make out what time of day it is. I have been warned about strange forests where I do not recognise the dangers. You should stay close to home, know what is what, understand the rules. Here I have no notion.

A perfume. I try to visualise a face that matches the aftershave emanating from behind my back, where I am sitting on a bench to regain my balance. A bitter aroma, something Yoel would never have used. But I recognise it, perhaps from one of Pappa's brothers, their various bottles of aftershave used to stand in a row on the bathroom windowsill. The advantage of old aftershave, I heard a friend of Yoel's once say, is that girls feel safe with someone who smells like their grandfather.

When I stand up with my map to ask for directions, he does not look at all as I had thought, my intuition has failed me completely. With his back to me on the bench a slender-limbed Latino is sitting, not much older than me, deeply engrossed in his music. Long legs stretched out in front of him, T-shirt and jacket, gold chain. Eyes fixed on a far-off point. He shifts his attention from the distance, straight into my eyes, not so much as a muscle in his face moving. If it had been a competition, I would have lost.

As I open out my map of Manhattan, he continues to focus on me, not a single glance at the street map I am holding out between us. Map-reading is a Swedish speciality, Yoel always said, Americans can scarcely make sense of a map of their own city, but they are completely au fait with all the streets, districts, underground lines, bus numbers.

Who are you? Brut? Jicky? Équipage? Eau Sauvage? Hypnôse?

When he makes no attempt to help me, I start to fold up the map. Then:

"Where do you come from?" he asks, without removing his earphones. He looks surprised at my reply, as if he did not really believe me. "You don't look Swedish. Swedes are usually tall, cold and beautiful.

I mean . . . well, you're not tall or especially cold." I give up folding the map and stuff it like a crumpled concertina into my bag. Ask for directions to Lower East Side, have no sense of what is even north and south here. Now he says that he is going to tell me something that I need to know to get my bearings:

"You see those towers over there, the two high ones, the highest in the city. You can see those from almost everywhere. As soon as you come out of the subway, you look for them. They mean downtown. The opposite direction is uptown. People would never find their way in this city without them."

When he finds out that I have just arrived and it is my first visit, he suggests a beer to celebrate landing. One beer will not be enough, but O.K. I am floating above the tarmac as I follow him along the wide streets, further and further from the station, as if he is trying to get me lost. Every district here is as large as a small town. Finally he stops at a surprisingly simple and anonymous place, the same as dozens of others we have passed on the way here. My eye wants to travel beyond the window to catch a glimpse of the pulsing streets out there.

"The New York sky gets electric just before it starts snowing. Do you know that?" he asks, lighting a cigarette. No. But I realise I have a certain weakness for people who tell me things like that. When I ask him what season this is, actually, he hesitates. He does not believe in seasons, he says – at least not in New York, it is mostly a question of weather.

"So you're one of those . . . reading types?" he asks then, with an eye on my bag, where a couple of travel paperbacks are sticking out. As though reading types would be a mutation of an otherwise sound human race. My response is a little evasive, as if it were an accusation I was trying to wriggle out of.

"I am too," he says unexpectedly. "Your favourite?" In his smile a gold tooth flashes like a portable life insurance. A gold tooth as well, I am thinking, and pretend not to hear his question, but he asks again. I squirm, say cagily that I do not have one. Have read far too little to have had a chance to have favourites, still reading everything for the first time, and anyway it is a very personal question.

"Sure you do. Come on, tell me." O.K., Bukowski, I say in the end. He is the only author I have read two books by.

"Bukowski? You mean *the* Bukowski? Like *Charles* Bukowski?" I nod, embarrassed that I feel embarrassed. Normal people do not find it more personal to reveal their favourite authors than their favourite cornflakes or their favourite air freshener. I am quick to throw the question back at him.

"Plath," he says without hesitation.

"Plath? You mean like *Sylvia* Plath?" I say, since I know her name.

"Yeah," he smiles. And then we start to laugh.

We laugh until he wipes the froth of beer from my upper lip with his thumb. And then we stop at once.

Desire and fear

Then we went back to his place. Or, to be exact, we took a taxi, because it was too far to walk, he lived up in Spanish Harlem. On a street full of litter that was called Pleasure Avenue, Pleasant Avenue, or something, where he asked the taxi to stop. The air from East River had an oily raw river stench, the staircase reeked of mould, cement and burned tostones. In the doorway a young woman was standing as if on guard, half-dressed, glared at me when he said hello. Behind us as we were going up the stairs I heard her say something about *chica blanca*, *coño blanca*, white girl, white cunt, he leant over the banister and hissed a warning to her.

"*Culo! Desgraciado!*" we heard her voice from below.

"*Puta!*" he shouted back.

"*Puto! Pato!*" she echoed, like cracks of a whip.

He clearly decided that could not be tolerated, he turned on the stairs and I managed to grab hold of him and whisper:

"Come on, let's go, it doesn't matter, I don't understand Spanish."

"Yes, you do! Do you think I'd let her insult us however she wants? *Carajo!* She'd never dare say anything if I was alone, she knows exactly what I'd do to her."

I recognised the swear words from Yoel's neighbours. When they thought their children were asleep they could stand on the balcony arguing for hours in a mixture of Spanish and Swedish. It was a

279

nuisance, but at least I learned all kind of foul words in the Spanish language.

Unsteady from the beer and his mood that exploded from one second to the next, I feel inclined to leave. Can I trust him? Do I have to trust him, is it at all possible to trust another person or should you just make a practice of assuming the worst every time? If Mamma had seen me now she would have said I was mad.

"Crackhead!" he screams at her, before we continue up the narrow stairs out of earshot of her filthy invective.

There is a lift, but you can be trapped all night in it between two floors if you are unlucky, and he seems to assume we would be.

"This isn't a priority district, you know . . . But you don't need to be afraid of the rats, they're not aggressive, there's plenty of food here," I hear him say as we pass a floor in darkness. Sense how they move along the walls.

The rats never scared me at home, I had no feelings for them, neither fascination nor loathing. Lukas on the other hand never got used to them. Intelligent eyes, he said.

"Do it quickly, for God's sake," he said, looking away as I drowned them. It was an act of love, I did it so that he did not have to, but I do not think he could love me as much afterwards. He may have been grateful that I did it instead of him, but he could never understand how I could do it at all, when it came to the crunch. It felt as though his view of me changed then, became more distant.

"They're only rats," I said.

"And you're only an idiot," he answered.

*

Thirteen flights I count, the lactic acid is building up in my legs, he does not offer to carry my case. I may have packed light, but it still feels heavy by the end. I do not have time to see much of his apartment before we reach our final destination, his bedroom, the moment when the whole world begins and ends in his narrow bed and the only air he lets me breathe is the air he has in his mouth.

"What's your name?" I whisper when he finally allows me some air.

"Don't talk so much." He is in a hurry to pull off the dusty clothes I have been travelling in and his own. Kicks off his trainers, wriggles out of his T-shirt and jeans and bores his way in with no caresses or frills.

———

Smells are like memories, they merge with one another and create new variations, Lukas merges with Yoel who merges with Luiz, who merges with Lukas again. Like the smell of water mixing with sandalwood, cement, African myrrh, geranium, iron, smoke. He smells of . . .

"Brut?" I breathe in against his smooth brown jaw as I sample a little bite. He nods. How could I guess? My tongue runs along the nape of his neck, which is one of the most beautiful I have seen, and I am after all a collector of beautiful necks, I have Rikard's, Lukas', Yoel's and some others whose names I have never asked and now Luiz's.

He does not object when I slide my hand into the gap between his groin and the mattress where his penis is resting semi-soft and spent and immediately it hardens again at my touch. Asks why I am here, in New York, and I tell him the truth: on the run. He looks surprised, a little worried, almost.

"A jealous sucker?" he asks, as though he took it for granted it was a man. From far away I can hear how sad my laugh sounds, like an out-of-tune piano in a cold room. Jealous . . . if only it were so simple.

"*Dámelo duro*," I whisper. Somewhere in my dubious Spanish vocabulary I find the phrase, and he looks at me in astonishment as if I do not know what I am saying.

"Forget it, kid," he whispers disapprovingly. Rolls over on to his back again and in the same movement slides me up on to him. "I really like you – inside and out." In Swedish it would have sounded impossible, but when he says it, it sounds completely right. This city, everything that is new . . . it is so unreal that it does not even make me think twice.

We roll another half-turn, our stomachs stick together and our breathing becomes one.

"You're such a beauty, do you know that?" I nod. And sturdy too, I can see in his eyes that he likes that, as his long sinewy body presses me halfway through the soft springs of the bed, before we go quite still.

In the kitchen some time later he strikes a match and lights the gas stove:

"Be honest . . . when you were doing it with me, were you actually thinking about him? The one you're on the run from?" he asks, revealing his gold tooth.

"Yes," I lie, though for the first time in ages I had managed to forget him for a little while, "and who were you thinking about?" He had no time to think, it was so quick, I was like a tropical cyclone in the middle of winter in Manhattan. Libido, the instinct for life, Thanatos, the death drive, loving or dying, the opposite of death is love. But let it not be a man, I am thinking, let it really not be a man, the light in this city is enough, the electric sky before the snowstorm.

In quick succession he breaks four eggs into a frying pan, the sizzling oil splashes up on his naked chest, but he does not react. A liberal American layer of mayonnaise on eight slices of spongy bread, with a practised hand he flips the eggs over and fries the other side. Salt. Tabasco. A few familiar movements. And the four double egg-mayonnaise sandwiches are ready. Am I sure I do not want some? He offers to make some for me too, but I shake my head. What he himself does with that amount of fat is a mystery that is solved when he tells me he only eats once a day. Mostly eggs, and eggs are practically vegetables, are they not? I have no appetite, my mouth tastes a little of blood.

"Four double sandwiches a day, and I haven't been ill since the day I was shot in the shoulder on the staircase five years ago." I had felt the scar against my lips earlier in bed. "Women with guns . . ." Luiz mumbles and examines me closely as he opens each of us a beer. "You're far too thin. Far too thin. *Flaca* . . . But it's O.K. I like thin girls." I look at my reflection in the night-dark window. Thin? This was a new accusation. But he is right, I hardly recognise myself, alarmed by how starved I look, lack of sleep, perhaps, giving me that intense, slightly swollen look.

After the food he cannot make love again. Does not even try. We just fall asleep together.

When I wake up he is no longer lying beside me. Out in the kitchen there is a woman with an intricate hairdo and wearing a torn coffee-brown dressing gown, sorting out small change.

"*Gringa* . . ." she says when she catches sight of me in the doorway, giving me a measured look, as if I were an exceptionally pale specimen. Feeling awkward, I ask where he is.

"Luiz? He's up in the Bronx, of course. Where else would he be?" *Bronx*? Why there? And who is she, his mother, sister, pimp, spider woman – his fate? No, his ex, I realise. I try to cover myself, though she has already seen my winter-white nakedness. "He went out an hour ago. He'll be in his apartment by now, with his wife, and who are you, his new whore? How old . . . let me guess, seventeen?"

My cheeks red with shame, I scramble all my things together as I hear her say that Luiz, the dog, only sleeps here when he has had a fight with his wife, he comes crawling back, has nowhere else to go when he has hit her and she has thrown him out. Then he comes here, and each time he has another slut in tow from the nearest bar, as if he thinks that will make him feel better, it just brings new problems. She gives me a look full of contempt, still counting coins with her two-inch nails.

"When he's calmed down – and the poor woman rings and forgives him – he goes back to her. He should be very grateful that I don't dish the dirt about his little comfort-fucks, then he'd find his bags packed outside the door when he came home . . . She has her limits. Just like I had once, when I still loved him. Now I don't care any more."

The bastard, bastard, bastard . . . the stairs down will never end, as I run I remember the sound of the telephone when I was half asleep. His wife must have rung, forgiven him for hitting her and then he went back to her without a word to me. Perhaps he fancied sleeping with two differ-ent women within a few hours. I emerge onto the deserted street in pitch black at three o'clock in the morning, the worst possible time, it is snowing now as he predicted. The weather will protect me, I think, not even dogs are out in this. I just have to walk, start moving – fast enough not to get stuck, but slow enough to keep my balance.

*

I hurry down the wide avenue, speed up past the dark side streets, without glancing in. After a while I discover that he has left a note in the pocket of my jeans. A telephone number on one side. On the other: "I never leave my number. Don't make me regret it."

I probably ought to sleep on it, but what you sleep on, you never do. I stop at the first telephone box I see, and I ring.

When he answers, it sounds as if he is on the other side of the world, not the other side of town. He does not apologise for his disappearance, does not even sound contrite, not a word of explanation about why he let me wake up in an apartment alone with his ex-wife. When am I going to see you again? he asks.

"Not as long as you're married," I reply.

"Married . . . O.K. . . . to a certain extent married," he qualifies, after a few minutes' silence. *To a certain extent?* It is not a question of degree or nuance. You are either married or not, I say.

"A marriage of convenience. Haven't you heard of it?" He has lowered his voice a little now . . . certainly, he is married, and certainly, they do live under the same roof, but they do not live as man and wife, they just keep up a front. A front – for whom, I ask. The authorities.

But how do you live so close together without something starting? That I have never understood. How . . . Luiz is silent on the telephone and when he finally answers he speaks even more quietly. Not with her, he says. I only married her to help her.

It could have been a fictitious sob-story, but if that were the case, he was very good at it. There is nothing wrong with her, he says, she

285

is a great girl, at least when she is not being a pain in the ass – but she has come here in the hope of getting treatment for her HIV, the marriage is just to help her and her two daughters. He tries to think of her as a sister, it is not easy, but he tries. You do not have to fancy your brothers and sisters to love them. That is how he feels about her. But lately . . .

He does not know if it is the illness, but recently she has changed. Has become temperamental and jealous, as if she believes he might leave. And he has certainly had that thought, increasingly. But he cannot. It is not he who hits her, it is she who hits him, so they are doing their bit for equality of the sexes in this country, he says: "Women know that men are stronger. But men know that women are harder." I stand with the receiver in my hand, my back against the glass, blue with cold, it has stopped snowing and now the wind is blowing instead, as cold as only wind in towns can be, through the wide empty streets. I am obliged to ask, insensitive, but it has to be direct. And what about him? Has he been . . . ?

"What?" he asks.

"Infected."

"Of course not."

"Sure?"

"Quite. And anyway we took precautions." Did we? Not that I remember. "No-one in this city has unprotected sex, for God's sake, especially not with a Swede," he bursts out.

But the violent kissing, blood on blood – I feel my heart racing. Drop the receiver. Go out into the cold. His words do not reassure me at all. I have been in New York for less than twenty-four hours and I am sure that I have already exposed myself to a fatal disease.

You are mad, Lo, Mamma would have said. It was also what Luiz said, as he distractedly caressed me.

"You're mad, girl, I thought that as soon as you started talking to me on the street, I could see it in your eyes; I know what mad girls look like, they look exactly like you, *nena*," he said and turned me over on to my stomach, "and I was even more sure that you were nuts when you came home with me without any persuasion . . . you must never, I'll say it one more time: you must NEVER go with strange men in New York, you should know that, for Christ's sake, didn't your mom teach you anything? You definitely must be kooky, babe, I was thinking, but O.K., I like crazy girls, so why not. And if you hadn't come home with me, you'd only have gone with someone else – and you don't know what maniac *that* could have been . . . so it was better that you came with me; I happen to be a reliable guy, one of very few in this city. Then you got straight into bed with me, when you were completely sober. I thought I'd have to waste at least half a bottle on you, but no, no . . . right into the bedroom, like a wild cat, I was speechless and it takes a lot for me to be speechless, you understand, but that's the way it is with mad girls and me, they're attracted to me, I knew that before."

———

Paralysed, I lay under a synthetic double quilt in a cheap hotel room in New York and thought about my own death. Numbed by a cloudy mixture of fear of dying and indifference. Tried to convince myself that I would not break down.

Not break down, but live hard and happy for the short time I had left before the virus led me to my doom. There are those people who can transform the most difficult experiences into something that strengthens them and helps them achieve maturity. Myself, I just wanted to be free of the pain. The quickest possible way out. Not cling to sorrow – but now it was clinging to me.

Something had to happen, I realised that, and it would not happen of its own accord. I lay in my hotel bed and listened to Nina Simone singing in almost unidentifiable French, *ne me quitte pas*, do not leave me, her voice was searing and pure – it hurt and then soothed – like a harsh big sister, like a winter bath, like a wound that is opened, emptied, disinfected and sewn back together.

I had taken out an advance on death and when I had done that, there was nothing else to be afraid of. The worst had already happened, I had no reason to be worried about anything now, I was as good as already dead. It made me feel safe. Safe and ravenous. As hungry as a wolf, I climbed out of bed and went out.

I bought a pair of boots I had seen in a shop window opposite the hotel. They awakened a yearning in me. To walk. Just walk. Over Brooklyn Bridge, Manhattan Bridge, Williamsburg Bridge, all the glittering bridges, cold and tempting, in the city that never sleeps. They were actually not my style at all, too smart and too expensive, made the rest of my clothing look cheap, but I was struck by such an inexplicable urge. A need to have them, like with some men, but with boots the craving is more compelling, all I have to do is throw enough money at them and they are mine. A pair of boots is a promise of movement – like a man is a promise, but of what you never really know. I walked everywhere, when people whistled at me by the river in the harbour district I just gave them a smile and walked on. Make no demands of life, just go your own way, intoxicated with your own fragrance, however stale it may be. Never stop, that seemed to be what this city was all about, perpetual motion, staying awake. Keep moving, it whispered, and I did. Until my money ran out.

When I reached home, Lukas' letter was still by the car windscreen, unopened. Winter had passed as if it had never existed.

The first one to look at me

I have been on the road for a long time now. Looking for European deserts, there are supposed to be seven of them, I have not even seen one. I travel cheaply and slowly, preferably at night, on trains that convey so much sleep back and forth between cities and countries. But Mamma never asks me about things like this – where I have been or where I am going to – she quite simply never asks. Instead: if I have cut my hair, if the car is working as it should, if I have enough money to manage on, if I am eating properly. Always the same questions, the same answers. Yes, Mamma, I am eating properly, large quantities and infrequently, you save time that way. I have enough money to manage on and if I have not, I sort it out, casual jobs, bread-and-butter jobs, tricks. You do not need to worry. I live cheaply, most of all when I travel.

Sometimes I tell her even though she does not ask. About the girl in Berlin going up and down the platform on just one roller-skate. She only had one leg, it must be a physical impossibility, but she did it anyway, gliding to and fro like the bubble in a spirit level. About the marionette museum in Nuremberg. A security man watched me, followed me through the rooms, showed me the store in the base-ment where we could be alone, warm and dusty with headless dolls hanging everywhere. Afterwards I thought – never again . . . was forced to go out into the town to buy new tights, black with red seams.

That night I dreamt about the one-legged girl again. How she defied gravity and all the other laws of nature about the hellishness of everything.

Work hard, live cheap, travel light. Bohemian, Mamma calls it, it sounds better in French, the simple life. However light I travel, I always have the letter with me in my luggage, but the opportunity to open it never presents itself.

I saw a butterfly whirling round like a shiny black chewing gum wrapper in the hot air above the rush-hour traffic in Warsaw. Then I stood on a train by an open window and smelled the same mixture of odours as in my childhood, caraway plants and wild cabbage, factory smoke, rotting toads, bonfires on the fields. At the station in Copenhagen a dog barked at me – not like dogs routinely bark at strangers, this one barked as if it really had something personal against just me. In Malmö I met a tourist, a young French woman who was laughing at the town. There was something about it she found comical. Pathetic perhaps. She kept repeating the word *mégalomanie* and I was uncertain what she meant. Delusions of grandeur? Yes, Malmö is a little town with a craving for status. A railway line that ends there like in the really big stations in the world. On the other hand: on holiday in Malmö in January . . . she must be slightly delusional herself, Malmö is a town for people, not butterflies – was there not something about that in her travel guide? Where do butterflies go when you do not see them, at night, in the winter, when the exhaust fumes and the sleet drape like a hangover above everything. They cannot always be twirling over city streets, childhood fields, the hot railway line out of the village, reality exists too, an everyday for all people in all places, life is not a string of pearls made up of lofty moments, it is only like that afterwards when you have kept the best pictures and deleted the reality between.

When the gods want to punish you, they answer your prayers. If you knew how many times I have wished him dead, she says.

Now he has been dead for three weeks, I find out when I ring home. His weak point was his heart. I sit on the edge of the bed and wait while Mamma weeps.

He has not lived with her in the house for a long time, not since the heart attack he had when a storm passed through the arboretum and he tried to save the sequoia. Gale warning, there was not even anything special about that tree, other than he liked it, but he liked all the trees. Remained in a hospital bed after that, did not get up again, did not come back, not as himself. Then he had one more attack, Björn's weak point . . . Mamma's tears subside and finally cease. The funeral? Have I missed it? No, not yet. The day after tomorrow, Lo – are you coming? No-one can be so far away on this earth that they do not have a chance to get home by the day after tomorrow, not if they really try. Is Pappa coming, I ask. Of course he is coming. Everyone is coming.

"Not me," I say.

"Do as you wish."

"Yes." She is silent.

"I love you, Mamma."

"I know."

We sit in silence for a while, she is the only person I can do this with. The morning air is cold in the room, I pull on my white skirt, the receiver tucked between my shoulder and my ear, rinse my face with the strongly chlorinated water. I have never been good at funerals and this is one funeral I would definitely not have been good at.

I cannot find my pants, or my wallet with the headache tablets either. The room is very small – only you could lose something in such a small room, Mamma would have said if she could see me now – and for a second . . . when she asks where I am, I do not know. I have to take half a step from the wash-basin to the window and draw back the net curtain. Do not remember the name of the street, but it is spring here, the silver birches in the rear courtyard of the hotel are coming out. Grandfather would have liked this town, full of trees, the air smells of Russian cigarettes after the war.

"Lublin."

"Dublin?"

"No, Lublin, between Poland and Ukraine. Lublin, L as in . . ."

"Lo," Mamma says, "come home." I will come. But not until after the funeral. When you wake up, I will be there, Mamma.

"Then I can't wait to wake up," she says, as if it were a long time since she had felt like that.

She will not be alone, people will be coming from all points of the compass, mostly from the north. And Pappa. A long time has passed since they last saw each other. He moved back north to the others a long time ago. I have really never been good at funerals and they will have to manage without me – Mamma and Pappa on either side of the aisle, who would I sit beside? He has lost his father, she has lost . . . well, who understood any of that, in fact? I am afraid that Mamma will start to weep during the service, not like the others, no, she will cry like a dog, between her teeth. Like she cried just now on the telephone when she told me he was dead.

I do not want to arrive too early. Make an unnecessary detour via Stockholm, collect the car and drive all the way down, it is so late when I eventually arrive that it is already light. I fetch the door key from the garden shed and go in through the cellar, creep up the long cold steps. My old bedroom is cold too, Mamma has forgotten to put on the heater, or else she did not believe I would come, in spite of everything.

Freezing, I go up to the attic for a couple of blankets that are always on top of the water tank. The scent of summer games and birch wood smoke reminds me of how we used to sneak up here and play at the princess and the pea, a game that Lukas never seemed to properly understand the point of, but his was only a supporting role: the footman who had to stuff the pea between the thick layers of blankets. I was made of genuine princess material, writhing on the wretched pea, more hollow-eyed with every night I was forced to sleep on the miserable bed. Lukas helped me put a streak of soot from the flues under my eyes to show how I grew more and more worn-out by the lack of comfort.

Once he pretended to be the budding prince who crept into the chamber to seek the princess's warmth – things had been shaping up for that, he had been forced to sit in the dark bored to death for far too long, waiting while I tossed around in a theatrical lamentation over insomnia. But a princess who cannot tolerate a golden pea underneath her can hardly put up with a nine-stone prince on top of her. I panicked, tried to knee him as he had taught me in self-defence, did not succeed and grabbed hold of a sharp, rusty implement instead, hit him right on the forehead with all my strength. He dropped on to me like a stone. If the blood had not looked so realistic, I would have thought he was joking. But it was pouring in a very lifelike way out of a bottomless gash and I had to wriggle free, tear off my dress and wrap it round the fountain of blood before running down to the adults wearing only my pants.

The unconscious prince was hauled down from the attic, driven to hospital and stitched back together. Afterwards he was dumped back at Gábriel's and threatened with the police. I do not know what Gábriel did with him next, but by the time I was allowed out again, he had started to gather moss.

And for me: lengthy interrogation until I nearly fell asleep from exhaustion standing up. Only if I admitted something would I be allowed to go to bed. Was I sure that *nothing* had actually happened? If I thought about it. Really thought about it. Pappa's mother was making hot chocolate and warming up meatballs and it made me feel sick. Did he touch you, did he touch you . . . he must have done – why would you have hit him otherwise, that is not like you. My aunts fixed their blue eyes on me until I told them the truth, that Lukas lay down on top of me when I was not expecting it, that I could not get any air, that I got hold of this thing . . .

"Thing? What thing?" Mamma asked, alarmed.

"The what do you call it? That hard thing . . ." They all stared at me. "The rusty thing. That I hit him with. I didn't mean to."

It was not your fault, Lo, he is the one responsible, they assured me.

The scar on his forehead afterwards. L-shaped with stitches that first reddened and then paled in the sun. Each time he looked at himself in the mirror he would see the initial of both our names.

Fall asleep, cold and fully clothed under double blankets. Woken a few hours later by a panting noise. When I wake up I never know where I am. I am tossed out of sleep with the sensation of colliding against something hard – another new day? Immediately wide awake. It is always like this. Wide awake, with no idea where.

It is the guide dog Mamma has unintentionally acquired as her final companion in life. It sniffs at the dust on the trousers I was travelling in, I smell of wild dog, they always rub against my legs, as if they want something. To belong, perhaps. I do not like her particularly, domesticated dogs unnerve me, I push her aside and climb out of bed. The house is silent. As if everyone had hurried away as soon as Grandfather was lowered into the earth. I had hoped that at least Rikard would still be here, it is such a long time since we saw each other, but his room is empty and Mamma's too.

Mamma, bitten by frost, sleeping on the veranda in one of the dilapidated summer chairs that ought to fall apart, but holds together at the seams just for her. So that she has somewhere to sit and nurse her urine infections, her bronchitis, freeze her fingers, dream deep-frozen dreams. She looks as though she is no longer part of this world, it is only when she opens her eyes that I know she is not dead. No emotion in her face, she does not even seem to be able to distinguish my silhouette. Snow-blind. It is a hideously bright day.

"Were you sitting there asleep? In this cold. There are quicker ways to die, Mamma." She gives a start.

"Lo?" It is nothing, she says, and pulls her hand through her hair, brittle with frost and static – nothing at all – she was born in much worse. Outdoors, where the cold belongs, she can enjoy it. Indoors she cannot endure it.

"Don't tell me you've been sitting here sleeping all night . . ." Mamma makes a dismissive gesture. But it looks as though she has, there are no footprints up to her chair. The snow must not have been forecast, often the case here in the remarkable south. You can go to bed on a warm spring evening and when you wake up the world has turned white during the night. I am cold in my flimsy dress under the thin jacket, it was spring in Lublin, spring all the way to Warsaw, it was spring all the way to Berlin too. In Copenhagen spring was beginning. Here it is winter, but starting to warm up with a smell of fresh green timber and newly fallen snow that is already melting. That feeling in the air when one season passes into another. Double dose of oxygen in every breath, I feel high, and low at the same time. Sweep the snow off the cane chair beside Mamma and sit next to her without touching. She looks as though she could fall to pieces, not from frailty, but from cold.

The summer before I was born they slept out here on the veranda, she has told me before. Because it was so hot, because Mamma was so big she could scarcely move from one chair to another, could not spend the night indoors, could not tolerate Pappa's brothers constantly pointing at her stomach and asking when she was going to produce this . . .

"How was it? The funeral?" Mamma squints into the light. Does not know, she says. Yes, she was *there*, but not quite with it. But it was nice. Rikard said it was nice. So it was. I nod. So it was. Even if she just sat and waited for the service to end, right at the back of the church – right at the back even though she ought to have been sitting right at the front. There is no obligation, I say. And Pappa?

He had aged. That is what the priest whispered to Mamma, who obviously could not see for herself how he looked. The priest was the same one who buried Grandmother Idun, the last time Pappa was here. Mamma did not remember the priest, but the priest clearly remembered Pappa. She had thought he was handsome when she saw him at the last funeral, now he had aged even though he was not so old, but what does age have to do with old at all.

Mamma had just waited until it was over. It was a short service, but it felt very long, with the children who had travelled down from the north and some old workmates from the factory. The coffin decorated with fresh branches from Grandfather's various trees in the arboretum – he would not have liked that, in fact he would have hated it – that they broke boughs off the trees. It was like breaking the arms off children, but he was dead now and had no say in the matter.

Anyway it was good to see the others again, even if she could not see them now. They had all come, but no-one stayed long. Rikard and Marina stayed the longest, had left on the night train a few hours before I arrived. Rikard looked just the same, had not changed at all, according to him at any rate. A few more sun- and laugh-lines around the eyes, that was all. New girlfriend, young, sweet, pregnant. They were all young, sweet and pregnant, Marina told Mamma – but no-one ever saw any children, they obviously took them when they left, because Rikard was one of those men women want to have children with, but not necessarily anything more.

*

I had bought a few packets of Silk Cut for Mamma on the way here. Take two out and light them. She sniffs at the air. Is it . . . yes, you cannot mistake the smell of light, mild tobacco.

"I don't smoke, haven't smoked since before you were born."

"Me neither," I say, "but with you I'm prepared to make an exception." She smiles.

"Well. That's alright then." Reaches forward with her hand ready for the cigarette. Still smiling when she cautiously inhales the smoke. But as it escapes through her frozen blue lips she becomes serious again. The trees in Grandfather's arboretum have a snowy side and sunny side, a brittle cracking sound when the ice slips off the branches; it is when something thaws from a frozen state that it breaks.

"Lo," she says hesitantly.

"What?"

The sloping ceiling

"Two weeks outside time and space and everything I was used to," Mamma tells me. Two weeks is nothing, two weeks is everything. Put up with it until it passes, Björn had said. But it did not.

She liked being alone with him in the new house as they waited for the others to follow with the vanload of furniture. As far as she was concerned, they could take their time. Perhaps she liked it too much, the new light made him look different, smell different, stronger. She looked different too, she could see it in his eyes.

Björn taught her how to cut wood. She had an energy that she had to channel into something sensible, he thought, and she learned quickly, as you do when you learn something that in fact you already know.

More than anything she liked doing nothing with him, they had never done that before – at home you always did *something*. But the new house was perfect, needed no attention at all, required nothing of them. They picked up snails in the arboretum instead, fat and shiny silvery-green. He had heard that they were edible, at least in France and here in the south they were already halfway there, pity to let them go to waste – boil them, or what? Butter? Salt? Mamma had no idea, but they had a try. It turned to glue. They laughed about it the whole evening. Seeing him laugh was an unusual sight and she liked it very much.

After she had taught him to laugh she wanted to teach him to swim, but he was not interested in that.

"Only animals swim," he protested.

"Aw, come on." She went first to show him. Up to her waist in the water. Turned round.

"Watch me – it's not dangerous." But Björn looked as though he thought it was dangerous to watch her.

"Are you scared?" When she said that he was forced to go out into the dark water. The words were a trap that had already closed around him.

"Lean back, I'm holding you. You have to relax, otherwise you'll sink."

He sank. As heavy as a black oak. As taut as a gun with the safety catch off.

But she held him.

She was strong and the water made her stronger.

The whole of his weight rested in her arms. His white underpants filled with water so he looked like a drowning Ophelia and she had to laugh at him – she had seen him more or less naked so many times in the old house, where they lived in such a cramped space, this sudden diffidence was something you had to laugh about.

Nothing could happen. The existence of a possibility did not mean that it was a real possibility. Not because Björn was like a father to her, the paternal type was the last thing he was, but Idun had always been like a mother to her, even more than her own. She had to put up with it, whether or not it passed.

After two weeks they were no longer alone, people in all the rooms. Karenina became Katarina again and Björn returned to his normal self, slower to laugh and other nonsense. He had to forget the swim he had taken with her and be content with viewing the lake from a distance. The lake that he thought with a little goodwill they could count as their own, like the cornfields and even the silver curve of the railway as it swept so assuredly through the countryside bearing its promise that the world carried on forever.

They were no longer alone, but the tension between them continued, soundless as a bird of prey. That someone might notice it, that it might suddenly strike with no chance of them stopping it, had been a nightmare. They had to avoid each other sufficiently to avert disaster – but not so openly that anyone had cause for suspicion.

With Idun leading the way, the new arrivals walked through the house, absolutely silent, struck dumb, until the children started to fight over the bedrooms on the upper floor. The upper floor for the children, the floor below for the adults, two pretty bedrooms with doors out on to the veranda. Veranda, it was like being in America. There was no limit to it all. *Three* toilets . . . Rikard, the youngest, ran around like an excited puppy and squirted into all three and flushed the cisterns so that it sounded as though an almighty torrent was running through the whole house. Björn shouted at his son, but Idun just laughed. Before they had had to manage with a communal dry closet, this was a luxury to laugh over every day.

The furniture was unloaded and carried in. It looked meagre in the large bright rooms. That was the disadvantage of trading up so dramatically, Björn said – not without some pride, because the move had been his idea from start to finish and this was the house he had found, crowned by the universe of exotic trees that spread out right to the edge of the fields of barley.

The shared bank loan, which had been much bigger than they had anticipated, was what held the four of them together now. Forever. As well as the past, of course. Children, memories, origins. And the fact that they were all now strangers in this new place. Björn, Idun, Anna and Aron.

And the bird of prey. The one that never struck. Doomed to carry on circling.

"Love is a *folie á deux*," Mamma says. What she has just told me is floating somewhere above my head, finding no point where it can sink in.

". . . Pappa, then? Why Pappa?" I whisper. Mamma is quiet in the brightness, hesitates so long I think she has changed her mind and does not want to tell me anymore. Then she gathers herself – the first one to look at me . . . she had thought.

———

The first time Mamma saw the pearl fisher's house it reminded her of a room decorated for a party that never took place. The feeling of an extravagant life. It was in such an inaccessible spot, it must have belonged to a person who wanted to avoid contact with others at any price. Even though it was cluttered from floor to ceiling with things from distant journeys, the house was echoing and desolate, as if everything had been hollowed out by time and vermin, like a walk in a dead forest. The way Mamma describes the place reveals that she does not know I spent my entire childhood there. As if I did not know every joint in the damp wooden floor, every fly speck on the wall in the alcove with the bed, exactly how the light filtered through the branches of the coral tree, the sour scent of the larch trees outside and the humid smell of incense and secret sleep.

In the alcove, in the middle of winter, bitterly cold. They must have kept their jackets on. Mamma was sure that it was that particular winter afternoon that I was conceived, because she had only been in there once and not returned. That my life had been created in there, in the iron bed where Lukas and I often slept our secret sleep, is an unreal thought.

No-one knew the pearl fisher, but everyone knew who he was and Mamma had decided that she would find the deserted house she had heard about. When she finally did, her first thought was that she would share the discovery with Björn. If anyone would understand, he would. They shared something that the other family members did not share, whatever it was, perhaps only a determination – for something more, something else, new, a striving, a dream, or several. And this was a house built by a dreamer, possibly a little mad, but he may not have been. Whether you are mad or not is measured by how successful you are, Björn had said, so when in the end, after much searching, she found the place, she went to fetch him.

He was the only one she wanted to show it to and she wanted to be alone with him there. Nowadays there was never the opportunity. It was perhaps best that way, her feelings for him had not passed, quite the reverse, they had grown and tangled themselves up in a knot of misery, no deliverance, no peace. She was twenty-one so it could hardly be seen as a harmless passing crush. No, nothing felt harmless any longer. They never spoke about it, but sometimes . . . he would cast a glance across the room. Only a glance, but if you know, a glance is enough.

*

It was a cold and beautiful day. She took a short cut over the winter fields and met him in the arboretum. He was standing there in his blue work trousers, no coat, but wearing a leather cap so ugly that you had to look like Björn to get away with it. Standing there doing something, as usual she did not know what, she supposed mostly standing and enjoying being between the trees. That was what he liked most about the arboretum, she had realised – not the trees themselves, but the space between them. The silence and the tranquillity that she could long for too.

Now he was watchful as he saw her coming in the distance. Even more watchful when she had come up close to stand in front of him, twisting and turning her mittens and her request. He shook his leather cap when she had finally managed to formulate the question that was so difficult to ask. No, Karenina. Do not call me Karenina . . . It is still no, he said. He did not want to. Without further explanation. Just no. Even though she could see he was not busy with anything. A sheath knife in one hand, that was all, a pretext in case he was caught red-handed doing nothing.

He did not want to. Not interested. Or perhaps terrified, she was not sure. Terrified? Yes . . . or whatever it might be called.

Her hopes were turned to disappointment. Sudden, strong, crushing disappointment. Without a word she turned and walked away.

The first one to look at me, she said to herself, without really under-standing where the idea came from. The thought just appeared in her head, unexpected and powerful, obvious and quite defiant, not to say insane, but nevertheless . . . appealing, yes, liberating, at any rate less impossible than other thoughts she had been having lately.

The first one, she thought as she walked up towards the house, her hands throbbing with blood and cold.

They were all there, Björn's four sons, busy with various things in the yard, the first sunny day for a long time. As it happened it was Rikard who looked at her first, from the open kitchen window where he was changing the draught excluder. Not Rikard . . . he was too young, the youngest of all the sons, no, not Rikard, she thought, slightly embarrassed. The next one to see her was Jon, but he was taken, he and his girlfriend were sitting on the step enjoying the winter sun. And then Isak, on the way to the compost with the day's slop buckets, but he did not count, he was her brother. She went up to Erik, who was bending over the engine of the broken-down Volvo, the eldest of Björn's sons and the one who resembled him most. But Erik was irritated and said: Can you not see that I have my hands full – where have you been anyway, you need to cycle down to do the shopping . . . milk, minced meat, soap, cigarettes . . .

She pretended not to hear. She had already turned to David.

There was only David left, the son who resembled Björn least. David with steam coming out of his mouth in the cold, on his way out to the winter fields to shoot small game, standing by the garage cleaning his gun.

"Come on," she said.

"What for?"

"Don't ask so many questions."

"O.K., O.K., stop nagging, I'm coming."

Everyone was used to her waywardness and perhaps David should have had his suspicions when she told him to come without any why and wherefore. But he had no objection to accompanying her. Help her with whatever it was she needed help with. He liked her, she was easy to like, he was the only one who did, but that just made him more convinced.

When they passed the arboretum, Björn watched them go. All the way down across the frost-covered fields, the same way she had just come and wanted him, Björn, to go with her . . . she was now walking with David.

"I don't know what he thought, I really don't know what he thought when he saw me go off with his son. And I've never asked."

At least she was no longer nervous, not with David. Not at all as she would have been if Björn had been at her side. Here. Now. Someone. She wanted nothing more. And what she was feeling and doing and why, she could not have explained, but she did not need to, because David asked no questions.

In the end she was the one who asked why he was taking his rifle with him. He did not need it where they were going, surely he understood that they were not going hunting, he was already caught.

"You never know," David replied, excessively vigilant. It also felt a little excessive when he suggested that they shoot off the lock when they reached the house and were unable to open the door. He took out a small pocket knife instead and worked it open. As if she had spent her life entering places that were not hers.

The chilled hide-out was full of remarkable things, but instead of paying closer attention to them or perhaps lighting a fire in the stove, she guided him into the sleeping alcove and disarmed him.

The gun propped against the old Calor gas burner beside the bed.

"What's got into you," he breathed when, still wrapped in her woollen scarf and without even taking off her mittens, she started to unbutton her cardigan. She had nothing underneath. He had seen her naked many times, but never like this, never for him, only him.

"Shhh . . ." she whispered, snuggling up to him in the creaking iron bed. She was quite calm and confident, sitting with her woollen hat and her white breasts. He was mortified and bewildered and was worried about . . . the others. How did she think they could keep this secret from the rest of the family? For they would have to. He did not want to think about their reaction.

"Shhh," she hushed him again.

He had always liked her, she knew that, maybe he looked up to her slightly. She was a few years older than him and had a way of making the age difference seem bigger. She was the one who always said what she thought, who even dared to stand up to Björn, something the others were wary of, with the exception of Idun.

When she tried to undress him she discovered a small home-tattooed star on one shoulder, newly done, not particularly attractive. She had not realised that there were things about him that she did not know – it was a start, although she had not exactly considered a sequel. Here. Now. Him. That was all she wanted, she could not explain it any better than that. David pulled his top back on, did not want to let her take his clothes off. No naked skin, perhaps it was too cold for that, and she had kept most of hers on too. His lips were dark with the cold, his pupils had contracted, she did not know what that meant, excitement, confusion, bedazzlement, all at the same time?

The quilts had a pattern of strange flowers she did not know the names of. And in David's eyes something else she did not know . . . a mixture of disquiet and lust verging on terror? He was probably a virgin. She was not. But she was not as experienced as she tried to appear.

David against Björn was like David's fight with Goliath. David was a boy compared to Björn, but he made her feel like a woman. On the sloping ceiling in the alcove over David's head hung the silhouettes of two Japanese dragons, cut out with edging scissors, she saw them only that one time, never forgot them. What sort of battle they were engaged in, whether they were mating or fighting, it was not possible to see. But they could carry on indefinitely, they were so evenly matched.

If Mamma could have seen me now she would have asked me what the matter was, why my eyes . . . I would not have been able to reply, but I wish she had asked. The love Mamma used to warn me about, I always wondered who it was she had loved with that sort of passion. There was never the right opportunity to ask.

"Lo, I love your Pappa, but I cannot bear to think about him," she answered when I tried. Her voice had a tone that did not invite further conversation. I pictured them as two animals equal in strength and wounds, who avoided each other so that they were not forced to tear each other apart.

———

When Mamma hears the familiar sound of the lighter, she holds her hand out automatically. Fingers poised for a cigarette. Her unseeing eyes sharpen. She listens to the sound of paper. A shadow of anxiety passes over her face. The sound of paper being ripped.

"What is it?" she asks. "Is is for me?" I hand her the lighted cigarette. No, it is for me, Mamma. I am opening it now.

Lukas' letter is as short as it is illegible. I stare at it and cannot understand what I am looking at. Unintelligible signs all mixed up together. It is obvious how hard he tried, how important it must have been, how impossible. His handwriting used to look as though he wrote up and down with his left hand and he never managed to get the letters in the right order.

The only feeling I have is of relief. Unbelievable relief.

No recriminations, at least none that I can interpret – there is no chance that I will be able to decipher this. I did not know that you could be so dyslexic, a whole page of illegible marks. Now at any rate I have done what I could, made the effort to look for the letter, found it, taken it with me everywhere waiting for a place where I could open it and in the end torn it open and read it, or at least tried. Only to find it impossible.

The muffled call of the bittern has been inside my head for so long and the moment I skim through the letter it glides out over the lake. Deathly quiet and a little heavy at the front. And my head is empty, light and calm.

Tomorrow never comes

When I have stared long enough at Lukas' incomprehensible words, I see ... at first only one word that stands out from the rest. Written with extra effort to make that at least legible. A simple word, and neverthe-less I do not understand it – why is he saying that to me? A feeling of disquiet spreads through me, just as when the bats in the attic unfold their dry wings after the winter and wake each other up, one after the other, until everything is fluttering. I rise out of the cane chair, tell Mamma that I have to take a walk, give her my jacket so that she does not freeze to death and leave her there.

Go in a wide curve down over the fields. The cold bites into my face and makes my eyes water. From a distance everything looks as usual, as I remember it. I have not set foot anywhere near Lukas' house since I left. See you in hell, Lo. Hell could be here, on the steps of the house where he grew up, it could be where we used to sit with a bowl of rice and his hand-rolled cigarettes and nothing special to do. It required intelligence to love like that, quietly and with no props, we grew up so under-stimulated, filled each other's field of vision so completely, breathed the same air, heavy with toads rotting in the rain.

He is not there, has not been for a long time, Mamma said, but I have to see for myself. No trace left of the fire, the exterior looks as though it has been restored, but only from a distance. When I come closer I see that there are no details in place, the interior looks crude and unfinished, bare partitions, no furniture, a front, that is all. The river rats must have their own empire here now with their own laws, move around as they please. If they stay here and keep each other in check, they will be left in peace. I look in all the windows and the tool shed and the garage, but everything seems to have been abandoned. Go down to the lake. The call of the bittern on a certain sort of evening, like the time Lukas had drunk too much and wanted to go home even though he was already at home. I have not been to the lake since then either, the last time I walked along this path was with Yoel, a stranger on a chance but momentous visit. I did not want to leave, but nothing held me back.

The dead forest and our hiding place. Yet childhood is not a place to which you can return, it is only that very short time in your life that you can never relive. Why Lukas – how many times have I asked myself this – because he and I were the people we were? The dead forest has risen up again, but the tender green shoots are just brushwood growing healthily between the trunks. I continue along the shore without finding our hide-out. Was it really so inaccessible and well concealed? There are no fixed points for my memory, everything indistinguishable, like the vegetation. I must have walked too far, got lost. Stop and look out over the lake, and there . . . with the lake water halfway up the broken windows, there it is. It is either floating or perhaps sinking, a little way out in the mirror-like water, about to be dragged even deeper. From a distance it looks like a rotting, half-sunken barge. Wherever Lukas is, it can hardly be here.

The sheltering trees around the house are gone. The beautiful little larch grove felled. Good timber, I remember Pappa's father used to say.

After the war he had travelled through Finland and when he came home he talked about the delightful larch forests and the impressively strong women, in that order, Grandmother laughed about that. Tall trees and hardy women, a longing for something that could compare with him.

I stand at the water's edge and see the light divide the lake, split it into the silvery surface and the dark depths. Giddiness, now or never, the water is deadly cold and muddy with sludge from the bottom, but I have to do it. Take off my clothes and wade out. When the water reaches my thighs I begin to sink. The bottom of the lake is so much muddier than I remember, or is it just my adult weight that pulls me down.

———

I should never have opened it. Should have left the seal of time and silence intact, had respect for it. The letter was not as unreadable as I had hoped it would be. After turning it over in my mind, in the end I could work it out, even though with every word it became harder to interpret, as if he had taken so long over each character that darkness descended while he battled with something that was impossible, too much, too bloody awful. *Forgive me*.

It was the last thing I had expected from him.

An accusation or a declaration of love or both, that was what I thought. Not this. *Lo . . . Copenhagen . . . forgive me . . . answer . . .*

The letter had travelled a long way. Lukas must have been waiting for an answer, fearful to begin with, then impatient, in the end resigned, no, in the end nothing at all. Taken my silence for a no, I do not forgive you. It only needs one to let go.

That explains why he never came up to Mamma's house when I

was at home. When he saw his old car standing there under the white birch. Not because he could not forgive me for going away – but because he thought that I could not forgive him.

The lake water is halfway up the peeling door to the pearl fisher's house. I am forced to enter via the broken window, haul myself up and clamber into the cold hall. A dull stagnation in the rooms, the moisture dampens both the light and the rustling in the winter reeds outside. The rooms are not flooded. Not submerged. The floors are damp, but the wood seems to have swollen with water from underneath and become watertight like boat timber. At first sight everything seems to be as usual. I find no food in the cool cupboard that might indicate someone's recent presence. At first I think I can feel a faint warmth coming from the cast-iron of the stove, but it must have been my imagination.

It is impossible to go back, the place I pictured only existed as long as we were here. The rest is just dead coral trees, an impression of wandering about in an artificially lit display.

I had slept the sleep of an inebriated child. An overtired youngster who had eaten far too much and Lukas could not stop himself – was that what he was trying to say in his letter? *This is a man's world . . . even in my sleep . . . but it wouldn't be nothing, nothing without . . .* intoxicated for the first time, teenage-drunk, sugar-scented, available, out of it, amidst the dark brown sheets. Dark brown, I remember that, have always had a memory for useless details, the curtains at the window were also dark brown, the entire hotel dark brown, like a bat, cheap and yet, I suspect, a fortune for him.

A memory for details. But I have forgotten what it is he is asking me to forgive. That he might have done something against my will. Surely I would remember that forever? You could not even drown the river rats, Lukas.

Memories and misgivings jumbled together until you cannot tell them apart. When I left you . . . was this the only explanation you could think of? That you once did something unforgivable that you were nevertheless trying to beg forgiveness for? Word against word, yours against mine, I say that it never happened, virgins do not rape virgins, Lukas, I only remember the tightening vice.

———

A few short seconds, that was all it took. The moment when I felt your weight and the knowledge that I would not have had a chance – if – and for a moment you did too, enjoyed the advantage before you regretted it. Held me like a dog holds a piece of meat he is prepared to fight for. I remember the sense of being at the mercy of your desire not to hurt me. *I did not want to hurt you*, you said afterwards. For me it meant that you could have done, if you had wanted to. *I could have hurt you, but I did not want to* – that was what I heard.

After that I saw the vice inside you, inside all men. But it provoked me more than it scared me. You know it, I know it, therefore it does not need to be said. And if we do say it, it changes nothing. I do not hurt you because I am not able to. But you do not hurt me because you do not want to.

I know that you cannot forgive me, but you must, you wrote. *If you forgive me you must reply. I am waiting until you reply.*

Time is a growing debt, impossible to repay.

Waiting until you reply. Waiting with what? Living? You should not have sent that letter. I should not have read it, not so many years too late. And I should not have asked Mamma to tell me the end of the story, but I am an insatiable type. Insatiable before you came into my life and took my dissatisfaction as something to do with you; it was not, Lukas – no-one else has sated me either. What you could give me was never sufficient. What I wanted from you was not sufficient either. And what I wanted to give you was not enough. I wanted to give you almost everything, but almost everything is almost nothing, you said.

What happened next?

How could Mamma have told me? The end. Tell me what happened next, I asked, and did not know what I was asking for. If there had been such a thing as fairy tales, there would be just a few for adults only, like the one Lukas used to tell me about the nightingale that sang most beautifully in captivity after its eyes had been poked out.

All Mamma knew about him she had heard from the doctor in the village. How she managed it, patient confidentiality and all that . . . But for the doctor Mamma was just a lonely blind middle-aged woman she could unburden herself to without risk. At any rate, after the fire Lukas had visited the village health centre, he had wounds that had become inflamed and needed to be dressed. He had eye problems caused by the smoke and the heat. He had a wear and tear injury from the factory. And some old injury that from time to time gave him migraine-like headaches. After a while pain in his shoulders too with the toil of building the house and a chronic respiratory infection. The pearl fisher's house that had become his temporary home was damp and draughty and winter was approaching. He suffered such a serious loss of appetite that he was not eating any food at all. Insomnia. And then the fire negligence prosecution hanging over him and an inquiry into his mental state. The only thing Lukas could thank his lucky stars for, if he had any, was that the house was uninsured. At least he avoided any suspicion of insurance fraud. And the fact that his Pappa had neither life insurance nor a krona in the bank meant that Lukas was never accused of increasing the morphine dose too quickly.

It was as if his body had suddenly seized up, all at once. Perhaps he just wanted to be looked after, the doctor thought. But not touched. Not that. No eye contact. He did not even want to take his top off in front of her when she needed to examine him. Difficult to talk to, unwilling to provide information about history of illness in his family, did not want to fill in any forms at all. He winced at any physical contact. A very reluctant patient, and yet he came and continued to come, with old injuries and new, his immune system had been destroyed, the degeneration of a human being – it happens sometimes – as a fellow human the doctor had followed it with horror, as a doctor not without fascination.

Then Lukas stopped turning up, suddenly and unexpectedly. Either he had been released from all his afflictions at once, or, more probably, he had gone under. Possibly moved, like so many others. At the leather factory where he worked there had been redundancies and lay-offs, the doctor thought that he was one of the many who left.

A long time passed with no sight of Lukas. When one day he was sitting in the waiting room again, it was not because he was ill, but to ask for a certificate of health. He requested it for a job he was going to apply for elsewhere. Visibly changed – or just more his old self – that was something the doctor could not determine since she had not met him before he became ill.

Specimens taken and routine tests. Everything was as it should be. He had regained not only his health, but also his physique. The doctor did not believe in miracles, but maybe . . . everyday miracles. When Lukas came for his next appointment to get his test results, she signed the health certificate and handed it over with the feeling that she was delivering a present. He should have a good chance, she said, of getting the job he was hoping for, on an oilrig somewhere in the Atlantic.

I looked at Mamma imploringly. As if she could turn back the clock, but no, even she cannot do that.

"*On an oilrig*? When you've been accused of arson?"

"That investigation was dropped," she reminds me.

"But – fire negligence . . ."

Well, if they did a check, Lukas managed to slip through regardless. He got the job. That was the last the doctor heard from him.

Lukas on an oilrig sounds like an evil fairy story, but there are no fairy stories, he said.

"Mamma, I don't know whether I want to hear the end."

"We can save it for tomorrow, Lo."

Tomorrow never comes. But I suspected anyway.

They say that a factor leading to pyromania may be homelessness during childhood. You and your bloody hand-rolled cigarettes, Lukas, only a lunatic would smoke on an oilrig, did your mistakes teach you nothing? Did you not sign a contract about fire safety when you got the job, had you not promised me to stop smoking, had I not promised you never to start? To whose lot does it fall to cast himself into the flame of guilt and put it out with his own body? An uncontrollable impulse. How often do you not think I have wanted to do it too? But it cannot be – you can only forget and carry on, forget and carry on, it is a blessing to be able to forget, but for you the blessing was that everything could burn.

———

As I was driving down here at dawn . . . I can still feel the tenderness around my midriff when I curl up in the alcove in the pearl fisher's house and shut my eyes. It was sunny on the motorway, the first light of day, a hundred and thirty kilometres an hour – too fast, too slippery, too bright – and suddenly: the oblique shaft that entered through the windscreen and transfixed me on the driver's seat. I was veering across a no man's land, straight into the light. Within its dazzling force was silence, the world was in slow motion, playing backwards, moving away. Not a sound, no metallic smell of blood, only something that was closing, my lungs emptied of air, there was no pain, it was beyond good and bad. If I survive this, I thought, if I survive, I will give our story a happier ending.